Praise for *I Am Thunder*

'Funny and clever – a perspective long overdue in British fiction'
Alex Wheatle, Guardian prize-winning author of *Crongton Knights*

'Fans of *Skins* and *The Hate U Give* will feel right at home here'
BuzzFeed

'This assured, hopeful debut feels unprecedented and essential'
Guardian

'An uplifting, empowering novel with hope at its heart' *Observer*
Children's Book of the Week

'This one is special . . . punches well above the weight of most
debuts' *The Times* Children's Book of the Week

'An incredibly powerful debut novel that brings the reader a
unique perspective . . . In order to foster tolerance and inclusiveness,
the world needs more books like this' *WhatsOn*

'No half measures – this is an important as well as immensely
assured first

Also by Muhammad Khan

I Am Thunder

KICK THE MOON

Illustrated by
Amrit Birdi

MUHAMMAD KHAN

MACMILLAN

First published 2019 by Macmillan Children's Books
an imprint of Pan Macmillan
20 New Wharf Road, London N1 9RR
Associated companies throughout the world
www.panmacmillan.com

ISBN 978-1-5098-7407-1

1 3 5 7 9 8 6 4 2

A CIP catalogue record for this book is available from
the British Library.

Printed and bound by CPI Group (UK) Ltd, Croydon CR0 4YY

To everyone looking for a best friend . . .
You are not alone

YEAR 5: WORLD BOOK DAY,

LADY TABITHA PRIMARY SCHOOL

'Who are you supposed to be?' asks Lee Garrison, ripping off his mask. Blond spikes stick out in a comic book explosion around his head.

I blink. For the last fifteen minutes, a steady stream of kids dressed as book characters has been arriving at my tutor room. Thankfully my costume is *still* the best. There's no way Lee doesn't know who I'm supposed to be. I'm rocking a movie-quality superhero costume. The kind that cost two Eids' worth of pocket money *and* an IOU on a third. Totally worth it though, because this year's twenty-pound book token is as good as mine. I get chills every time I think of all the comics I'm going to buy with it.

I fling out my arms, and my cape whips and billows like the sail of a mighty ship. Thanks to some clever stuffing in the costume, I'm looking every bit as muscly as my comic book idol. My voice drops really low, and I do the squinting thing heroes do when they're about to drop a great line. 'I'm *Superman*.'

The other kids nod approvingly. Pitch perfect and on point. After five years of obsessive practice, you'd expect nothing less.

Lee glances round at the gathering crowd, eyes bulging, lips vibrating as spit comes whooshing out of him.

'Ilyas, mate!' he cries dramatically.

Hate when people make my name sound like *Elias*. But I'm done telling them it's *Illy-yaas*, because then I just get called 'silly arse', which is about ten times worse.

'Just no, seriously!' Lee continues, cringing.

The back of my neck starts to prickle, and in about three seconds, I know I'll be blushing, but I don't have a clue what he's on about. Unless I've peed my super-pants? Discreetly I give myself a quick feel. *Houston, we do not need a diaper.*

I stiffen as Lee snakes an arm across my shoulders. 'Look – who am I?' he asks.

'Spider-Man,' I say, without hesitation. 'Just like I'm—'

'Exactly!' he says, cutting me off mid flow. 'And who's Ryan, then?'

My eyes lock with Ryan's. The idiot stole my limited-edition floaty Superman pen in Year 4. Payback time.

I shrug. 'Mary Poppins?'

'I'm Willy Wonka, you idiot!' retorts Ryan.

Course he is, if Willy Wonka got dressed in the dark and ended up in his mother's wardrobe.

'He still doesn't get it!' Alice chuckles. A lipsticked scar zigzags across her forehead, and huge plastic glasses sit at the end of her nose. Unfortunately four other people had the same idea, killing her chances of taking home the book token, or ten points for Gryffindor.

'Know Blade?' Lee asks.

I nod, perking up at the mention of the coolest vampire hunter in comic history.

'OK. Now imagine I came as *him*.'

'That would've been wicked!'

'It'd be fricking *dumb*,' he says with disgust.

Everyone falls silent.

'Look, you *can't* be Superman, mate,' Lee continues. 'Superman ain't no brown boy. You get me?'

'Why didn't you come as Aladdin? Or Mowgli?' asks Alice, tapping her chin with her wand.

'Cos they're not superheroes,' I say in a small voice, palms growing sweaty. I hope I'm not stinking out my suit. Amma warned me this costume was wipe clean only.

'That's racist,' says my best mate, Daevon. In a red-and-black-striped hoody, with an aluminium foil sword, he's nailed Thresh from District 11.

'Shut up, I'm racist!' Lee snarls, practically foaming at the mouth.

Daevon backs up so fast he nearly sits in the bin.

'Superman is *white*. Facts!' Lee looks around for support.

'You're *all* lame,' says Vidya snarkily, shimmying her shoulders, setting the sequins on her blood-red sari ablaze. 'Dress-up's for babies! I've come as the best person ever: ME! And before you say there's no book about me, *there is*. It's called a *diary*, people. Look it up.'

Vidya's gang of fashionistas have completely ignored the rules for dressing up on World Book Day. These girls are channelling Bollywood big time. They sashay into the corner to give each other makeovers with a jumbo box of make-up.

'Oh my days!' Lee shout-laughs, making everyone jump. 'Only way he's Superman, yeah, is if he flew head first into a big pile of poo!'

'Or flew up a cow's bum!' Ryan adds. He starts making mooing and farting sound effects while flapping the back of his mum's purple coat.

Laughter and squeals of disgust ring out. Even Daevon can't clamp a hand over his mouth fast enough.

'It's Pooperman!' shrieks Alice, pointing her wand at me like a spear.

Humiliation spreads over me like a rash. My lower lip trembles, and I bite down hard. *Boys don't cry* – that's what Dad says. That's what everybody says. Can't let them win. 'I *am* Superman, though. Got myself a tan, innit.'

'Superman can't tan, you fool!' Lee shouts. 'His super-strength comes from the sun, and a tan would block it.'

'Dickhead!' A wand punctures my suit faster than I can react. The strained squeal of ripping fabric fills my ears as it's tugged back and forth. My impressive right pec sags, a cloud of stuffing tumbling to the ground taking my heart with it.

'Ew! It's Pooperman's booby!' cries a Gangsta Granny, booting the fluff away. Throwing her lilac cardigan over her head, she runs around like she's scored a goal at Wembley.

The laughs are coming thick and fast now. Any last hopes of manning up are drowned by a sea of tears. Ms Lipscombe enters the classroom – cheeks flushed, apologizing because her train got cancelled. She finally senses something's up, but it's too late.

The good kids tell her what Lee said; tell her that it was Ryan who damaged my suit with Alice's wand. She banishes the lot of them to the Learning Centre, but the damage has been done. Not even Amma's needle and thread can fix this.

Everyone listens in subdued silence as Ms Lipscombe, having placed a box of tissues on my desk at the back of the room, goes off on a major rant.

'I am *thoroughly* disappointed in you, 5ML!' she tells us, shaking off her suede coat. Blonde corkscrew curls bounce angrily on red-and-white-striped shoulders. 'I expected so much more from this form. We're a team. The A-Team! You must look out for each other.'

Twenty-two pairs of solemn eyes follow her every gesture, occasionally swivelling round to gawp at me sobbing. Realizing that Dad will be angry with me for blubbing, I cry even harder.

'Who are we to tell someone they can't be Harry Potter or Katniss Everdeen just because they're a different skin colour or gender?' she demands.

'Miss, what's *agenda*?' asks Vidya, her eyelids caked in gold and green.

I tune them out. The part of me that has loved Superman from as early as I can remember just died. And unlike issue number seventy-five – *The Death of Superman* – there's no coming back from this. When I get home tonight, this costume is going in a large box along with the rest of my Superman merch. Come Saturday, I'll be dropping it off at Cancer Research.

If I can't be Superman, I'm going to be someone better. I'm making my own superhero, and he's going to be AMAZING. He'll have light brown skin, love lamb biryani, and pray at the mosque every Friday. He's going to be British *and* Pakistani. His name will be . . . PakCore.

But for now, I'm just going to sit at the back of the classroom in my torn Superman suit and cry.

YEAR 11: LAST DAY OF AUTUMN

HALF-TERM HOLIDAY, SOUTH LONDON

CHAPTER 1

A squillion coloured diamonds.
  Winking, melting, morphing.
  Spinning, faster and faster and —
  I'm flying! I'm flying!

Snapping open my eyes, I gasp for air. A wasp is buzzing in the centre of my brain, and my tongue is foaming. I'm crammed inside a wooden box with three other boys, our knees bunched tightly around our ears. The night air is thick with smoke and stinks like a heated swamp. To my right, a portal frames a collapsed see-saw and a swingless swing set.

How did I get here?

The wasp shifts from my brain to my pocket, buzzing furiously against my thigh before I realize it's actually my phone. I'm about to answer it when a trainer kicks my left hip and then my right thigh as Imran straightens his long legs, tilting his head back. He's directly opposite me, one hand holding a steaming vape mod, the other a joint. In the moonlight, his face is all angles and edges. His fade is fire; his topknot perfection. Right there and then, I make the massive decision to reboot my PakCore comic book series. This time using Imran's handsome face.

I'm excitedly designing the cover for issue number one in my head when a halo of fog comes sailing out of Imran's lungs. His palm nudges the delicate creation into the world as he blows a fist of vapour at it. Punching through the middle, the fist opens, coiling wispy fingers round the smoke ring. The ghosts entwine, sprout tendrils and glide forward as one.

My mouth hangs open as the vapour jellyfish swims passed the window, moonbeams plating it in silver.

'See that?' Imran says smugly. 'Man's got tricks for days!'

Daevon raises his phone and takes a snap. 'Nice one,' he says, stroking his cornrows.

'Fire!' Noah agrees, then starts giggling like a crazy person, his face going as red as his hair.

This is my mandem. Noah and Daevon couldn't be more different. Noah's skinny as a rake and meaner than a switchblade, while my boy Daevon loves his mum's Caribbean cooking and is the closest thing I have to a best friend. We're sitting inside a wooden castle in the local kiddies playground. Nobody comes here any more. The equipment is mashed up, dicks and swears are scrawled over every available space, and used needles hide in the tall grass. The council condemned the place a while back, but it takes more than a sign and a locked gate to keep us out.

Imran's eyes settle on me. My heart beats just a little bit faster, my Adam's apple swelling in my throat.

'What you reckon, Ilyas?' says Imran. 'Epic or nah?' His pupils are spreading like crop circles.

'Killed it,' I agree.

The mesmerizing smoke creature flickers once, then winks out forever. The awe I felt is replaced by an unexpected sadness.

'Look, look, look!' Noah says, gesturing with his chin, eyes as bright as headlights. 'Lickle Ilyas is crying like a *gyal*.'

'I ain't crying!' I protest. Only I am. And I have no clue *why*, just as I have no memory of climbing inside this Claustrophobia Tank with these three.

'Relax. His eyes are just going pee-pee,' mocks Imran, voice deep as a rumble of thunder.

My mates crack up, and the joint tumbles from Imran's

long fingers. Noah and Daevon dive for it at the same time, knocking heads and laughing like fools.

'You brung my tag?' Imran asks me, popping a couple of pieces of gum in his mouth. The square wings of his jaw ripple as he chews.

'Yeah, course,' I say, hurriedly whipping out a scroll of paper.

Drawing is my superpower. Back in nursery, when kids were still sketching stick figures floating about randomly on a page, I was drawing Dad setting up his store front, laying out exotic fruit and veg in eye-catching displays. I didn't know their names (not then, anyway), but I discovered that if I closed my eyes, I could make each and every one of them appear in 4K clarity. My teacher was gushing when Amma came to pick me up.

'Oh Ilyas loves his drawing,' Amma cooed. 'My other children always wanted toys. But give this one pencils and paint, and he's happy as Larry!'

Imran unfurls my scroll now, giving me butterflies. After studying gang tags, tribal art and Urdu calligraphy, I experimented for days, looking for the perfect blend. Of course my mates will never appreciate any of this, but for me drawing is sacred. Go hard or go home.

Imran traces out the D and the M for DedManz, the name of our gang. He frowns, squinting at the brown-skinned character with the killer cheekbones. Yep, you guessed it: Imran immortalized in street art.

'Rahh . . .' whispers Noah.

'Sick!' says Daevon, steam trailing from his lips like dragon breath.

Silence from Imran.

The butterflies in my stomach mutate into killer bees. He's our fearless leader, captain of both the basketball and football teams, so cool even teachers suck up to him. Basically, his opinion is the only one that counts.

Thick eyelashes – the ones that drive girls crazy – flick up, and Imran's intense eyes bore into mine. Now his fist comes sailing towards me. Just in time, I make one of my own, and we fist bump. 'One hunna,' he says. 'I'mma make you famous, bruv.' He tucks something in my pocket.

Pulling out the fifty-pound note, I blink in disbelief. 'What's this?'

'Man's gotta take care of his mans, innit? You did good.'

Suddenly my dream of owning a sixth-scale figure of Star Lord with Baby Groot seems a little less impossible.

'He's only gonna spend it on something gay, like comics or toys.' Noah rolls his eyes.

'As opposed to premium porn sites?' says Daevon.

'Everyone knows how to get that shit for free. I need that dollar to buy quality ganja.'

'Got you covered, bro,' says Imran. 'DedManz gonna rule these ends. Money, drugs, women.'

'We gonna have like an initiation?' Daevon asks, clearly impressed.

'What you on about?' I say, snatching glances at my vibrating phone. Ten missed calls from Amma. *Oops.* Unfortunately calling my mum back in front of these guys would be like whipping out a bunch of My Little Ponies and braiding their manes. Amma will have to wait.

'Every gang has one,' Daevon explains, passing the joint to me, which I palm off to Noah. 'To show solidarity and that? Like the Triads have to drink a bowl of their own blood. Sons of Malcolm X bust a cap in some loser's ass. Hell's Angels piss on each other . . .'

'Acid attack!' Noah says, clapping his hands with psychotic glee.

'Shut up, man!' I say with disgust. 'You wanna end up in prison?'

'Pussy!' he spits.

'Ilyas has a point,' Imran says, taking a toke on his vape. 'All that running from the feds? Nah, bruv. Think smarter.'

'We could steal stuff?' Daevon suggests. 'Latest iPhone?'

Easy for Daevon. His dad is loaded so he could just go out and buy one.

'Nah.' Imran closes his eyes and exhales. Smoke swirls between us like a dancing *jinn*. His fist snaps round it, snuffing out its life. 'Got it.'

We exchange glances.

'If you idiots want to be proper DedManz, it has to be for life. Bros before hoes. Understand?'

We nod under his fierce glare.

'So if you want in,' he continues, 'gotta prove your worth. You're gonna get some girl bare-arse naked and film the skank making a fool of herself.'

'What if she don't want to?' Noah asks.

Imran shrugs coolly. 'Up to you, innit?'

My stomach ties itself in knots. I know what he means. Imran's eyes are on me in a heartbeat.

'You up for it?'

'Nah, man,' I say quickly. 'I'm out. Naked girls are haram.'

'Don't count if she's a thot,' he says, grinning.

The word hangs in the air like a bad smell. *That Hoe Over There*. Noah goes into another fit of giggles, then bucks his hips, moaning like a porn star. *Idiot*.

'Your boy ain't doing it,' Daevon tells Imran, and for a moment I think he's sticking up for me like he used to when we were small. Then I catch the eye-roll, and my last hope dies.

'Course he is.' Imran grins. An ambulance rushes by in the night, the emergency lights temporarily bathing him in red. 'Me and Ilyas gonna go mosque after and smooth things over with

God.' He takes a long drag, then holds the joint out to me. Three pairs of eyes study me intently. Melting under their gaze, I accept the joint and take a toke.

I trip up my street. One minute, I'm walking along, minding my own business; the next, I'm stuck in someone's hedge. My phone buzzes in my pocket. Crap – I *completely* forgot about Amma.

'*Assalaamu alaykum*, Amma,' I say, all casual, like she hasn't been blowing up my phone.

'Ilyas! Oh thank God. I've been calling you for over an hour. Where are you? Why haven't you been answering your phone?'

'I told you. Hanging with mates.'

Disappointed silence.

'Come home, please, *beyta*.' Amma sounds scared. It makes me want to slap myself.

'On it,' I say, hanging up.

When I finally rock up, I see golden light spilling into our street, and Amma standing in the doorway with her shawl over her head, hugging herself in the chill night air. Nervous puffs of fog escape her lips. Catching sight of me, she comes flying out.

'You had me worried sick! I don't want you hanging around with those—'

'Sorry, Amma,' I say, dodging the hug and the lecture as I vanish up the stairs. 'We had two-ninety-nine burger meals, and I gotta puke.'

Can't let her touch me. Can't let her get a whiff of the weed clinging to me like sweat. It will break her heart. No way am I doing that to her.

Locking myself in the bathroom, I crash on to the toilet seat, holding my pulsating head. Snot swings from the tip of my nose like a wrecking ball. How I hate Imran and Noah and . . .

Daevon? My homie, my hype man, my brother from another mother?

There was a time I would have done anything for the big guy, but now it's like he's gone Skrull – replaced by a shape-shifting alien. Cos the mate I knew, the boy with the heart of gold, would not be down with humiliating a girl for some dumb initiation challenge. And since when did taking drugs become a thing?

I wipe away my snot. Zigzags of it streak my cheek as the shakes kick in. The bathroom tiles begin to pulsate, and my eyes tear up. Even though I don't want it to, my mind forces me back to the moment Imran and Noah entered my life . . .

'Stop hanging round the house like a flipping girl!' Dad would say with disgust, watching me colouring in my Spider-Man picture. 'Go play football with the other lads!'

So I traded art for freezing my nuts off in a game of street football. Wouldn't have been so bad if I could play for shit. All I got were kicked shins and grazed knees. But the really humiliating part was getting shouted at by Noah and Imran every time I missed the ball. They made me feel like a factory reject.

Coming home, Dad would ask how many goals I scored. I'd lie, and he'd smile.

Tonight, those lads Dad wished I was more like have got me doing drugs and want me to humiliate a girl.

Wiping my eyes, I wonder what life might have been like if I'd turned out as smart as my brother Amir – killing it at Harvard in business management, sponsored by a Fortune 500 company. Or like my sister Shaista – girl boss and vlogging genius.

But I'm just Ilyas Mian: the girly-boy who draws stupid comics that nobody will ever read.

CHAPTER 2

'Amma!' my eighteen-year-old sister yells at 7 a.m. 'Ilyas is doing *stuff* in the bathroom. He's been in there for over twenty minutes.'

Shaista's downstairs, but her jarring voice still manages to seep through the crack in the bathroom door.

'Well, who doesn't do stuff in the bathroom, *beyta*?' my mother replies, exasperated. 'That's what it's there for.'

'Oh don't be so obtuse, Amma. He's doing haram stuff to himself.'

I can imagine the dirty hand gesture Shaista must be making.

'No I'm not!' I shout from the doorway, only it comes out all garbled because I have a toothbrush jammed in my mouth. I needed to brush my teeth twice to fix my skunky breath.

'You aren't the only one rushing around trying to get ready this morning,' Amma grumbles.

'But I *am* the only one juggling studying Level Two Hair and Beauty with running a successful vlog and earning an actual income.'

'A little empathy wouldn't go amiss,' Amma tells Shais. 'You and Ilyas were thick as thieves when you were small.'

I twist the tap, blasting every last blob of toothpaste down the plughole, then breathalyse myself into cupped palms. *Result*. Snagging a towel, I skitter down the stairs to end this diss-fest.

'*Thief* being the operative word!' my sister retorts. 'Ilyas stole every diary I ever owned and scribbled pictures in them.'

'Not like you ever used them!' I shoot back, wiping my face as I join them.

'Not the point,' she persists. 'I happen to like blank diaries. Blankness is very therapeutic.'

Amma and I exchange glances.

'You're siding with him again!' Shaista is looking furious now. 'God I wish I was a boy so I could get some respect around here.' She storms upstairs and slams the bathroom door for dramatic effect.

'Sorry, Amma,' I say.

My mum shakes her head, a wry smile wavering on her lips. She takes her large glasses off, polishing the lenses with her cornflower-blue *dupatta*. 'Have you fed and watered Sparkle?'

Sparkle is Shaista's Mini Rex rabbit. Nine years ago, Shaista announced that she wanted a 'teeny-weeny blue-eyed bunny, with velvety-soft white fur' for her birthday. (She actually wanted it to poop Skittles, but that was never gonna happen.) Dad drove all the way up to Derby to pick up Princess Shaista's dream gift. Except a year later, Amma and I were the ones left looking after poor Sparkle.

I nod. 'Yeah, course – at 6.30 a.m., straight after praying *Fajr*. I'm like clockwork.'

Amma frowns at me, yanks the damp towel from my hand, and attacks my face with it. I protest, but she grips my chin, fixing me in place. 'See?' she says holding out the corner of the towel for me to inspect. 'You would've turned up to school with toothpaste smears on your chin, and some bright spark would've made a crude joke.'

My eyes widen. Amma is a part-time librarian, full-time family wrangler, and without her, I'd probably be an even bigger loser than I already am.

'I love you, Amma,' I say, and I mean it.

Amma draws me into a hug, and suddenly I'm four years old again, lost in the soft jasmine and spice scent of her on a warm summer's day.

'Foz, no huggy-huggy,' Dad says, coming out of the kitchen, raking stubby fingers through salt-and-pepper stubble. WORLD'S BEST DAD is printed on his mug. 'The lad's nearly sixteen.'

Slipping out of Amma's arms, my cheeks prickle with shame.

'Ilyas will *always* be my baby –' Amma sticks her nose in the air, *dupatta* slipping from her head to her shoulders – 'even when he's married with ickle babies of his own.'

Dad looks like she just told him she'll be a contestant on *Love Island* next week. 'You're making him into a target for bullies, Foz. Tough love – that's what boys need. Trust me, I was one.'

Sloping off, I leave them to argue over the correct way of parenting me.

'Oi! Don't forget to mow the lawn tonight,' Dad calls, pointing at his eyes and then at me, letting me know I'm under surveillance.

'Mow the lawn on your face first,' Amma quips.

In the hallway, I unzip my backpack, making sure my finished homework is inside. It's not. Panic detonates in my gut before I remember it's still on my USB. I glance up as Shaista thunders down the stairs. Honey-blonde hair flat-ironed, hazel contacts, face powdered like a corpse, and candy-coloured rose-patterned vintage heels (a love letter to the Grim Reaper) on her feet.

'What are you staring at?' she demands.

It's like I'm looking at her through a Halloween Insta filter.

'Nothing,' I say quietly. 'Can you borrow me your printer?'

'Sorry, I don't speak Street. Proper grammar or out of my way.'

I try again. 'Can I borrow your printer, please? Only I need to print off my history homework, and there's always this massive queue at school.'

She folds her arms across her narrow frame, shifting her dead-fish-eye contacts from me to the memory stick, like it's a poisoned stick of gum or something. 'First, answer me one question.'

'Er, OK?'

'What were you thinking just now when you looked at me. And don't even *think* about telling porkies.'

I shift from foot to foot, scratching my upper arm through my school blazer. 'Um . . . something dumb.'

She rolls her scary eyes. 'Want the privilege of using my printer? Then spit it out.'

I try to invent something, but my mind defaults to comic book mode. All I see is an alien race of fish-eyed zombies demanding one thousand human souls in exchange for not invading the planet. A pointy-toed shoe taps impatiently.

'Um, your hair . . . your skin . . . and those eyes . . .' I say, as if that explains anything.

'*You* have hazel eyes!' she snaps. It's something she has never forgiven me for.

'I can't help it, though. But you, with that foundation . . . it's like you're trying to be . . .' I trail off, shaking my head. If I don't shut up now, I'll be banned from using her printer for life.

'What?' she says, getting in my face. 'Trying to be *what*, exactly?'

'White,' I finish in a tiny voice. Man it's like she used the Phoenix Force to get the truth out of me.

'Dad!' Shaista hollers, batting her eyelids, contacts sliding around like frogspawn. 'My sweet little brother just called me an Uncle Tom.'

'No I didn't! Why you lying, though?' I say, backing away because I know Dad will take her side. Being the only girl in the family has its perks. 'I don't even speak like that.'

'What's that?' Dad says, voice trailing from the kitchen where Amma is now quoting parenting skills from Mumsnet at him. That argument escalated quickly.

I cuss under my breath, grab my bag and fly out the front door. I really don't get Shaista. Mad at me when I wouldn't answer her question; and even madder when I actually did. Big Sister Logic.

My bike is old and dinged, but blazing with twenty-one superhero emblems I spent half-term painting on its frame – the twenty-first being PakCore's very own shooting star. I pelt out into the street making rocket engine sounds. Out of nowhere, a car brakes sharply, its grill roasting my thigh as it screeches to a halt. I swerve to the side of the road and freeze, my mouth hanging open as the horn blares.

'Soz!' I say, raising a hand in apology.

The car is a silver BMW, one of those classy hybrids that cost about a million pounds. Through the windscreen I watch a blonde woman release the steering wheel to fling her hands in the air like a seriously pissed-off mime. Beside her is a girl from my year – Kirsty or Kimberly? – one of the popular girls. She glances up at me, then back down at her phone. Course she does. I'm not on her level.

The lady lowers her window, and I wait patiently for the earful that's coming my way. 'MOVE!' she shrieks.

Veering back into the street, I pump the pedals hard, anxious to put as much distance between me and the BMW as possible.

At the traffic lights, my phone pings. I fumble for it in my pocket and pull it out: a message from my brother Amir. I stuff it back into my pocket, unanswered. I'm still blanking him. After promising Dad he'd expand the family business when he got his management degree, Amir's decided he's too good for it, and is planning to work for some big US company instead. I wouldn't even mind, except taking over the family business has now become *my* responsibility when all I want to do is make comics.

The green light comes on, and I pedal fast. No time to hang about. Stanley Park Academy is cracking down on latecomers this term. A 'late', even if it's your first one, now equals a break-time detention. Like that's gonna change the Ofsted inspectors' minds. Mrs Waldorf needs to retire. She's been around since the dinosaurs, even if she does dress like a teenage contestant from *RuPaul's Drag Race*.

As I wheel through the gates, our deputy principal, Mr Gilchrist, flings out a beefy arm and clamps a paw around my handlebars, making me lurch against them. Dude is *stronger* than my brakes.

'*Oof!* Sir!' I complain, rubbing my chest. 'You nearly killed me!'

'Well then, I'll just have to try harder next time, won't I?' He starts chuckling for some reason. 'Now off your bike – you know the rules. *Properly*. That's it. Good man!'

Gilchrist is so extra. Thinks the moment you come through the gates, you lose the ability to control your bike. Two years of riding, and I've never had an accident. Not including the near miss with the hybrid just now . . .

'Hey, gorgeous!' says a female voice.

In my world, female voices do not say amazing words like this.

I glance up in hopeful surprise and nearly have a heart attack. Jade Henley-Peters is girlfriend goals. Her long blonde hair hangs like a curtain of pure silk, framing wide butterfly blue eyes. She's biting her lower lip right now, the tender flesh losing its rose-pink colour beneath her perfect white teeth.

Back up! my brain warns.

Good advice. I've seen enough teen movies not to fall victim of the old they're-talking-to-someone-behind-you moment. So I glance over my shoulder. But nobody *is* behind me. 'Me?' I say, looking back at her in surprise.

She laughs. 'Of course I mean *you*.'

No lie: she is looking directly at me.

'Oh my God,' she says, placing a delicate hand at the dip in her throat. 'I picked up some super-sexy underwear at La Senza.'

'Yeah?' I say, stroking my jaw thoughtfully, acting like my circuits aren't overloading.

'Just come round after school and watch me try it on. Swear to God, the bra does amazing things to my tits.'

'Sounds great,' I tell her, making my voice deep and squinting like a superhero. 'Whereabouts do you live?'

Her pupils shift no more than a millimetre, but it's enough to tell me something is very wrong with this picture. A gust of wind sweeps away her platinum hair exposing an earbud wedged in her delicate ear, a mic hovering beside her lips.

The air becomes ionized.

'*Keep going, babes,*' comes the tinny voice of the friend from her earbud.

I duck my head and wheel my bike off as quickly as I can. If anybody heard me, I'd *never* live it down.

'We are ready to start,' warbles Mrs Waldorf into the microphone.

No one gives a shit. After all these years, exactly why this still baffles Mrs Waldorf is a mystery. She taps the microphone in case it's malfunctioning. The irritating whistle of feedback makes people no more than glance her way, before resuming their conversations. Her bloated face fills with alarm as she looks to her senior teachers for assistance. Mr Gilchrist bounces up onstage and grips the edges of the lectern, like he's about to Hulk out and fling it into the audience.

'Good morning, children!' he booms. He's just about the only person who can make a greeting sound like a death threat. Conversations end; egos self-destruct. 'Right, much better.' He nods at Mrs Waldorf, who gives a grateful girly back-kick.

'That woman is butters!' whispers Daevon, surprising a laugh out of me.

'Good morning and welcome back to Stanley Park,' Waldorf mutters into the microphone, barely moving her thin red lips. 'I'm sure you all had a lovely half-term break, but it is time to refocus and get back into the flow of things.'

A flutter of grumbles spreads through the rows. The innocent Year 7s glance round in horror. They're such newbies.

'It gives me great pleasure to welcome Mrs Wallington to the stage. She's going to be taking assembly today with the assistance of some wonderful Year Eleven students who went on our highly educational trip to Morocco before half-term. Let's all give them a big Stanley Park welcome!'

Mrs Wallington smiles assuredly as she canters up to the lectern to lacklustre applause. Every year is the same. A bunch of privileged kids go to a developing country to gawp at how primitive brown people can be. Said privileged kids muck in, take rides on camels, sample the culture by wearing colourful kaftans and pulling off some dodgy dance moves, which we're expected to laugh at, and then there's a whole montage of them hugging little kids or giving them piggybacks, and some 'hilarious' pictures of teachers in their pyjamas pretending to look shocked. And the soundtrack is Taylor Swift. Every. Single. Time.

'White Saviour Barbies, fam,' I whisper to Daevon. We both kiss our teeth and shake our heads.

My sour grapes are instantly sweetened as Jade's beautiful head appears above the lectern like the rising sun. I could stare at her all day. A carousel of Jade and her pretty friends and some smug-looking boys acting like they got lucky in the dorms take it in turns to read cue cards about how the trip has changed their lives forever.

Projected on to the screen is an image of Jade looking flawless next to some grinning guy in a fez. Standing in the souk, they're posing in front of a whole galaxy of glittering lanterns of every shape and colour. *I could be your brown guy, Jade.* I think wistfully. *You wouldn't need to buy a lantern off me to make me smile.*

Must've been drifting, cos when I come to, I sense major awkwardness. The Morocco-trip kids have stopped speaking and are looking vexed.

The doors fly open dramatically, and standing there with red cheeks and windswept hair is the girl whose mum nearly mowed me down this morning.

'Oh! Kelly, perfect timing,' says Mrs Wallington, throwing an arm out like a ringmaster.

The girl flushes as she clambers on to the stage while a grumpy teacher closes the doors behind her. She's wearing red Dr Martens, which look like they belong to her dad. Jade flashes the girl a death stare, thrusts a cue card into her hands, and walks off, hair swishing.

This Kelly girl starts reading like a pro. I can legit imagine her reporting for the BBC.

'These rich kids, fam,' Daevon whispers, shaking his head. 'It's like they're a whole other species. They're gonna end up with all the top jobs, lording it over the rest of us.'

Daevon likes to pretend he's ghetto cos he thinks it's cool. His dad is a barrister, and his mum is a primary school teacher. Speak slang in their presence and suffer the consequences.

'*You're* rich,' I remind him.

'My dad is,' he corrects. 'I'm just a wasteman.'

Only he's not. Daevon is smart and funny when Imran and Noah aren't around.

'So here are some of our best bits and a few of our bloopers too!' one of the boys onstage finishes, making us glance up at the screen. I prepare myself for a montage of bullshit, consoling myself that at least this means the cringe-fest is nearly over.

A rhythm and a beat start up, and almost involuntarily I begin flexing to the irresistible sound of Afrobeats. Cheering and whooping flare around me. Shakalewa's 'Rotation' is a real crowd-pleaser. Some kids raise their arms up to dance, hands clapping, fingers clicking; others sing the words, voices soaring up to the rafters. The fresh beat reaches into the very foundations of Stanley Park and gives it a good shake. Suddenly the cringe photos on the screen or the fact that us poor kids never get to go places like Morocco doesn't matter. There is a rippling energy in the hall that frees us from the mundanity of being in school, gives us permission to cut loose. Man, I want to get up and bust a move, but I bob my head instead.

The video comes to an end, and a tsunami of applause follows. A few kids sing the chorus on loop, not ready to let go of the good vibes just yet.

'RESPECT!' I shout, raising my fist into the air.

Daevon does the same. 'Mad ting!' he adds, grinning from ear to ear.

Some of the Year 10s start ululating and whooping, but they're trying too hard. Their head of year starts taking names, which shuts them up fast.

Mrs Waldorf smiles superiorly as if the love in the room is all for her. 'Well!' she says, trying to get everyone's attention. Good luck with that. 'Didn't they do well? Let's have another round of applause for the Morocco-trip students and Mrs Wallington.'

Afrobeats gives me life. The La Senza Scandal is forgotten, banished to the darkest reaches of the multiverse. Roll on, period one.

CHAPTER 3

I'm in the lower set for maths. My whole mandem is, but I bring the algebra. To be honest, it's kind of distracting always having to pass my book over to Imran, Daevon and Noah so they can take pics, then copy my answers. Plus, every time I get one wrong, I'm guaranteed a smack. Maths is starting to give me concussion.

Our teacher is Mr Gordon, a lanky, grey-haired dude with a nose like a parrot's beak, and a moustache the size of a USB port. Gordon resents having to teach a lower-ability set. That's what I think, anyway, but Imran has other ideas. Reckons the man's a racist cos apparently he spotted him on this anti-immigrant march one time on the news. I think Imran's just pissed off cos Gordon keeps giving him detentions for not doing homework. Besides, guys like Imran don't even watch the news.

'Here he is!' says Imran, announcing me as I enter the classroom. He's wearing a claret-and-gold Cleveland Cavaliers hoody, a pen wedged behind his ear. Gordon is going to be vexed. Imran knows hoodies are banned, but I suppose arguing about it means less time doing maths.

'Oh shit!' Daevon says. 'You done the homework, bro? Cos I totally forgot.'

'Forgot, or couldn't be arsed?' says Noah, chuckling.

'Look, guys,' I say, trying to muster up some courage. Having practised my speech in the bathroom mirror every morning of half-term, the words should roll off my tongue. Only mine are a jumble of letters, melting on my tongue like Alphabetti Spaghetti. 'If you copy from me all the time, yeah, what you gonna do when it's the actual exams?'

'Don't hold out on us, fam.' Imran glares at me, hand extended for my book like it's a foregone conclusion.

'I'm not,' I say quickly. 'But you guys know what Gordon's like! Copy one of my mistakes, and we all get detention. Or a phone call home.'

'Let us worry about that,' Imran says, fingers flexing for my book.

I feel blood rise to my face, dew forming on every strand of my fuzzy moustache.

'No,' I say, raising a finger.

The room falls silent, and I am suddenly aware of dozens of pairs of eyes watching us.

I lick my lips. 'Amma is sick of getting calls from Gordon saying I copied you when it's always the other way around. I ain't doing that to her no more. She's had enough stress with my big bro pissing off to America.'

Daevon has the decency to look ashamed. 'Yeah, yeah – you're right. I'll take the L.'

Imran's eyes flash at me, and it's as if he's casting a spell over my hand. It slips into my bag, ready to hand my homework over – the homework I spent ages doing by watching a ton of YouTube videos presented by teachers who could actually teach, instead of confuse-the-hell-out-of-you Gordon. *No, no, no!* I scream silently at my hand. *You have to stand up for yourself.*

'Oi! Hand it over,' Imran barks, boiling over with impatience.

'Well, what a nice surprise!' Mr Gordon says in his nasal voice, misinterpreting the tense silence in the room. 'We're certainly getting off on the right foot this term, aren't we? Guess you lot have finally realized you only have seven months left to scrape through with those Fives. Stranger things have happened . . .'

Imran's basketball-honed hands shoot out and grip my bag.

I cry out in surprise as he rips it from my fingers, giving me burns.

Gordon traps me in his crosshairs. 'Nice to see you on your feet, Mr Mian. No, no. Don't sit down. Your genius has finally revealed you're a cut above these dunderheads. You're being moved up two sets. Cheerio!'

I blink in surprise as Gordon sits down behind his desk and unlocks the computer.

'You still here?' Gordon asks, looking like he's just swallowed a kangaroo anus left over from last year's *I'm A Celebrity*. 'Skedaddle, Mr Mian. Skedaddle!'

'Sir, are you saying I'm in set two?' I stammer, unable to believe it, because good stuff *never* happens to me.

'Cor blimey!' he sneers. 'If you can't even subtract two from four, then perhaps you shouldn't be moving up at all.'

'My boy's moving up to Ms Mughal's class. Represent!' says Daevon, fist pumping in celebration.

I throw him a grateful glance. Imran shoots my bag at my chest, and I catch it, absorbing the impact with my puny arms.

'Go on then. Piss off,' he hisses.

'Language, Mr Akhtar!' Gordon trills.

'Oh sorry,' Imran says, canines glinting like daggers. '*Dafa ho, panchod.*'

My mouth drops open at the insult.

'Speak words we can all understand!' snaps Gordon.

I leave them to it. The first day of term just got a whole lot better. Without my mates dragging me down or Mr Gordon confusing me, maybe I can get a decent grade in maths after all? Everyone knows maths and English are the subjects you need to pass if you don't want to end up cleaning toilets for the rest of your life.

I gangsta walk it to my new classroom, feeling little explosions of happiness going off in my chest. In my mind, I'm PakCore, patrolling Stanley Park, keeping these ends safe. At the first sign of danger, my hands will swing out, making the *Sign of Wahid*. This, I imagine, is how I'd summon mystical energies from the universe to aid in my fight against evil. Fingers raking through the air, snipping apart atoms, setting off a chain reaction of incredible power. A dazzling glow will envelop me, replacing my civilian clothes with a totally dope superhero costume. Jade and black leather, studded with silver Urdu letters, and a glowing green trim that accentuates every muscle and supercharges them. Approaching the door, the knock I give is anything but ordinary. It's a super-knock.

CHAPTER 4

'Come in!' a friendly voice calls.

I don't know Ms Mughal all that much, never been lucky enough to be in any of her classes, but I've seen her around, rocking her black hijab/jilbab combo. She's up at the interactive board, waving long, slim arms at a colourful display. On it is an algebra question; one I have zero clue how to answer. *Uh-oh . . .*

'Stormzy!' I cry, pointing at the bottom-right corner of the screen in surprise.

Her large green eyes glance at the image, and she smiles. Wow — I never noticed before, but Ms Mughal looks like a supermodel. 'Oh, Mr Omari's a regular here.' Turning to face the class, she says, 'Everyone, this is Ilyas Mian, who's joining us today. Be nice and say hey.'

'Hey, Ilyas Mian!' the class says in unison, waving.

'A'ight.' I nod, keeping it icy.

'Ilyas, can we have you next to Kara, please,' Ms Mughal says, pointing the way.

'Oh hell naw!' Kara says, making me blush. She's a mixed-race girl with tight cinnamon curls, prominent freckles, and eyes the colour of honey.

'Don't worry, Kara. I'm sure *he* won't mind,' Ms Mughal replies with a mischievous wink.

Everyone bursts out laughing as Kara blushes. Soon she's giggling too, moving her bag off my designated seat. And suddenly I realize there's a vibe in this class I haven't seen since primary school. People are actually cool with each other. Man, did I luck out.

The hour goes by in a crazy blur, and it's nothing like a regular maths lesson. Turns out Stormzy isn't the only celeb Ms Mughal's mates with. Taylor Swift, Kwamz, Zayn Malik, Ed Sheeran, and Maya Angelou all put in appearances on her slide show. The thing is, it's still all about the maths, just a thousand times more relevant to our lives. By the end of the lesson, I'm solving simultaneous equations like a pro. This has me low-key believing I might actually be on my way to hitting a grade six.

'Your homework is online. Do it, or else.' Ms Mughal's warning finger swings out like a shotgun, and people chuckle.

Ray, a tall blond kid who sits at the front, clutches his chest and hits the ground. 'Miss just shot me! Tell my family I love them.'

Ms Mughal throws open the door, and everyone waits patiently as a Somali girl in a motorized wheelchair rolls down the aisle. 'See you tomorrow, Nawal!' she says brightly.

'Beep-beep, people!' Nawal says zooming into the corridor. 'Out the way, unless you want me to run you down.'

'OK, off you go, beautiful people!' Ms Mughal says as the pips go, sweeping us out of her room with a wave.

I watch the rest of the class say bye to Ms Mughal on the way out, but feel too weird doing it myself. So my watch becomes the perfect distraction.

'Hey,' she says, stopping me. *Not* the perfect distraction. 'How was it?'

'Yeah, yeah. All right,' I mumble, scratching behind an ear. 'Like, good.'

'You ever feel you don't understand anything, you're always welcome to come see me for extra help. OK?'

'Thanks,' I say, ducking out.

Suddenly the corridor has shrunk to the size of a crawl tunnel. I stumble along, feeling too big and clumsy for the world. I hope Ms Mughal doesn't think I'm a rude boy, but talking to teachers is just another thing I'm crap at.

Jade's galdem are gathered by the lockers. A girl wearing her hair in space buns is holding her nails out for her mates to admire.

'Totes amazing, Melanie!' squeals one of her friends.

'Right?' agrees Melanie, demonstrating a variety of sexy Catwoman poses.

'Where'd you get them done?' asks Jade.

'There's this place on the high street called Flawless. Oh my God, like all the workers are Asian girls who can't speak a word of English!'

'Yeah, what's up with that?' Jade says, nodding.

'The Viet girl who does mine is really pretty!' Kelly says. 'Like Jennie from BlackPink.'

Her friends wear blank expressions.

'From K-pop?' she offers.

'Not to discourage you, hon, but your nails look a little rough,' Jade says sympathetically. 'You should try Flawless.'

'It's not the nails; it's her man-hands,' says Melanie. 'They're too chunky.'

'Mel!' Jade shakes her head at her disapprovingly. 'Don't be mean.'

'So anyways, I read somewhere that they all get human-trafficked from North Korea.'

My jaw drops. Kelly spots me and blushes. One by one, the other girls clock me too.

'Yes, can we help you?' Jade asks pointedly, placing delicate hands on a size-zero waist, burning me with her laser vision.

Jade just spoke to me for the first time since Year 7. This is supposed to be the greatest day of my life.

I drop my eyes and hurry off, hearing her say, 'Honestly, I see that boy everywhere.'

'Oooh! Jade has a stalker.'

They burst out laughing.

CHAPTER 5

At break-time, I see my mates playing football on the field with a bunch of scary-ass sixth-formers. Noah and Daevon hold back a little, but Imran is fearless. He dribbles the ball towards a meathead, feints left, then thunders right, the ball tracking his foot like magic. Two players try to tackle him, but he's already sprinting towards the goal, topknot flapping in the wind, muscles vibrating. Imran is drama incarnate.

Before I even know what I'm doing, my phone is out, and I'm snapping pics of him. Noah glances up at me, which quickly brings me to my senses. I turn my phone round and start talking into it, walking off as fast as I can.

With nothing better to do, I head for my safe space: the gap under the stairs in the science block. Unfortunately a supply teacher is on guard, banishing anyone seeking shelter. The woman must be descended from those stingy innkeepers who wouldn't give Mary and Joseph a place to crash. But if DedManz has taught me anything, it's Finessing 101. Rule number one: act like you're doing something perfectly legit, and people won't bother you.

'And where do you think you're going, young man?' booms the woman, intercepting me immediately.

Rule number two . . .

I give her Shocked Face, which is guaranteed to cause extreme levels of self-doubt. Use with caution.

'Ms Wallington told me to come for detention?' I make it sound like a question, as if she should already know this.

'Oh I see,' she says momentarily softening before thinking

better of it. 'And where is this detention?'

Rule number three . . .

I point up the staircase, 'Room thirty-three G, third floor. Come up with me if you want?'

'No, that's all right,' she says, as if I just asked her up to my bedroom or something. 'Just hurry up then.'

Giving a salute, I meander towards the stairs. Once her back is turned, I skid into the dark place under the stairs. Thirty seconds to make sure I haven't been seen, then I silently unzip my bag and pull out my sketch pad.

Flipping to a blank page, I arrange my special art pencils in a semi-circle close to my right thigh and pull out my phone. I swipe through the pictures I just took of Imran, searching for the perfect look – that unique mix of bravery, determination and cockiness that is SO PakCore. Not easy when you don't have the guts to ask someone to pose for you. Really I should man up and ask him instead of going all stalkerazzi. Maybe he'd be flattered by the idea of having a comic book hero modelled after him?

Yeah, and pork chops are halal . . .

My finger hits the perfect shot.

Placing my phone on the floor, I sketch a skull shape on my pad, then go in with a softer pencil, marking in the hollows of the eyes, the strong bridge of the nose, and the squareness of the jaw. As I'm doing all this, I begin to imagine what it must be like to be Imran. A natural-born leader, a *gyalis* like no other, and the undisputed MVP of Stanley Park Academy. What does the world look like when you're so tall, your head is practically saying 'Yo!' to the clouds? What does it feel like to fear nobody – bullies, teachers or parents?

Working my way down the torso, chiselling away at his abs with a medium graphite pencil, I find myself thinking about Imran's family situation. It's hard to feel sorry for the guy everyone wants to be, but actually his life is kind of sad. His dad walked out on them when Imran was only seven. Rumours have it he ran off with some *desi* babe half his age, but Imran's mum claims he's a huge landowner in Pakistan, regularly sending cash over to support them. While it's true Imran's never short of a few quid, I once overheard Auntie Simrat telling Amma that something seriously dodgy is going on with vans regularly bringing stuff in and out of their house under cover of darkness.

As I add shading to PakCore's eyes, I realize this is the one and only bit of myself I'm transferring over to the character. Hazel eyes gleaming through his black eye mask, the ties at the back of his head rippling in the wind like cobras attacking in tandem. Ten minutes in, the image has become my best yet. If I had one shot to present PakCore to the world, this picture would be it. My heart races, imaging PakCore becoming the Next Big Thing, licensed for comics and movies and action figures.

Reality check: if Amir won't take over the family business, I have to. Haji Mian & Sons has been in the family for three generations. It's survived riots, recessions, and competition from supermarkets. Who am I to turn my nose up at all that history?

The pips go, and I gather up my stuff.

CHAPTER 6

Sunday afternoon, I'm hanging with the guys in somebody's muddy alleyway, wishing Dad hadn't answered the door to them after I'd told him not to.

'What's this?' I ask, as Imran tosses a drawstring gym bag at my feet. It lands with a metallic clang. Inside are shiny cans of spray paint and a small packet of caps. I look up at Imran, but already know the answer to my next question.

'That gang tag you come up with for DedManz? You're gonna do a nice big one right there.' He points at a pristine double garage door, the roller kind made of thick strips of metal.

'Who lives there?' I ask. Vandalizing somebody's property is next level, but I can't think of a way out of it. Delay tactics are the best I've got.

'Shah Rukh Khan,' Imran says sarcastically. 'Just do your thing, and we can bounce.' He pulls out his designer vape pen and starts puffing mini rings that smell like watermelon.

'How do you even do that?' Daevon asks.

'Double Os? That ain't nothing. Watch this,' Imran says, loading his lungs with vape.

We stand back and give the man some room. With luck, Imran's ego will get so bloated, he'll forget this tagging madness, and we can go chicken shop.

Imran opens his mouth and blows a big-ass cloud of steam. His hands fly out, sculpting it into a white sphere. Without missing a beat, he surrounds it with a stream of mini rings, then sweeping his hands like Mandrake the Magician, creates a vape solar system before the whole thing dissipates.

I gasp. 'Man, that is fire!'

'One hunna,' Noah agrees, filming it on his phone.

Imran laps up the praise, then tucks his vape pen inside his leather jacket, and my heart sinks. 'All right, Ilyas. Back to work, my younger.'

'I know the perfect place,' I say, turning on my salesman pitch with what I hope is a winning smile. 'Big massive wall, peng black finish—'

Imran's fists make bunches out of my hoody, yanking me so close, I'm afraid he's going to headbutt me. 'Stop pissing about and get spraying or I'mma paint this garage door with your brains. You feel me?'

'Hey,' Daevon says, placing a restraining hand on Imran's shoulder.

Imran glares for a second longer, then releases me. 'You got five minutes.' He sets the timer on his Apple Watch.

I look back and forth, searching for a way out of this mess. Wish I was PakCore in real life. Right now I'd use my amazing parkour skills: flip myself up on to the roof of the garage, take a running leap on to the next one, scuttle along the corrugated metal and—

'Do it!' Imran booms, jets of vapour blasting out of the double barrel of his nose and the corners of his mouth. The man looks like Satan.

I obediently flip the cap off a can and give it a good shake. The glass bead rattles around inside, setting my teeth on edge. Experimentally, I press the top. A fine mist of brown squirts out and splatters the silver surface of the garage door. I swirl the can in circles to get the basic head shape down, getting a feel for the pressure. Noah whoops, pulling a bottle of vodka out of his backpack. Next, I grab the red can for the baseball cap, testing it with the gentlest tap. Thick red paint, dark as congealed blood, oozes out. Harder to control than the brown, but changing to a super-skinny cap fixes that. By the time I grab the gold, I'm actually enjoying myself. My artistic soul handsprings and backflips across this huge canvas.

'Call me Pak-Asso, cos I'm bringing desi back,' I quip, totally in the zone.

'Listen to this one!' Imran says, reaching out for Noah's bottle of vodka.

'Pick up the pace, cuz . . .' Daevon says, his voice as tense as a bowstring.

'You all need to hush yourselves,' I tell him, living in the canvas. 'Art cannot be rushed.'

Then I hear it. A door creaking open in the distance, somewhere beyond the wooden fence. It takes a moment for me to realize the owner of this garage door – the one I'm tagging – is approaching.

'Oh shit!' I whisper, tossing the cans back in the bag.

Imran's eyes drill into me. 'Finish it.' He shoves me so hard, I nearly kiss the wet paint.

With no choice but to continue, I spray on the D and the M, my heart hammering in my chest. The sound of slippered footfall grows louder.

'Who's there?' asks a man on the other side of the fence.

Imran's fingers curl over my shoulder like lever arches, fixing me in place. I can barely see through the sweat waterfalling over my eyes, but I keep going, adding accents and highlights.

'I'm warning you! I've got a gun!' the owner shouts, and suddenly I recognize the voice and nearly piss myself. It's Mr Gordon, my old maths teacher.

Imran's fingers burrow under my collarbone sending fresh jolts of pain skirting across my chest. Completing the tag, I hurriedly toss the cans back in the bag.

The side gate begins to rattle as multiple bolts are pulled back, each one like a gunshot. 'Who's there?'

Daevon's hand finds mine, and he tugs. Suddenly I'm stumbling after him, being dragged away from the scene of my crime. Imran swings the bag of cans over his shoulder and runs like the Flash, practically hurdling over fences as he makes a smooth getaway. Noah charges up behind, blindsiding me with a massive shove. I catapult into some squelching mud, practically bodysurfing over it as the metallic scent of rain and rotting leaves fills my nose. Noah cackles, running in the opposite direction, shouting the filthiest cusses about Gordon's wife. Clammy mud clings to me like a whale's tongue, swallowing my hands and sucking at my jeans.

'Get up, you idiot!' Daevon hisses, yanking me to my feet. 'Run!'

'YAAARGH!' roars Gordon, finally charging into the driveway.

My heart crashes in my chest when I see his rifle. Then the illusion fades. Mr Gordon is wearing a dark red dressing gown over stripy pyjamas and brandishing nothing more dangerous than a brolly. At any other time, I'd have died laughing. Daevon throws my hood over my face, spurring me on.

'I've got you n-OOOOOOOW!' Mr Gordon yells in surprise as he slips and goes down. His back hits the wet earth with a slap, and his grandad slippers go flying. The umbrella pops open. Gordon wriggles about in the mire, an overturned woodlouse trying to right itself.

'Daev, we should help . . .' I say, slowing down.

'Help!' Gordon wails. 'Somebody help me, please! I've broken my back!'

'Keep moving!' Daevon shouts, shoving me. 'Man's bluffing.'

As I pump my legs, keeping pace with Daevon, I realize I've been played. Imran must have got into another argument with

Gordon at school – something worse than the usual – and this was his idea of payback. Only now I'm an accessory. And if Gordon's not faking, if his back is legit broken, I can add GBH to my growing list of crimes.

CHAPTER 7

When I get home, I call out, but no one answers. I look up the stairs longingly, imagining clean water rushing over my sweaty body, washing away the custardy mud. First things first. I quickly rinse my hands and head out into the garden to let Sparkle stretch her legs.

'Hey, girl!' I say, lifting up the thick tarpaulin that covers her hutch. 'Wassup?'

Sparkle glances over a polar-white shoulder, two beautiful blue marble eyes checking me out. She bounces over, rising on to her hind legs excitedly, nose twitching. I unbolt her door, but I'm too slow for her liking. Sparkle attacks the wire mesh window like a ninja bunny.

'Easy! I gotcha,' I say, opening her door.

My rabbit glances up at me expectantly, sniffing my hand, flipping it upside down with a nudge of her pink nose, searching for the hidden treat that I don't have. I gently lift her up and carry her over to the rabbit run Dad bought Shaista. Nine years down the line, it's starting to look shabby, but it does the job of keeping the foxes, cats and ravens out.

'Man,' I whisper. 'All them bad tings trying to eat you. The Bunny Life ain't good.'

Sparkle begins to work her strong hind legs free and kicks as we approach the pen. In her excitement, she scratches the insides of my wrists.

'Easy there, Sparks . . .' I say, cradling her in the crook of an arm and popping open the lock on the run. 'There ya go!' She vaults through the door in a perfect arc. Her paws have barely touched the ground before she does a double lap of the pen, and binkies with pleasure. I chuckle. 'See you in a bit.'

I grab the wire brush Amma keeps in a ceramic pot on the patio and perch on the stone steps to scrape the mud off my trainers.

Back inside, I pull open the fridge door and make a grab for the orange juice. My hand hits a jug, and it comes tumbling out, spilling its contents down the front of my clothes.

'Shit!' I'm covered in a thick green mess and start to cough, realizing one of the main ingredients is finely chopped chillies. Need to get out of these clothes FAST.

'Amma? Shais? Anybody home?'

Silence.

Ripping off my gloopy hoody and jeans, and peeling my muddy socks off, I bung the lot in the washing machine, creep along the hallway in my boxers, and bound up the stairs.

Suddenly there's a fire in my pants. Panic grips me as I see the chilli sauce has soaked right through. Yanking my boxers down, I'm about to step out of them when I hear a laugh. Nearly giving myself a wedgie, I whip round.

There at the foot of the stairs is Shaista, holding up her phone, a Halloween-pumpkin grin carved into her over-powdered face.

'Omigosh!' I squeak, hugging myself. 'Tell me you did not just see my bum.'

'Bum?' Shaista says, brow furrowed. 'That's the least of your worries.' She places a hand on her hip. 'What on earth will your "mandem" say when this appalling vision is shared across social media?'

'You wouldn't!' I break out in goose pimples.

'Wouldn't I?'

'Come on, Shais, man. Posting nudes is haram,' I plead.

'So are the websites you go on. Yeah, I checked your browser history, Mr Haram Police.' The gloating switches to confusion. 'Got to admit, I am a little disappointed. Always figured you were gay.'

'Come on, man!' I'm literally begging now. 'Taking pics of your naked little brother is rank!'

She yawns languidly. 'Oh I'll happily delete it, but on one condition. Amma asked me to hoover the house before she gets back. *You* do it.'

'But Dad told me to mow the lawn!'

'Well then, you'll just have to do both. That is unless you want your pathetic mates laughing at your even more pathetic unmentionables.'

'I-I-I called out, and no one answered,' I say foolishly, as if I can logic away the last five minutes.

'And that, right there, was your downfall. Don't be so trusting, ickle Ilyas. The villains shall inherit the earth!'

'*Assalaamu alaykum*, kids!' Amma calls from the corridor.

Shais skips along to help with the shopping. 'Are you all right, Amma?' she asks, shoving the heavy bags at me and smirking. 'Notice anything?'

Amma studies us both – looking for war wounds (mine are all psychological) – then glances down. 'Oh the carpets are clean!'

'Of course,' says Shais. 'I'm the perfect daughter.'

'Yes you are!' Amma says, planting a kiss on my evil sister's cheek.

Oh well, I think. *At least I get to keep my privates private.*

'I mowed the lawn, Amma,' I point out, angling for some love.

'Did you, though?' Shais asks, glancing back at me sternly.

I look at her in shock before understanding how this is going to play out.

'No,' I mumble. 'Shais did that too.'

'Goodness me, we have been busy!' Amma says, grinning at Shais. 'Well you've earned your favourite meal tonight. Ilyas can you put the shopping away, please, since you got your sister to do your chores.'

I open my mouth, then close it. Amma is watching me closely. 'Sorry, Amma.' I lumber to the kitchen with the bags.

Shais pokes me and grins. 'How does it feel, ickle Ily?'

'Least we're even.'

'Not even close.' She winks and sashays away.

The weekend rolls around, and I'm up in my room working on my latest PakCore story arc. The pictures come easy. The words? Not so much. Right now, all I know is I want PakCore to burst into a massive wedding hall, hot on the heels of a double agent, with tables, chairs and canapés flying like a hurricane hit them. I picture PakCore leaping over an enormous wedding cake, the ruffles of his mask flapping in the wind, right leg scything forwards.

I lay a few guidelines down on a blank page, trying to pin down my chaotic imagination. Gradually it starts to come together. It always does, but even after all these years of drawing, there's still that paralysing self-doubt. It's always crap till it's finished.

Good. Great. Now for the face . . .

I pull out my phone and flick through my photos. Imran playing basketball. Imran playing football. Imran climbing a tree. Imran smoking shisha. Imran vaping O's.

Guilt bubbles in my belly. I don't want to be creepy, and I would totally base PakCore on my own looks if I could, but who'd want to read a comic about a skinny kid with a big nose? Even nerdy Peter Parker is shredded. Let's face it: Imran lucked out on both the genetics lottery and the confidence thing. It's like he believes in himself so much, he's got the entire universe believing in him too. That's the superhero life, not *my* life.

The last time I showed any of my friends my comic was back in Year 9.

'Cool pics, bro,' Daevon had said in a way that meant the exact opposite.

'*But?*' I said, sensing unsaid words teetering on the edge of his sentence.

He looked at me and smirked. 'Come on, man. We're not kids any more. Comics are for losers.'

'No they're not!'

He gave me a look. 'OK – if they're not, then how comes Comic Book guy from *The Simpsons* is a fat old loser who everyone laughs at?'

'That's just stereotyping . . .'

'You know it ain't. You're lying to yourself, mate.'

'I'm not! All the biggest movies are based off of comics.'

'Yeah that's *movies*. Normal people with normal lives watch movies. It's freaks and geeks who camp outside the cinema for the premiere, then go online and bitch about how much they switched things up from the original source material. Those are the kinds of people who live, breathe and die comics, fam.'

'Comics *are* cool,' I said, refusing to let it go. 'I'm telling you: it's a fricking goldmine.'

Daevon sighed, cracking his knuckles. 'OK – if you're telling me drawing comics isn't major cringe, how comes you're not showing this stuff to Imran or Noah then?'

I shrugged. 'Noah's a prick.'

'And Imran?' He placed a hand on my sagging shoulders. 'Sorry, man, but the sooner you get your nose out of comics, the sooner you'll land an actual girlfriend. You do not want to end up fapping over Power Girl for the rest of your life. Facts.'

It hurt more than it would if it had come from Noah or Imran. Daevon was my first friend, but while he kept changing, I was stuck with being me.

CHAPTER 8

'So,' Imran says, his voice like a strummed double bass. 'Ms Mughal, eh?'

We're hanging in the playground before maths, sharing a bag of chips Imran blagged off some Year 8 fangirls.

My boys are upset because Gordon's giving them a test next period. Apparently he was lying about breaking his back on Sunday. He's in school and saltier than ever.

'Yeah, lucky me,' I say, shrugging. 'She's the realest teacher in this school.'

'Looks like a supermodel,' Imran says, caressing his lower lip in a way that makes me uncomfortable. 'I like her big juicy . . . lips.'

'Stoppit, man!' I snap. 'She's a hijabi.'

'More like hija*bae*.' Imran grins hungrily, stroking his abs.

'Come on, bruv,' Daevon says. 'You wouldn't be saying stuff about a pretty nun, would you?'

'Ms Mughal knows how to get the D,' says Noah, making grabby hands.

Imran slams him against a wall. 'Taking it too far, man.'

Daevon and I exchange a surprised look.

Noah nods, flushing. Boy got owned. This is how Imran rolls: from time to time, he'll get rough with us, just to remind us that it's him who makes the rules, and he can change them without notice.

He and Gordon aren't so different. Gordon's setting his class a test he knows they'll fail. Classic shake-up strategy. Remind people who's top dog through fear and humiliation.

'Laters,' I say, using the awkward moment to make a quick exit.

'Oi, listen!' Imran says, making me wince.

I turn around, and he sticks some money in my pocket. Two fifties.

'Nah, you keep it.' I pull the notes back out, feeling guilty enough about wrecking Gordon's garage door without taking money for it.

He snatches the notes out of my hand and slips them back inside my pocket with a firm pat. 'This weekend, we're hitting up more places. DedManz for life, yeah?' He makes the bro hand signal: little and ring fingers extended, hand held to his heart.

My shoulders slouch as I return the signal. How did I ever get involved with these sexist clowns? *Oh well*, I think. *Maybe I can pay Shais off to stop her from leaking my nudes?*

That evening, I'm chilling with a bag of Wotsits and a chocolate doughnut watching CBBC. The programme is cheesier than the corn puffs, but watching kids' TV is therapy. Adults don't get how stressful being a teenager is. Sometimes you just need to kick back and remember the days before life got complicated.

On the show, there's a gang of misfits getting bullied by this nasty senior who everyone loves because she's captain of the cheerleading squad. The kids put itching powder in her uniform. She goes on to perform a cheer, which predictably goes wrong, and the entire pyramid of girls comes crashing down. It's always fun to watch the bully get wrecked.

Laughing along with the misfits gets me thinking, and before I know it, I'm hatching my own fiendish plan to get even with Shaista.

I leave the TV playing as I sneak into the dining room. Inside the cupboard is a plastic tub we store medicines in – plasters, painkillers and ancient vitamins nobody uses any more . . .

'Gotcha!'

Glancing over my shoulder to make sure I'm not being watched, I skim the instructions. The plan is to get Shaista out of my face, not to kill her. I pop out a few tablets from a blister pack, grinning. Operation Nude Photo Deletion is well under way.

At dinner-time, I hover around the kitchen, being extra helpful, looking for an opening to execute my plan. Finally the perfect chance presents itself, and I pull out the balled tissue in my pocket containing the crushed tablets, liberally seasoning Shaista's dinner plate and giving it a good mix.

'My – you're being helpful today!' Amma says.

'No!' I say, before realizing this is every guilty person's first response ever. 'What you saying, Amma? I'm always helpful.'

'And I thank Allah for it every day,' she says, making the chai.

I carry Shais and Dad's plates through to the dining room, reminding myself that it's all for the greater good.

'Lovely jubbly!' Dad says, rubbing his hands together, inhaling the warm aroma of basmati rice and chicken ginger *karahi*.

'Amma!' Shais cries, making my stomach drop.

'Yes, *beyta*?' Amma says, peering through the serving hatch between the kitchen and dining room.

My sister waves her hands with excitement. 'This tastes even better than Auntie Ambreen's version.'

I'm a regular Gordon Ramsay. It's all I can do not to burst out laughing.

An hour and fifteen minutes later, and Shaista still hasn't answered the call of nature. What's her stomach made of – cast iron? She's locked in her room filming a video for one of her hair-and-make-up vlogs. With over twenty-one thousand subscribers to her channel, that's an awful lot of impressionable girls being led astray by my evil sis.

I lurk outside her door, hearing her laugh at her own jokes as she serves up beauty 'hacks'. The more I listen, the more confused I get. A zombie alien speaking an intergalactic language, she's on about 'dupes' and 'glass skin', 'jade rollers' and 'Kabuki'. Don't even try telling me that's normal.

Suddenly she goes quiet. The sound of an almighty fart permeates the silence. I hear the frantic hiss of perfume being squirted like a full-on fumigation mission. Her door flies open before I can duck and run. Shaista spots me but is too preoccupied with holding her stomach to realize how high-key suspicious this all is.

'Don't go in my room,' she snaps, brandishing a nail like a scalpel.

'Like I'd want to!' I call after her as she crab-walks to the bathroom.

'I'm serious. I've hooked up my vlogging camera and—' Her stomach gives an unholy gurgle, and the look on her face is priceless. 'Just don't!' She slams the bathroom door.

The door has barely shut before I hear her cry out in surprise. A sound like a trombone blares out.

'You left me no choice, sis . . .' I whisper under my breath, trying not to laugh. If she'd taken the tag money I'd offered this morning, the laxatives wouldn't be necessary.

I sneak into her room, scanning for her webcam. It's in its usual filming spot, but the green button is flashing, which means it's on pause. I hurry over to her purple-and-gold chaise longue, from where she presents her weekly vlogs like a true diva. A massive glowing halo of light dazzles me. Apparently Kim Kardashian started a trend with the promise that good lighting gives the same effect as all her plastic surgery. My eyes settle on a clutch of egg-shaped sponges in clear plastic cups.

'Embryos,' I mutter. 'Girl's growing an army of mutant zombies.'

Sometimes companies send Shais free stuff to try out for a video review. Apparently this boosts sales. Guess they must specialize in Halloween merch.

I hunt for her phone, looking high and low and everywhere in between. It suddenly occurs to me that she might have taken it into the bathroom with her. Frustration grips me before I spot her familiar diamante phone charm, glittering brightly on a table. Pressing the home button, I'm immediately prompted for her passcode. No problem. From all the years' experience of stealing her diary to draw pictures in, I know that she *always* writes her passwords and pin numbers in the back. Within seconds, I've found her diary, and the passcode is mine.

The squeak of a tap makes me gasp. Time is running out.

Sweat beads my brow as I flick through her photos, trying to locate the nude of me she had no business taking. There are literally a million filtered selfies of her pulling weird faces in a thousand different poses. Then – worse than all of that – an image of my sister in a *bright orange bikini*.

Going through her private stuff is so wrong. But desperate times . . .

The phone rings, and I nearly hurl it out of the window in surprise. Getting it under control, I catch the caller ID: Zaman. The only Zaman I know is Imran's cousin who works at Dad's store. But that guy is a legit gangsta.

Last summer, I caught sight of a dog tattoo on Zaman's abs while he was changing a light bulb. He started acting seriously sketchy when I asked him about it, claiming it was something he did for a dare when he was younger. Of course, being a lifelong sufferer of Nosy-Kid-itis, I immediately searched for it online and found out the tattoo belongs to DX Dingoes – one of the roughest gangs in south London. I told Dad, but he said it wasn't right to judge a person by their past.

Still, the caller *has* to be a different guy. Shais is too high maintenance to date somebody with a gangsta past.

The sound of rushing water startles me. Guess the laxatives worked a little *too* well.

'Stay focused!' I tell myself, swiping like a lunatic, keeping my eyes peeled for the photo that has given me sleepless nights. Finally I hit the jackpot. Only it's worse than I thought. Shaista hadn't just taken a picture – she'd filmed me bounding up the stairs like some discount stripper. What kind of twisted person would do that to their own flesh and blood? It confirms everything I have always suspected: my sister is a member of the Illuminati.

The flush goes, jerking me back to reality. With a couple more taps, the shameful video is banished to the Twelfth Dimension. Mission accomplished, I sprint out of the room.

CHAPTER 9

'What you got there?' Daevon asks at break-time in the cafeteria.

'Lamb samosa,' I say, holding the tub out to him. Four golden envelopes of crispy deliciousness sit inside a nest of kitchen towels.

'Nice one!' Noah says, snatching the tub and grabbing three samosas.

'Give 'em back!' I roar.

He locks eyes with me and licks, saliva linking the samosas together like savoury bunting. I yank my tub back a second faster than he can defile the last one. His drool splatters the table instead.

'You're an arsehole!' I say, fuming. Then turning to Daevon, I offer the solitary untarnished samosa.

'Nah, blud. I'm on a diet,' he says gloomily.

'Why?' I ask, tucking into it myself, savouring the rich and spicy taste. Daevon has always been a bigger guy, and honestly it suits him. Trying to imagine a skinny version of my mate does my head in.

Imran crashes at our table, chuckling. Everyone stiffens. 'If man's changing his habits, gotta be a girl involved.' He chucks a stick of gum in his mouth, the mouldy stink of skunk radiating off him. 'How you getting on with the DedManz challenge, lads?'

'Yeah, so me and Denusha went Westfield cos she needed some new kicks,' Daevon says reluctantly.

'Big mistake,' Imran says sagely. 'Don't let some girl boss you around, fam.'

Daevon droops. 'Long story short: we end up in the toilets,

and she's grinding on me. Man gets hot. So I start filming. "You filming me?" she says. "How'd you like it if I filmed your *fat belly*!" Then she starts beating me up. Telling you, man, I could not get out of there fast enough!'

'Daevon got Solanged!' Imran says as everyone cracks up.

Daevon bristles, jabbing Noah. 'What you laughing for? Like *you* got any.'

'From yo momma!' Noah says, nodding.

I roll my eyes. 'Ignore this fool. No woman's ever letting him within a mile of her.'

'Except one did,' Imran says, stretching. 'Noah sent me the video, and I uploaded it to a porn site.'

Noah and Imran fist bump.

'What about you then?' Daevon asks, wrapping his arms around his stomach.

'Me?' Imran says, wide-eyed and innocent. He leans back and shouts. 'Yo! Jasmine! Over here, *gyal*.'

Jasmine blushes as her group of friends giggle and poke her. Hastily running fingers through her hair, as if getting ready for a selfie, Jasmine trips over to our table. 'You all right, bae?' she asks.

The look in her eye, the tinkle in her voice: *Uh-oh*, I think. *This poor girl is in love.*

'Where was I last night?' Imran asks, his hand spanning the width of her waist as he draws her closer. Her skirt has been rolled so short that the sudden movement gives us a flash of mint green knickers.

Jasmine's eyes widen, glancing at me and the boys nervously as if to remind Imran they have company.

'Forget them,' Imran says, vanquishing us with a flick of his wrist. 'They ain't nobody. Now, where was man last night?'

She flushes, shoulders rolling like pistons. 'We was together.'

'And what did you do for me?' Imran asks, like the skunk has given him amnesia.

'Allow it,' I say, feeling for Jasmine.

'You *know*,' she says, giggling nervously. Her eyes are glossy, and sweat is making her foundation gather at the corners of her nose.

'Wanna be my girl, Jas?' Imran asks, squinching like a supermodel, thick eyelashes framing his narrowed eyes.

'I *am* your girl . . .' she whimpers.

Imran has reduced her to a baby afraid of having its rattle snatched. This is so wrong.

He spreads his long legs like the jaws of a shark and pats his left thigh. Jasmine obediently climbs on. Imran casually plants a hand horribly close to her crotch, and I'm silently begging for a teacher to spot them and bring an end to this madness. But this is the DedManz corner of the dinner hall, specifically chosen for being a major blind spot.

'The sort of girl I want isn't ashamed of her man. So, let's try this one more time. What did you do for me last night?' Imran stares into her eyes, his face predatory and handsome.

'I . . . showed you my moves . . .' she says, hanging her head so her hair forms a modesty curtain between us.

Imran shoves her hair back and lifts her chin. '*Moves*? What, we in primary school now?'

'But *you* know.' Jasmine pokes his chest in a horrible combination of desperation and playfulness. 'Why do I have to—'

He grips her jaw with a viciousness that makes my heart jump into my throat. 'Cos I said, innit? If you want to be my woman, spell it out for my friends here.' He twists her head round to face us, but I'm the one blushing.

'I gave Imran a lap dance,' she says reluctantly.

'What kind of lap dance?' he asks, practically chewing her ear off.

'A naked one,' she admits.

His hand slides up her chest till I'm afraid he's going to make her do it again right here in the dinner hall. 'Now get off me. I don't date sluts.'

Jasmine looks at him in horror seconds before he gives her a shove. She hits the floor with a thwack, mint pants on show for the world to see. The humiliation in her eyes is unbearable.

Noah starts hooting with laughter, snapping pics. Daevon covers his mouth, but within seconds, spittle and laughter burst through. Having witnessed the whole thing, Jasmine's mates rush over to help her up, blasting Imran with death stares.

'What?' he retorts, but no one challenges him.

Nobody ever challenges him.

'Mission complete!' Noah says, saluting Imran.

'Nah, rules is rules,' Imran says. 'Didn't think that bitch was worth filming. I'm picking someone better for the Challenge.'

I grab my stuff and run from the scene like a coward, wishing I had the guts to call Imran out.

CHAPTER 10

Maths is after lunch, and it's such a relief. Ms Mughal's classroom has become my sanctum sanctorum. So it comes as a nasty surprise when I see each desk bearing a little sheet of fluorescent yellow paper. Nothing screams *Fail!* louder than a surprise test on radioactive paper.

'Turn that frown upside down, mister!' Ms Mughal says wagging a finger at me. 'It's a game, not a test.'

'Oh, bingo!' says Kara happily, unhooking her backpack from her shoulders. 'Yay!'

'What's bingo got to do with maths?' I ask quietly as Ms Mughal calls the register.

'Are you serious? We play it, like, *all* the time. Who was your teacher before?'

'Mr Gordon.'

'Whoa! My cousin's in his class, and every lesson, she feels like she's actually getting dumber.'

'Your cousin ain't wrong.'

'Hey, wait. If you came from Gordon's class, you must be some kind of genius to jump two sets.'

'I'm no genius,' I say miserably.

'OK!' Ms Mughal says, minimizing the register on the screen and springing up from her chair. 'Who's going to remind us of the rules?'

As she says this, she sidles towards the door and executes a solid back kick, slamming the door shut without breaking a sweat. I glance around, but nobody else seems impressed by this. Tough crowd.

Ray puts his hand up and explains the basics of maths bingo.

'Thank you, Ray. OK – who wants to start us off?' Ms Mughal says, holding up the largest die I have ever laid eyes on. 'Ilyas, how about you?'

The red inflatable cube flips through the air, and I catch it. 'Can I keep it?'

Ms Mughal laughs, shaking her head. 'One throw is all you get.'

I stand up, and put a spin on the die as I throw it, narrowly missing the lighting.

'Come on, lucky five!' I say rubbing my hands together.

It lands on a two. On the interactive board is a set of multicoloured buttons with numbers on. Miss taps a two, and a question pops up on the screen inside a balloon.

'Solve the question, then cross off the answer if it's on your bingo card.' Ms Mughal is bouncing on the balls of her feet enthusiastically.

I know it's only a revision game with no actual prize, but I *really* want to win. Channelling Black Panther's sister Shuri, with her genius-level intellect, I work through the question as quickly as I can. Ms Mughal is crouching beside Ray, discreetly helping him with the answer. I compare this to Gordon's method of drawing the lesson to a grinding halt, followed by some naming and shaming.

After a heated final between me and Kara, the pips go, marking the end of the lesson. As we're packing up, Mr Gordon strolls in like he owns the room.

'Well, Ms Mughal,' he says, eyeing me critically. 'How's Mr Mian faring in your set? You know you can always send him back down if he requires a *sterner approach*.' He makes a fist, like he's volunteering to punch my lights out.

'Actually, Ilyas is doing really well, Mr Gordon,' she says, smiling proudly. 'He's a credit to you. Enthusiastic *and* smart.'

Cheeks burning, I pack my stuff away, only suddenly I'm ten times clumsier, and my bag seems to hate me.

Mr Gordon looks disappointed. 'Hmm, well I suppose it's early days yet. Don't dawdle, boy! I believe you have PE now.' Mr Gordon turns back to Ms Mughal. 'Hooligans, the lot of them,' I hear him say as I scurry out of the door. 'Honestly, you'd be better off working in a girls' school. Easier to handle.'

I'm in no rush to get to the changing rooms. PE is the last lesson of the day – like a final-level boss waiting to torture me for my freedom. I imagine having Quicksilver's powers, and time warping straight to 3.10 p.m. That would be so dope.

'Honestly, Kelly – what were you thinking?'

My ears perk up at the sound of Jade's voice.

'I'm sorry . . .' Kelly says, her cheeks flushing red, her back up against a noticeboard.

'Are you? Because sometimes it seems like your sole purpose in life is to make us look stupid.'

'Yah! And what is up with those boots?' Melanie snipes in her almost-American accent. 'Swear to God you nicked them off a tramp.'

'I happen to like these boots,' Kelly says, her lower lip protruding. 'We have history.'

'The boots can stay,' Jade says promptly.

Melanie's eyes bulge mutinously.

'What? They're supposed to be ironic.'

'Fine.' Melanie gives a thwarted sigh before turning back to Kelly. 'But cut back on the frappés, Carbi B. I'm getting stretch marks just looking at you.'

I move along before they report me for stalking.

*

The changing room is filled with boys talking shit as they get into their PE kit. Topics include all the standard stuff: girls, PS5 vs Xbox One X, how lit the latest *Call of Duty* game is, some diss track that has gone viral, and a sex act they're doing stateside that has got ten people hospitalized and one person killed. I glance at everyone's bodies, feeling like a donkey that stumbled into a stable full of stallions.

Drawing as little attention to my wimpy self as possible, I quietly get changed into my football kit.

The pitch is a cold, damp nightmare. I zone out for no more than five seconds, imagining an epic battle between PakCore and the Quintet: an elite group of five highly skilled supernatural assassins. Unfortunately five seconds turn out to be a lifetime when you're in the middle of a football match with half of the school's elite squad involved. My nemesis takes the form of a spinning black-and-white orb. The ball smacks me in the middle of my face with the sound of a punched pig's belly.

'You all right, bro?' Daevon asks, jogging over.

'I'b fyb,' I say, eyes watering. Making sure my nose is still there, my fingertips come away stained red with blood. I take it back; I'm the exact opposite of fine.

'What are you two doing here?' snaps Mr Kumar, our PE teacher. 'Back in the game, you slackers. Now!'

'He's proper mashed up his nose, sir,' explains Daevon.

I smile apologetically, and blood gushes from my nostrils, drenching my shirt.

Mr Kumar shakes his head. 'It's always something with you, isn't it, Mian? Go on. Get yourself down to the medical room.'

'Shall I take him, sir?' Daevon asks.

Clearly the answer is an eye-gouging no.

I march myself off to the school nurse, debating whether a

busted nose is a fair trade for getting out of PE on this blustery afternoon.

Twenty minutes later, I'm back in the locker room, holding an ice pack to my throbbing schnoz. Dad, Shaista and me all have the famous Mian family nose. Large and humped. It's the reason my sister spends forever with her make-up kit, contouring her nose to make it look 'smaller, thinner, sexier'. It's actually the subject of one of her most-liked YouTube vids. I once heard her tell Amma she's going to get a nose job when she's eighteen. So Amma gave her this long lecture about loving yourself the way God made you.

'Don't be so old-fashioned!' my sister had replied. 'If people can get boob jobs and gastric bands on the NHS, then why shouldn't I fix my nose with a little nip and tuck?'

'Your dad has the same nose.' Amma looked offended.

'Yes, and he should have kept it instead of passing it on to his glamorous daughter. What was he thinking?'

Amma is a superwoman to put up with all our stupid problems without going on a killing spree.

Experimentally I lift off the ice pack. The inside of my nose feels like it's been burned with a flame thrower, but the outside is numb with frostbite. *Result!* Now the only thing left to decide is whether to go back on the field or hide out here for the next forty-five minutes. No contest. Grabbing my sketch pad and pencils, I quickly lose myself in my art.

In the creative zone, time and reality are meaningless concepts. So it's a shock when I hear loud banter as the lads barge back into my private art studio. I quickly hide my drawing in my bag as Mr Kumar marches over to the communal showers and turns the water on.

'Good game, lads! But you stink like skunks. In and out of these showers double quick, then off you go. No hanging about,' he barks.

'Come on, sir,' Imran says, bashing his football boots together like boxing gloves, scattering mud all over the floor. 'Tell us who your Man of the Match was.'

Mr Kumar gives him a withering look.

'It's all right, sir,' says James, who's vice captain of the school team. 'I know it's me, so . . .'

Imran bops him on the head with a boot.

James touches his hair and inspects the mud on his fingers. 'Oi, you wanker!'

'Man of the Match was –' Mr Kumar uses his beer belly to give a drum roll – 'Imran Akhtar!'

Imran raises his arms, throwing his head back with delight. 'Thank you, fans!'

I roll my eyes, then do a double take. The expression on his face, the hazy lighting and the Christlike pose is *perfect* for a PakCore victory sketch. I reach for my phone, then stop. If someone catches me taking a picture in the boys locker room, I am so dead. But damn, that pose is *too* good to miss. Imran sheds his clothes and heads for the shower.

'Out the way!' he bellows, shoving a kid from the prime spot right at the front.

I pull out an aloe vera shower wipe and rub it over my chest, then scrub my pits. Amma wrote the school a letter informing them that as a practising Muslim, I wouldn't be showering communally. Thank God, because compared to these dudes, my body is jokes. The bullying would never end.

'Who do think is the fittest teacher in school?' James asks.

Same shit, different day.

The boys in the shower begin throwing out names. Someone

says Mrs Waldorf, to bellows of laughter and disgust.

'You got granny problems, mate,' Imran says. 'Me? I got a boner for Ms Mughal.'

I flinch. Thought we'd agreed Ms Mughal is off limits. A teacher like that is not wank material; she's like the older sister you wish you had. But this is Imran changing the rules again.

'That teacher is fine as hell,' James agrees. 'I'd bang her.'

James and Imran play one-up, laughing about the increasingly disturbing things they'd like to do to my maths teacher. My heart beats faster, stomach churning with lava. Jasmine's face flashes before my eyes – her mint-green knickers and tears of shame. It's not my fault – *I* didn't do anything . . .

But I *should* have done something.

'SHUT YOUR MOUTH!' I roar.

Imran turns his head slowly, observing me through the deluge of warm water. 'You say something?'

'You heard,' I reply, my voice cracking, my breath coming in panicked little gasps.

'Ooooh,' some little stirrer says. 'Kid thinks he's hard.'

I square my chicken-bone shoulders as Imran continues to stare at me over a bulging deltoid.

'Hush yourself, unless you wanna get bodied.' He turns his back, dismissing me.

'Then don't talk shit about women!'

Imran steps out of the shower and glares at me. 'I'll talk about who I want, when I want. Understand, little man? *And* about your mother and your sister.'

'Do that and watch.'

Every head turns to look at me in surprise, but nobody is more surprised than me. *Why can't I shut up?* In two minutes, the pips will go, and I could go home alive instead of zipped up in a body bag.

Imran's large wet feet slap the locker-room floor as he strides towards me, completely unconcerned by his nakedness. My life flashes before my eyes.

'Come at me, bro,' he says, raising his chin.

'Look, I ain't starting nothing,' I say, dropping my eyes, because frankly I don't want to die. 'Just don't talk so much shit about women, OK? Pisses me off, bro—'

His fist connects with my jaw, whipping it so fast, I think it might actually have spun round twice. The locker room swims in and out of focus. Punch-drunk, by some miracle I keep my feet. My throbbing lips are another matter. Touching them paints my palm in red making this the goriest day of my life.

'Don't ever disrespect me, fam,' Imran growls. 'Understand? Even when I'm on your sister, you shut your mouth and enjoy the show.'

Laughter explodes around me, boys' faces melding into one nightmarish creature – a bloated demon with a thousand cackling mouths. Tears fill my eyes, and my skull creaks, straining against a rapidly swelling brain. *Kablam!* A detonation behind my eyeballs sends shockwaves of adrenalin fizzing through my body.

Finally I have become PakCore, the destroyer of thugs.

As the superpowered instrument of Imran's comeuppance, I rush towards him, an unstoppable force—

I trip and spill, forehead striking the centre of Imran's chest with a *schlap* before I rebound and hit the floor. I close my eyes, bracing myself for the biggest shit-kicking of my life. Hope Amma doesn't miss me too much . . .

A united gasp forces my eyes open.

The next few seconds happen in a fast-cutting blur. Imran's left foot is planted in the middle of the looped handle on his sports bag. His ankle shifts, and the strap snaps taut with the sound of a whip. His right foot clumsily stomps on Noah's mud-caked football boots, the exposed studs stabbing his sole. Then he's falling, all six feet of him, muscular legs whooshing up into the air. *One!* The back of his head strikes a clothes hook. *Two!* It cracks against the side of the bench. *Three!* His head slams against the moulded floor tiles with a reverberating thud. Only the sound of Thor's hammer could be louder.

Stunned, we all stare at Imran lying flat on his back, eyes closed for business.

'You all right, bruv?' someone asks.

No answer.

I scramble up and nudge Imran with my foot. He doesn't move. My heart drops through a bottomless abyss. This cannot be happening.

'What have you done?' booms Mr Gilchrist.

I turn round slowly. Mr Gilchrist stands with his feet apart, blazing with fury. I glance back, hoping Imran's unconscious body was nothing more than a revenge fantasy I cooked up in my stupid, comic-obsessed brain. But it's still there, only now his head is surrounded by a crimson halo of blood.

Shit. I just killed Imran Akhtar.

CHAPTER 11

My mind begins to unravel. In confusion, I grab my bag to place over Imran's exposed junk. That's when Gilchrist loses it and pulls me away. My bag hits the ground like a sack of potatoes. In hindsight, I realize it looked a lot like I was trying to finish the job instead of spare Imran's blushes.

'Right, you little terror!' Gilchrist booms, dragging me along the corridor. 'We'll have your parents in, and you can explain this to the police.'

'Anything I can do?' Mr Kumar asks, scratching behind an ear, eyes twitching nervously.

Mr Gilchrist secures me in a headlock as I thrash about.

'For God's sake, man!' he yells. 'Call an ambulance and send the other boys home!'

Live teacher-on-teacher rage. Shit got serious. The fight goes out of me, and Mr Gilchrist hauls me to his office like a rag doll.

I'm sat in between Amma and Dad, on the opposite side of the table from Mr Gilchrist and the police liaison, Officer Pryce. I'm still in my bloodstained PE kit, knobbly knees knocking together, holding an ice pack to lips that look like freshly done butt implants.

'We're so sorry,' Amma says. 'He's never done anything like it in his life. I promise you, he's the gentlest boy in the world.'

'I can't believe it!' says Dad, trying to rub off the last of his thinning hair. He's still in his grocer's apron. 'Imran's a good lad and twice this one's size.'

'Good lad, my foot!' Amma says, snorting. 'The Akhtar boy is nothing but trouble. Terrorizes his own mother!'

'The point is,' Dad says, 'how could Ilyas have landed a blow on Imran? That's David and Goliath right there!'

All this time, Dad's been telling me to stand up for myself, and when I finally do, he sides with the enemy. I hate my life.

'I didn't, though!' I say. 'It was an accident, Dad. He was mouthing off, saying all this stuff about . . .' I pause – can't bring myself to repeat the dirty things Imran said in my mother's presence.

'Sticks and stones, young man!' says the officer, leaning forward. With bulging biceps and silky black hair, the woman looks perfect for the role of She-Hulk. 'You're in high school,' she continues. 'If you're going to be assaulting every kid who calls you a nasty name, you'll end up in prison before you're eighteen! Do you understand?'

I grunt. Amma gives me a sharp prod.

'Yes, miss,' I say, sulkily.

'Well,' says Mr Gilchrist, eyeing my written statement distastefully. Beside it are another two. They could literally be from anyone. No shortage of offers to back up golden boy Imran against a wasteman like me. 'It appears the attack wasn't altogether unprovoked. But violence is never the answer, as Officer Pryce has just outlined for you. Now according to Stanley Park rules, there are sufficient grounds for a permanent exclusion—'

Amma gasps.

'But,' he continues, raising a finger, 'we take a liberal approach here, and I do believe Ilyas is a good lad at heart – current actions notwithstanding. If we don't give our own another chance, then what sort of a school are we? I'm going to recommend to the principal and governors five days of suspension, effective immediately, followed by one week of hour-long after-school detentions with me.'

'But what about his GCSEs?' Amma looks fraught. 'He can't afford a week out of school.'

Dad nudges her and shakes his head. She ignores him, large eyes imploring Mr Gilchrist to reconsider.

'The school has a legal obligation to provide work for your son to continue his studies at home. It will all be uploaded to the school's virtual learning environment, Mrs Mian.'

'Come on, Mr Gilchrist – you know as well as I do that his studies will suffer. How can a fifteen-year-old self-motivate for an entire week?' Amma blinks like a sad owl.

'Your son is the cause of another student missing out on his classes for who knows how long,' Gilchrist points out. 'The medics have advised us they are on top of the situation, and Imran should have no lasting damage, but one simply cannot underestimate the negative impact this will have on *his* GCSEs.'

What about smoking pot and disrupting every class he's in? I want to shout. *What effect will* that *have on the idiot's results? And what about what he did to Jasmine? What will that do to her GCSEs? And let's not forget Imran never does any homework, anyway. You're only giving him a free pass cos of all the cups he's won for the school.*

'I'm so sorry,' Amma says pulling a tissue out of her handbag to dab at her eyes.

'Please don't cry, Amma!' I beg, reaching for her.

She stiffens. 'I'll stop crying when you thank these nice people for giving you a second chance.'

'Chance? One week's suspension and five hours of after-school detentions! How is that a *chance*?'

Amma waits for my rude outburst to cease before continuing. 'And you promise me –' the rebuke in her eyes is painful – '*promise me* you'll never raise your hand to another student ever again, no matter how much they provoke you. What's the point of your teachers making allowances for you to do your Friday prayers if you're going to attack people?' She sniffs. 'I thought we raised you better than that.'

My own eyes fill with tears of frustration. I don't want to let Amma down, but if only she knew the truth, she'd see that I was trying to stand up and do the right thing. But the world in my head – the one in which PakCore swoops in and saves the day – is not the world I live in.

On the drive home, I sit in the back, sinking lower and lower as my parents argue over why I'm such a screw-up.

'No more hanging out with the bad boys! You're grounded until further notice.' Amma catches my eye in the rear-view mirror, her brow like a scrunched-up paper bag. 'I don't care how cool it makes you feel. Associate with skunks, and you start smelling like one.'

'Now wait a minute,' Dad says, hanging a sharp left that sends me sweeping across the back seat and banging my head against the window. 'Hanging around with Imran's what taught him to be assertive. It's miles better than hanging with artsy-fartsy anoraks and sissies.'

'Oh for goodness sake! It's not the 1950s, Osman,' Amma snaps. 'Ilyas isn't like you or Amir. He's a gentle, intelligent sort of boy.'

'You 'avin' a laugh? Amir was so intelligent, he got summoned by Uncle Moneybags himself! S'why the selfish git buggered off.' He shakes his head. 'Promised his old man he'd help out with the family business so I'd pay his college fees, then pulled a fast one.'

On and on it goes.

Gently squeezing my throbbing nose, I lower my head till my tears gather into a massive droplet on the tip. I'm not manly enough, clever enough or even gentle enough. Not only am I completely useless, but I'm wrecking my parents' relationship too.

CHAPTER 12

Daevon texts me on Saturday.

> Yo, what's good?

I've been thinking about Daevon a lot. Wondering how Gilchrist of all people suddenly appeared in the boys' changing room. Daevon was standing at Gilchrist's elbow with an expression I didn't recognize at the time. Now I'm thinking it was guilt.

> Why you snake me out to Gilchrist???

> When it all kicked off, I went to get help.
> Figured Imran was going to merc you!

> Thanks! Fam hate me, got suspended. Detentions for LIFE!!!!

I wait for a reply, getting madder and madder by the minute. When it finally comes, I boil over. It's the middle-finger emoji. I hurl my phone across the room.

'Oi!' Dad says, appearing out of nowhere. 'Want me to confiscate your phone 'n' all? In case you hadn't realized, you're in the doghouse, mate.'

Silently fuming, I go over and pick up my phone, wiping off the dust bunnies.

'Wanna work your way back into me and your mum's good graces? Well, you'll be working bloody hard, I can tell you! Ten minutes. Get dressed, powder your nose, then you're coming with me to the store. It's time you started to learn your future.'

'But I gotta revise!'

My protests fall on deaf ears. Dad blinks at me threateningly, retracting his thick neck into his shoulders. 'Di'nt you hear what I just said? Pull your finger out! Ten minutes.' He points at me for emphasis, then shuts the door.

Man, I hate going to Haji Mian & Sons. All these rude people everywhere, talking loudly, stealing the plastic bags cos they can't be bothered to spend a pound at Tesco. And don't get me started on the abuse of the produce. Sniffing, poking and scratching. *Wanna make out with a mooli? Buy the damn thing first!* Of course I learned the hard way to keep my trap shut. One time, I caught a woman taking marrow biopsies with her nails and asked her to stop. She went and complained to Dad, who clipped me round the ear. Respecting elders is how we roll, even when they're wrong.

So I spend the whole morning in an itchy white coat stacking shelves and trying to help customers who seem to assume I can speak all five hundred Asian languages just cos I'm brown. And you should see the look on their faces when I ask them to repeat it in English.

'Ilyas!' Dad shouts for the tenth time in two hours.

He's up at the till serving a long line of customers. They all turn round to stare at me as I scamper over, rubbing at my war wounds. Turns out stacking shelves is a lot like playing with knives.

'Yes, Dad?'

'Fetch a mop and clear up this mess.'

I look down and see a glass bottle floating in a sea of garlic sauce. Lovely.

In the back room, I fill a bucket with water and bung in a few drops of pine disinfectant. Grabbing a mop, and tucking a kitchen roll under one arm, I carry everything to the till. I cover the puddle in swathes of kitchen roll. The beige sauce soaks straight through, reducing them to a soupy sludge.

'Pick up the bottle first, you div!' Dad snaps. Then, turning to the woman who must be responsible for the spill, he says, 'Honestly, what do they teach 'em in school these days?'

This may surprise you, Dad, but cleaning floors isn't on the curriculum. In fact, it probably counts as slave labour, since you're making me do it for free.

'Why's he not in school today?' Ms Nosy inquires.

'This one picked a fight with a kid nearly twice his size, would you believe!'

'No!' she says, giving me evils like Dad had just told her I kill kittens for fun.

'It's why he's got them ugly bruises under his eyes. Punched on the hooter.'

The woman continues to stare. I take my aggression out on the floor with the wet mop.

'Schools have gone soft,' she concludes. 'Spare the rod and spoil the child. That's what my dear mother used to say.'

Your mum was a psycho.

'Exactly!' Dad says, reaching into her basket and pricing a packet of curry powder. 'Used to give my elder son licks with the belt. Now he's at Harvard studying business management!'

'Ooh, you must be *so* proud,' the lady coos.

Apparently, getting beats off Dad was the secret of Amir's success.

'Thank God, don't I? But my old woman won't let me teach this one any manners. She's all "Mumsnet this" and "Supernanny that". All that modern malarkey!'

'Heavens!' says the woman. 'The internet has made us into a

nation of deviants. All this sexy-camming and selfie-shooting, I ask you! What've we got to show for it? Nothing but mental health problems, stabbings and suicides!'

'A woman after my own heart!' Dad says, going all dopey.

'Married the wrong girl, didn't you?' She chuckles.

I hurriedly clean up the mess before I add to it with my own vomit.

'Listen,' says the woman in my ear, nearly making me jump out of my skin. 'Make your dad proud. He's a good man, and children always learn too late that parents won't be around forever.'

How about you learn not to break bottles and mind your own business?

'Yeah, thanks,' I mumble. Two minutes of bantz with a middle-aged Romeo, and this woman thinks she's got my family sussed.

As the morning wears on, Dad works me harder than any of his employees. Then his workers get in on the act too, bossing me around like a sweatshop boy. I think about contacting Childline, but I'm in enough trouble as it is.

At lunchtime, I go and hide in the stockroom to eat my sandwiches and flip through some rough panels I sketched for my comic. The pictures are fire, but now there's a bitter aftertaste because PakCore shares faces with Imran – the reason I'm in this mess.

'There you are!'

For one horrible moment, I think Imran has made a miraculous recovery and is here to deliver the arse-whupping of a century. It's actually Zaman, his older, less attractive cousin. As he steps towards me, my eyes dart around nervously, searching for an escape route. Or a weapon. *Does a can of fly spray count as a weapon?*

He grips my arm.

'Piss off!' I yell, flapping my arms like a turkey trying to take off.

He crushes my windpipe between his dry worker's fingers. 'You put Imran in hospital. The only reason I'm not choking you now is because Uncle Osman is the boss.'

'Except you are choking me!' I squeak, pushing a palm at him, imagining I've summoned a mystical mandala like Doctor Strange. 'Plus, it was an accident. Imran tripped over his own bag.'

Zaman processes this new bit of info, then sneers. 'Obviously. As if a tiny maggot like you could take my cousin in a fair fight!'

'Everything OK?' Yunus asks, standing at the threshold.

Zaman releases me and ruffles my hair in a mildly threatening way.

'All good,' I lie.

Yunus gives us some side-eye, then grabs a couple of boxes of soap powder from the shelves. Zaman flashes his eyes at me, then retreats to the shop floor. A minute later, Yunus follows him out.

My sandwich goes in the bin, the thought of Imran's return killing my appetite. On that day, I'll be a sitting duck. I think about asking Dad for help, then remember his answer to everything: *Man up!*

Grabbing my navy-blue parka, I head out. Up on the shop floor, Dad is holding a mug of tea, telling dirty jokes in Punjabi to two of his workers.

'Dad, just nipping out to see Amma, 'kay?' I say, beelining for the door.

'No, absolutely not,' he says. 'Can't go running off to your Amma every time life gives you lemons. Man up.'

'I'll be right back. Just for lunch, yeah? I need to apologize for letting her down.'

One of the workers chips in. '*Ainu jaan dhey* – let him go. When his mum greets him with slaps, he'll come running back.'

Jogging to the library, I feel ice crystals scrape against my cheeks. I can't even remember the last time it snowed, like, *proper* snowed.

Crossing the street, it comes back to me. Year 6, school playground, me and Daevon having this great idea of building a snow Batman. We were so proud of our sculpture, until Lee Garrison and his mates beat us up for building a 'snow boyfriend'.

The memory makes me nauseous. An uncomfortable idea drops into my head. Is this the reason Daevon started making tough mates like Imran and Noah? Did he start seeing me as a bully magnet and a threat to his own safety?

At the end of the road, the frosted glass apex of our local library pops into view, and as I travel down the decline, the rest of the pyramid appears to rise. Our library was a total tip when I was small. Then Amma got involved, mobilizing a group of shouty parents, who campaigned for renovation and funding, arguing that every child deserved access to books. Amma can be fierce when she needs to be. She bullied the local MP, Theodon Papadakis, to take the war to Westminster. Funding finally went through, and we got our shiny new library.

The sensors pick me up, and the doors hum open.

'Hey, Ilyas!' says Mohamud, the security guard. We fist bump. 'Why aren't you at school today?'

Mohamud fled Mogadishu about four years ago after pirates hijacked his family's house. Came for them in the dead of night with guns and knives and messed-up intentions. Trouble is, things got worse when his family arrived in Britain. He lost his mother and three sisters in a fire started by faulty electrical wiring. Mohamud only escaped that night because he'd been praying *Tarawih* at the local mosque. The thing is, the guy still has a hundred-watt smile. Whenever he lights the room up with it, I feel guilty for complaining about my own stupid problems.

I fill Mohamud in on my temporary exclusion.

He sighs. 'Mate, why are you doing this to your mum?'

I shrug, too sad to give my reasons; too exhausted to explain that *I'm* the victim here.

'Seriously, brother, you don't know how lucky you are to have access to free education and two loving parents.'

I'm standing in a tar pit, sinking lower and lower with every word he speaks.

Mohamud puts a slim hand on my shoulder, and leans in close. 'Look, I can see you're sorry. That's half the battle won. Now go give your mum the biggest, cheesiest hug you can manage. You're her favourite, you know?'

'Ya think?'

'Ye-ah!' he says, appearing surprised that I'd doubt this. 'Auntie Fozia's always telling everybody about your drawings and how kind you are. She said you look after an abandoned rabbit better than some parents look after their own kids.'

A jalapeño fieriness spreads across my cheeks. Teenage boys and bunnies aren't supposed to mix. This gets out, I'm dead.

'Don't be embarrassed,' Mohamud says quickly. 'Allah placed mercy in your heart. You're like a young Abu Bakr, the first Caliph of Islam.'

I give him a seriously doubtful look.

'He was all about the baby camels. Abu Bakr literally means "Father of the Camel". Maybe we should call you Abu 'Arnab!'

Sparkle's Daddy? I chuckle in spite of my current mood. 'Thanks, bro.'

Inside the library, Amma's sitting on a beanbag in the 'interactive section', reading a picture book to a bunch of hypnotized little kids. She's doing all the voices and everything, just like she used to when I was small. Warm bath first; mad wailing as she'd scrub my crusty heels; then marshmallows and a dope story, snuggling up on the sofa together. Man, I miss those days.

Amma notices me, blinking behind her large glasses, then asks a worried-looking lady to take over. I raise my hands and shake my head furiously, but it's too late cos she's coming over.

'What's the matter, *beyta*?' she asks, taking her glasses off and massaging the bridge of her nose. 'I thought you were helping Dad at the store today?'

'Yeah, I was. I am. I just . . . I feel crap, Amma. I don't want you hating on me.'

Amma strokes my cheek, her eyebrows dipping. 'Silly boy. I could never hate you. You've disappointed us, and I'm sure we're partly to blame . . . but *hate* you? Don't ever think that again.'

I shake my head. 'This is all on me. Imran's been pushing me for *time*. But I didn't have to get into it, right? I could've just walked away and spared you the embarrassment.'

She nods. 'They've stitched his wounds, and he's on the mend. Thankfully it wasn't as bad as it could've been, but his mother is still worried.'

'I'm sorry . . .'

'Are you?'

Her questions catches me off guard, and I shake my head.

'He could have died, Ilyas. Or ended up with permanent brain damage. How would that have made you feel?'

'But he was seriously out of order—'

'You have to stop thinking with your fists. No matter what your father might say, there's always a better way of handling things.' She looks over her shoulder. The kids stare back with eyes like fishing rods. 'Better get back, love. Chantelle doesn't like doing the voices.'

I want to say more, want her to help me figure stuff out, but I realize Amma has a life outside of our family.

She turns back briefly. 'I want you to go to mosque and think about how you could have handled things differently. And if you get stuck, I want you to speak to the Imam.'

Wish I could be the son Amma deserves, but every time I think about Imran chatting shit about her, I want to smash his pretty-boy face in with a cricket bat. Truth be told, my life would be a million times easier if he never came back.

Carrying a ton of self-loathing on my back, I head back to the shop.

CHAPTER 13

'Aren't you scared for your life, dating the boss's daughter?' Yunus asks Zaman, an inch of ash dangling from his cigarette.

I'm standing on a stool, quietly replenishing the various packets of Laziza Masala mix on the shelf, when this bombshell drops. Shaista and Zaman: my bougie sis and Imran's ex-gansta cuz? No freaking way . . . though it would explain the weird call to her phone the other day.

'What's to be scared of?' Zaman says, flexing his rotator-cuff muscles with a smirk. 'I'll probably marry her.'

'Osman *bhai* would never allow it. She's his princess,' Yunus says, waving his fag in the air like a conductor's baton.

'Uncle Osman will have no choice when she's carrying my baby.'

Yunus stares aghast at Zaman, then shakes his head tutting.

I grip the shelf, steadying myself. Zaman has to be lying. Shais would *never* date a gangsta.

But the idea refuses to go away.

That afternoon, I pluck up the courage and confront my sister.

'Shais, can I talk to you?' I ask, hanging in her bedroom doorway.

'Only if it's not in Street,' she says, sitting in front of her laptop, designing a flattering thumbnail for her latest video.

'Look, man, this is serious!'

She rolls her eyes. 'So is basic grammar. Why are teenagers so obsessed with speaking in increasingly stupid ways, anyway?

Soon enough, you'll have to learn to communicate properly, or nobody's going to employ you.'

I shrug. 'Are you . . . um . . .'

'Incredibly beautiful and talented? Why, yes. Do I have over *twenty-two* thousand followers on YouTube? Yes again. Am I available for Hollywood film roles? Speak to my agent . . .' She pauses, like she just got a whiff of something rotten. 'Unless you're one of those casting-couch directors, in which case, please hand yourself in to the nearest police station.'

'Shais!' I snap. 'This is important.'

She knits her painted eyebrows together, about to unleash grammatically correct fury when she detects the edge in my voice.

'Are you dating Zaman?' I blurt.

She's searching for a comeback, her false eyelashes fluttering like feathers. Exposure has fried my sister's brain.

'So it *is* true,' I say, shaking my head sadly. 'Man is talking trash about you.'

'What?'

'When everyone takes breaks at the store, Zaman sits there boasting about you being his girl. Real personal stuff he ain't got no business telling others.'

She narrows her eyes. 'Like what?'

I look down, my face roasting with shame. 'Said he was going to get you . . . um . . . Make you have his baby, so Dad would have to let him marry you.' The last bit comes out in a whisper cos I feel dirty just saying it.

An uncomfortable silence foams around us, worry momentarily flashing over Shais's forehead.

'You are a terrible liar.' She dismisses me with a flick of her nails.

'*Wallahi!*' I say, placing a hand over my heart.

'Get out. I've got work to do.'

I hover for a moment longer, but she goes back to editing the thumbnail graphic. I feel like the World's Biggest Arsehole.

'Where's your sister run off to?' Amma asks at dinner-time. 'Her lasagne's getting cold, and she won't eat stringy cheese.'

'I'll get her . . .' I grumble, scrapping my chair back.

I'm about to go up the stairs when a cold draught tickles the side of my face. Glancing to the right, I see a sliver of light, and realize the front door hasn't been closed properly. Peering into the street, there's no sign of Shais. About to shut it, I notice two figures on the opposite side of the street, partially hidden by the conker tree. Dropping down to all fours, I slip out in stealth mode, taking up a recon position behind our wall. Now I'm PakCore, engaging the advanced tech in my bodysuit, thin silver lenses clicking into position behind the eyeholes of my mask for some old-school magnification. A giggle cuts my imaginings, and Shaista scampers away from the tree. A hand flies out, gripping her wrist. Instinctively my jaw tightens. A second later, Zaman steps out from behind the tree, pulls her into his arms and presses his lips to hers.

The gross sight makes me want to gouge my eyes out. Then something worse happens. Zaman's hand slips inside my sister's jeans. She tries to pull away, but he's locked on, like Killer Frost sapping Superman's powers with a death kiss. Her hands close over his arm, and I can't work out whether she's trying to push him off or living her best Bollywood life.

'Ilyas?' Dad's voice drifts towards me. 'You found her?'

Shais may be Dad's favourite, but if he catches her now, he's guaranteed to hit the roof. Switching to Damage Control Mode, I scuttle back inside.

'She's OK, Dad,' I say, intercepting him in the corridor,

directing him back to the dining room. 'On the phone to one of her gal pals, innit?'

Amma raises her eyebrows disapprovingly. 'What sort of time is this to be phoning a friend?' She starts to rise, ready to give Shais a piece of her mind.

'Allow it, Amma,' I say quickly. 'One of her mates is having a massive meltdown. Shais is giving life-saving advice.'

'That's my girl!' Dad says proudly, stuffing a spoonful of lasagne into his mouth, a spatter of sweetcorn and mince raining back on to his plate. 'Always thinking of others first.'

I sigh inwardly. Crisis averted. For now.

Later that evening, I catch Shais on her way to the bathroom.

'Are you in love with Zaman?' I say with subtleness of a meat cleaver.

'None of your business,' she says, making scary eyes before stepping past me.

'I saw you guys, by the tree.'

She freezes, shoulders hunched. I can imagine the expression on her face, a volcano in the early stages of erupting. 'Are you *blackmailing* me? Threatening to go public to Amma and Dad?'

'No, never. I just . . . I need to know he isn't bullying you into doing stuff you ain't comfortable with. Cos . . . that's what it sorta looked like.' I twiddle my index fingers nervously.

She looks at me, sadness tweaking the corners of her lips. 'Look, appreciate your concern, but *not* the spying. Do you honestly think there's a man alive who could take advantage of *moi*? Razor-sharp wit and vitriolic put-downs, remember? You're the one who needs saving all the time, ickle Ilyas, not me.'

Strutting over to the bathroom, she's projecting power, but I sense fear under the cracks. There's something about living with a person your whole life – you just *know*. Without saying a word about it, Shais has just told me everything I need to know about her relationship with Zaman. And that makes everything ten times worse. No point in telling Dad; Shais will only hate me for the betrayal. The only way I can rescue her is to expose Zaman. Shaista's got to be the one to kick him to the kerb.

CHAPTER 14

Dad's trying to talk down an irate customer who's more wound up than a cuckoo clock. The old man's ranting in Urdu about credit-card fraud. Like Dad would ever get involved in something like *that* no matter how bad business might be.

After a couple of days waiting, I finally see my chance to expose Zaman. While my dad's distracted, I dart towards the back room.

A woman blocks my way.

'Can you help me?' she asks, looking me up and down, the corners of her lips dipping doubtfully.

'Uh, not right now. But—'

'Do you work here?'

'Yes . . .'

'Then it's your job to help me.' She adjusts her glasses. 'Get me the ingredients for *Nkontomire*, please.'

I open my mouth to apologize and tell her I have literally no clue what that is, but I catch the look in her eye and realize going there is suicide. I gulp.

'Er, you wanna sit down while I sort it for you?' I ask, grabbing her a chair.

'Now that's a much better attitude!' she says, dusting the seat with a hanky before sitting down. 'And don't take too long.'

After giving her an ingratiating smile, I dive into aisle three and whip out my phone. Thank God for Google. *Nkontomire* turns out to be spinach stew. I memorize the list of ingredients, grab a basket, and whip round the store like I'm on *Supermarket Sweep*, while the woman chuckles on her phone with a mate.

Spinach, plum tomatoes, onions, garlic, ginger, chilli . . . What the heck is egusi?

'Yo, Yunus!' I call. 'We got *egusi*?'

He looks at me like I stuttered. 'Eggs?'

'No, deffo *egusi*.'

He shakes his head.

I glance in the direction of the customer, and she's staring right back, nodding forbiddingly with the phone pressed to her ear.

Seeking refuge in aisle five, I check my trusty phone to see if *egusi* has an alias. 'Melon seeds!' I say triumphantly.

'Don't need them,' the woman calls out.

I proudly present the basket of *Nkontomire* ingredients with a big smile. The lady points at the floor without missing a beat of her telephone conversation. Placing the basket at her feet, and making sure Dad's still occupied, I shoot for the back room.

Dad's office is small and messy, and the combined stink of cigarettes and Old Spice hangs in the air like smog. Stacked in front of me are four CCTV monitors with different views of the shop.

I spend the next ten minutes trying to figure out the system. Once I've got the hang of it, I'm away, searching for evidence of Zaman talking shit about my sister. Moments later, I stumble across something ten times worse.

'No freaking way . . .' I whisper.

I hit rewind. And again. A fourth viewing confirms it. Ilyas Mian has found his smoking gun.

Back on the shop floor, a massive queue has materialized, snaking round the aisles like a conga line. Dad's looking stressed, and there's no sign of Zaman or Yunus anywhere. I hop on a till, and between us, me and Dad clear the line.

'Blimey!' Dad says, mopping the sweat on his brow. 'Lord knows where all them customers popped up from. Not that I'm complaining.'

My eyes give the place a sweep, making sure Zaman hasn't returned as I psych myself up for the big reveal. 'Er, Dad, can I show you something? It's kinda urgent.'

He humours me with a smile as I pull out my phone.

'This better not be some dirty video you downloaded off the interwebs . . .' Dad falls silent as the video plays.

I study his face, watching his frown deepen when he realizes it's footage from the shop's CCTV, then switch to stark confusion. On the screen, Zaman saunters over to the till. He makes an almost cartoonish left-right sweep of his head, before hitting the button that opens the till and pulling out a bundle of twenties. Shocking, right? Well Zaman's not done. He connects a small device to the credit-card reader. A red LED pulses like a heart-rate monitor. He looks nervous, then startled as he turns his head. *Be with you in a second!* he calls to someone off camera. A green light comes on, and he quickly disconnects the device, making it disappear inside his coat.

Dad's lips shrink to a thin line, his face becoming a midnight thunderstorm.

Zaman and Yunus come in laughing, polishing off the last few fries of their two-ninety-nine burger meals from the local chicken shop.

'Oi, Zaman!' Dad says, then makes a sound that's halfway between a whistle and a whoosh as he heads to the back room.

Zaman looks up as Dad walks in. 'Yes, boss. Just hanging my coat up—'

'Nah, don't bother,' Dad says, grimacing.

You'd need to be dumb not to realize he means business.

Zaman and Yunus exchange dark glances. Zaman smiles ingratiatingly as he follows Dad over to his office. '*Han-ji*, uncle-*ji*.'

Two *ji*s in one breath? Man smells trouble.

Licking excess salt off his oily fingers, Yunus accompanies them. A few seconds later, I follow at a safe distance. Dad settles into his boss chair, Zaman leaning over his shoulder, his face tinged blue in the glare of the incriminating CCTV footage. First, his eyes widen; then, his jaw muscles ripple. Finally he looks into Dad's accusing face, his eyes all watery and apologetic.

'Uncle-ji, I only took the money because I needed to borrow it. I was going to pay you back later,' he says, shaking his head remorsefully.

In some parallel universe, violins are playing. In mine, it's party music.

'How many times?' Dad asks.

Zaman swallows thickly, his lips twitching as if he's trying to think of a number that doesn't sound too bad. 'Twice.'

Dad cackles. 'Funny, cos I've been scratching my head for a while now wondering why the accounts don't add up. Figured it was me, what with having failed my GCSEs and all, but you've clearly been pulling a fast one for *months*. And all those customers complaining about credit-card fraud too! You conned an old man whose wife recently died. You're a nasty piece of work, Zaman Akhtar.'

'Uncle-ji—'

'Don't call me that! Family don't steal from family.'

Zaman glances up, and I duck out of sight fast. If he realizes I'm the one who showed Dad, I am so dead.

'Why'd you do it?' Dad asks, refusing to take silence for an answer.

His Adam's apple bobs twice. 'For Shaista. We're getting married—'

Dad's fist slams into Zaman's belly so fast, I never even see it happen. All I hear is the sickening *thwack* and see Zaman's eyes bulging.

'My daughter's never marrying a thieving *kuta* like you!'

Zaman clutches his stomach, gasping. 'You're lucky I want to marry Shaista. Who else is going to marry a pregnant girl?'

'Dad, don't!' I yell as Dad grabs a broom, ready to bash Zaman's brains out.

Then we all freeze.

Zaman has pulled out a seven-inch M9 bayonet from God knows where.

'Come on!' he says, waving Dad forwards. 'Do you really think a fat old man like you can touch someone like me? I've got an army of Dingoes. What do you have?' He points the blade at me, and my heart stops. 'One son who's a coward, and another who ditched his family for greed. Oh yeah – and one sweet, sweet daughter who worships my dick.'

Dad takes a swipe at Zaman's head. Zaman parries the blow with the side of the blade, before swirling around and nicking the heel of Dad's hand.

'*Yara*, stop it!' Yunus calls.

'Or what?' Zaman replies, now pointing the blade at Yunus.

The sound of a siren can be heard approaching.

'You didn't . . .' Zaman says, looking unsure.

Yunus grins, even as a bead of sweat drips down the side of his face. 'Are you sticking around to find out?'

Zaman points his blade at each of us in turn. Then as the sound of the siren rises to a scream, he darts off, vanishing out of the back door, crashing into the bins.

'Dad, shall I call an ambulance?!' I ask, panicking.

'No, you numpty. Just get your ol' man a plaster from the first-aid box.'

I hunt around for the green box. The sirens blare loudly, then rapidly recede, as the ambulance apparently drives on towards another emergency.

I gawp. 'You didn't call the police then?'

Yunus shakes his head.

'Neither of you are mentioning a word of this to the missus, OK?' Dad says, ripping open a plaster. 'You let me handle it my way.'

That evening, Shaista sulks all night up in her bedroom. I overhear her phoning friend after friend, telling them how *oppressed* she is. She's in denial about just how dangerous Zaman is. The rest of us sit around the table, picking at our dinner in an uncomfortable silence.

'My own flesh and blood!' Dad says, shaking his head. 'My precious little princess!'

'Give it a rest, Osman. She says she didn't do anything,' Amma says.

For the past five minutes, I've watched *khichri* migrate from one side of Mum's plate to the other, one rice grain at a time. Poor Amma: all her kids turned out shit. She deserves better than us.

'Yeah, well that's all right then, innit?' Dad says, pouring on the sarcasm. 'She's a real bastion of honour. A virtuous virgin.'

'Oh for goodness sake! What do you want her to do? Take a pregnancy test?'

'That'd be a start!' Dad lashes out like a wounded bear.

'Look, I know you're hurt,' Amma says, topping up our glasses with chilled water. 'Allah gave us three children, but what you have to remember is that they're on loan. You do your best, then you let go. Do you want to lose her as well as Amir?'

Unable to listen to this, I carry my plate through to the kitchen and stick it in the dishwasher. From as early as I can remember, whenever Amma and Dad have argued, I've ended up with this large rock in my belly, mashing up my guts, making me feel sick. It's been happening so much lately, the rock's upgraded to a boulder.

I traipse up the stairs, reminding myself that I did what had to be done. How was I supposed to know Zaman was going to throw Shaista under a bus to save his own skin?

'You!' Shais stops me on the upper landing, smudged make-up transforming her into The Crow. 'I'll *never* forgive you. From the day you were born, you've been hell-bent on destroying everything I love.'

'Shais, it weren't like that!' I protest. 'Zaman's been nicking money.'

Her eyeliner dribbles like engine oil down her cheeks. 'It's not Zamz's fault Dad didn't pay him enough. Do you even know where the money went?'

I shake my head.

'To *ME*. He's been wooing his lady with gifts. And since I'm Dad's daughter, technically it wasn't even stealing.'

'I know you love him, but he's bad news . . .'

Her eyes fill with tears. 'Amir had the right idea, pissing off to America. I'm going to run away too, then I'll never have to deal with you Love Nazis again!'

The door slams in my face. I stare at its blank surface until my own eyes start to prickle. Shais is hard work, and sometimes I can't stand her, but I'd be lost if she left.

I make my way downstairs, where Amma and Dad are still rowing.

The sound of the phone makes me jump. I make a rush for it, but Dad beats me to it.

'Yes?' he barks down the receiver. Then his face drops, and he swears under his breath. 'Are you sure? OK, OK. Be there in five.'

'Dad, what's up?' I ask.

He looks at me, his eyes pools of worry as Amma creeps into the hall.

'Osman?' she says.

Dad shakes his head, pinching the flesh between his eyebrows. 'There's been a petrol attack on the shop.'

'Oh my God!' Amma says, a hand fluttering to her mouth.

'Nothing like *that*,' he quickly reassures her. 'Thank God Yunus was looking out of his window, nosy bugger. Says he saw a bunch of hoodies gathering, so he raised the alarm before they could do any real damage. The police and fire service have it under control.'

'Why would anyone do that?' Amma asks. 'We've never hurt anyone . . .'

'It was Zaman!' I blurt.

My parents look at me, astounded, before Dad shakes his head. 'They're saying it was racially motivated. Little fascists sprayed slurs on the roller shutters, di'nt they?'

Amma stares into the distance – her eyes look haunted. 'Amir leaves us, Ilyas gets suspended, Shaista gets involved with a bad boy, and . . . now *this* . . .' Amma blinks, dabbing at her eyes with her *dupatta*. 'I think God might be trying to tell us something.'

'What, by visiting us with the Ten Plagues? Don't be daft!' Dad scoffs.

'I'm coming with you,' Amma says, steeling herself.

'Me too,' I grab both our coats off the hooks.

'Nah. You lot stay here and keep an eye on Shaista.' Dad's eyes rise to the darkness at the top of the stairs. 'Make sure she doesn't do a runner with her fancy man. I'll sort this.'

CHAPTER 15

The next day, after dropping off a bowl of Amma's *palak paneer* at Auntie Simrat's house, I decide to take a stroll past Haji Mian & Sons to check out the damage from yesterday. Turns out the petrol attack was worse than Dad let on. A lot worse. Temporary repair film clings to a mosaic of fractured glass. An ugly board has been nailed over a second window, and the third set of roller shutters are completely blistered. Yellow and black graffiti streaks across them, screaming outdated racist BS. I want to cover it up with a nice mural. One of Dad smiling, surrounded by the freshest produce, glistening with dewdrops.

I'm about to go in and ask him when something catches my eye. My breath comes out in a low whistle. Hidden within the offensive swirls is a pair of gleaming yellow eyes. The thugs' tag boy, whoever he was, had obviously just started to leave the gang's calling card before either being stopped or remembering to keep things on the down-low. A mistake so small, nobody would notice it. Nobody that is except for another tag boy.

With a sigh, I go inside to find Dad checking out the extent of the damage.

'Dad, the graffiti outside . . . it wasn't a racist attack. It was DX Dingoes.'

Dad hushes me quickly, then leads me into the back room. 'Look, you can't say this stuff out loud or I'll end up with a whole bunch of resignations on my hands.'

'Dad, are you mad at Shaista?'

'Course I am. Thanks to her, I'll forever be looking over my shoulder, worried that Zaman's crew might try to hurt one of you.'

'She doesn't know he's a legit gangsta.'

He sighs, then nods. 'Guess I should blame myself really. Sometimes you see one of your own struggling, and you feel sorry for 'em. I gave Zaman a chance, believing his lies about putting Dingoes behind him. More fool me, eh? Can't invite the Devil into your house and not expect to get burned.'

'Can't we tell the cops?'

He shakes his head sadly. 'You watch the news. If the Old Bill can't stop kids from stabbing each other, how are they going to handle an organization as big as DX Dingoes? Nah, mate. Best we can do is live our lives on the quiet.'

Back at home, I'm researching climate change for a geography assignment when I start thinking about the current climate in my house. Greenhouse gases swirl around in my belly, bringing a soup of guilt and remorse to the boil, till I finally grab my art pad and stare at the picture I drew earlier. Shais's favourite Disney princess, Aurora, stares back with an apologetic finger in her mouth and the word 'SORRY!' printed above.

Swallowing my pride, I rip the page out and begin scrawling on the back.

Shais,

I'm sorry for destroying your life. Tbh I think you're kind of cool Ok. Not everyone has a YouTuber for a sister, right? Me telling Dad about Zaman was never about the money. I was trying to protect you from a lying supposedly ex-gangsta who wanted to get you in trouble.

You might not be nice to me all that much, or ever really, but you deserve a proper Bollywood hero.

Ilyas

Now comes the hard part. With lumbering steps, I head to her room like a very reluctant postman. The familiar sound of her telling-it-like-it-is to her thousands of fans drifts towards me. I wait a minute but she's in full flow, so I tuck the letter under her door and head back.

CHAPTER 16

You'd think the shop drama would've made me forget about Monday morning. Just thinking about facing Noah and Daevon has me bricking it, knowing I'm in the Traitor Zone. Pulling a sickie for the rest of my life and staying home to protect Amma and Shaista seems the wisest option to me. Sadly Mum's having none of it.

'You've already missed a week of school!' she says. 'You can't afford not to go and end up like these thugs.'

At the breakfast table, I practise swiping the fruit knife, just for protection. I can totally see Noah trying to beat me up at school. Pulling a knife on the bastard would stop him in his tracks. But then what? Stab him? Like I'd ever do *that*. Besides, knowing my luck, I'd probably get caught carrying and end up in a Young Offender Institution before lunch.

Instead, I grab an apple from the bowl and set off out the door.

Spotting Mr Gilchrist standing at the school gates. I jump off my bike, trying to avoid eye contact. Given he's the size of a small mountain, that ain't happening.

'Morning, Ilyas. Hope you've had a chance to think about your actions?' He deliberately blocks the gate with his bulk.

'Yeah, course,' I say, placing a hand over my heart. 'I'm steering well clear.'

'Don't forget to come down to room F10 at 3.10 p.m. sharp for you first detention.'

I nod gloomily. He steps aside, and I wheel my bike in, then glance back over my shoulder. 'By the way, I'm sorry, yeah. For real.'

'We'll determine that at 3.10 p.m. Have a good day.'

It's an order.

My day turns out to be hell. I get all the stares and whispers. I've transformed into Notorious I.L.Y.A.S. – the kid everybody chats shit about.

'Is that the guy who . . .'

'. . .one crazy mutha-f . . .'

'Looks like a homo. How could he . . .'

'. . . heard he tortures kittens . . .'

'. . . jacked up on LSD and went batshit with a knife!'

Room F10 looms in front of me, like the gateway to hell. I knock on the door, tired from a day of being stared at.

'Sorry I'm late, sir. We had Spanish on the other side of school last period.' I spot another student in the classroom, only her head's on the table, drowned beneath a sea of auburn curls.

'Take a seat, please, Ilyas,' Mr Gilchrist says, directing me with a hairy hand. 'As you've no doubt just realized, there are two of you. A pair of rusty nails spoiling the otherwise perfect veneer of Stanley Park.' He turns to the girl. '*Sit up, please,* young lady!'

The girl slowly winches herself up off the table and folds her arms. I'm shocked to see it's Kelly, Jade's friend – the posh girl with the battered DMs. Just like Imran has always been the school mascot for Sports, Jade's crew are squad goals for overachievers. What on earth could a girl like that have done to end up here?

'I don't need to remind you how dire your situation is,' Gilchrist drones. 'Never in all my born days has any student displayed such disregard for the rules. You've both *violently* assaulted another member of the school. Needless to say, we'd be well within our rights to permanently exclude you. Do I make myself clear?'

I nod. Kelly shrugs. The girl is brave, I'll give her that.

'Take out your best writing pens,' he says, placing two sheets of A4 lined paper in front of each of us.

I raise an eyebrow. 'You making us do lines?'

'No, that would be pointless. Didn't work for old Dolores Umbridge now, did it?'

Gilchrist is a *Harry Potter* fan? Somebody, *Avada Kedavra* me right now.

'I'd like you to join me in a reflective task. You've had a week of suspension to contemplate the error of your ways. Hopefully you've arrived at the conclusion that violence never pays. With this fine idea in mind, you will pen a letter of apology to your victims.'

'What?' Kelly and I blurt simultaneously, then look at each other, before quickly looking away, because having a 'moment' is major cringe. Me and her run with different crowds.

Mr Gilchrist places gorilla paws on the desk, elbows jutting out. 'Ms Matthews, Mr Mian – refuse and you leave us no choice but to pursue the path of exclusion.' He pauses for effect. 'Perform the task successfully, and I will recommend to the governors that we expunge the incident from your permanent record. And may I point out that with an incident of this severity against your name, it would be unlikely that any college would consider taking you on.'

I swallow. No college would definitely mean being stuck working at Haji Mian & Sons till kingdom come. And worse still, Amma's disappointment.

'Do you have something to say, Kelly?' Gilchrist asks.

'No . . . It's just, I don't really see the point of this. You kicked us out for a week – obvs assuming here . . .'

I realize she's talking to me, and I nod.

'So,' she continues, 'seems like overkill. We did the crime, we've done the time, and we're better people for it. Can't we all go home now?'

'It's *that* attitude that got you into this mess in the first place, young lady! A perfect academic record blighted by a single, but very serious, error in judgement.'

'OK, OK – I get it. But you haven't even listened to my side of the story yet,' she says reproachfully.

'You are walking on very thin ice here.' Gilchrist flashes his steely eyes in warning. 'We're bending over backwards giving you a second chance. Write that letter of apology or I'll have your mother in again.'

Kelly looks away, shaking her head like she's being blackmailed. Gal's got me intrigued. Who did she hit and why?

'Begin!' Gilchrist orders.

> ~~Dear Imran,~~
> ~~Yo, bro!~~
> Imran,
> Sorry I hit you. Violence is never the answer.

I pause, because it's the *only* answer in every single superhero comic ever.

I glance up at Gilchrist, who is either involved in an intense WhatsApp session, or could be on the final level of Candy Crush.

'Damn!' he says.

His eyes flick up, and I immediately drop mine. Satisfied that Kelly and me are not going to kill each other, Gilchrist walks into the corridor to speak privately on his phone. We hear him slowly plodding away.

The air grows thick and stale, each minute drawn out like an hour. My ears begin to ring. Five sessions of this seems impossible. Why couldn't they have stuck me in the Phantom Zone instead?

'What's that?'

I glance up, getting an eyeful of Kelly's long shaggy mane, which smells of fresh apples. Her fingertip rests on the picture of PakCore I must have unconsciously sketched in the middle of my letter. *Shit!* I turn the page over protectively.

'Nothing,' I mutter.

'Really?' Kelly says, raising her eyebrows. 'Well it was an awesome nothing then. That character looks like he could leap off the page.'

I keep quiet, hoping she'll go back to her seat. I get that I'm the only other human being in this room, but in five years, we've never spoken or even smiled at each other. Doing it now is so fake. She's part of the elite crew, and I'm a wannabe gangsta. Plus we have a job to do, and it doesn't involve talking.

'So have you written anything yet?' she persists, sitting on my desk like I invited her over.

'What? No. Look you better get back over there, else Gilchrist's gonna exclude both our arses.'

She rolls her eyes. 'Don't be basic. If they were going to exclude us, it would've happened back when they summoned that She-Hulk police officer.'

I blink in surprise. Calling Officer Pryce 'She-Hulk' was an inside joke that never made it to the outside. With all that long red hair, this girl is definitely giving me Jean Grey vibes. Maybe she *is* a mind reader?

'I've written a story,' she announces proudly. 'Would you like to hear it?'

'No.'

'Rude! I said I liked *your* drawing.'

'PakCore.'

'Did you just call me a whore?'

'What? No!' I say, nearly falling off my chair.

'Good, cos I have a mean left hook, mister. Just ask Melanie.'

I recall her pretty band of friends, zooming in on Melanie with her Chun-Li hairdo and her Catwoman poses. 'Why'd you hit her?'

A stern look sweeps over her face. 'Because I have anger-management issues, I guess. These fists were flying, she got in the way, so *ka-pow*.' She gives a quick left-right combo, making the table quake.

In spite of myself, I smile. '*Ka-pow*? As in comics?'

She nods. 'But with smaller tits.'

I blush. 'Not all comics are like that . . .' But even as I say it, I know they mostly are.

'I prefer speculative fiction, where you get to imagine the heroine without a massive pair of jugs crammed into a tiny bondage suit. Yep, science fiction and fantasy are my jam.'

'What, like *Star Wars*?'

She grins impishly. 'Also like *that*.' In a single fluid movement, she flips over my page, a stubby nail coming to rest on PakCore's bulging pecs.

'Stoppit, man!' I growl.

'Why? If I could draw even half as good you, I'd be drawing all over these walls right now, sharing my talent with the world.'

Her words give me flashbacks. Leaving the DedManz tag on private property all over the town I was born in. The dirty money Imran's been paying me to do it.

'Who taught you how to draw?' she asks.

I shrug. 'Everyone can draw, innit?'

'Not like you, they can't.' She clicks her heels together – Dorothy, but with battered man-boots instead of ruby slippers. 'My mum taught me how to write. Aged three.'

'Seriously?' I say, ninety-nine per cent sure she's exaggerating.

'M'hm. Mum has always had these insane ambitions for me.'

'I always figured it was just Asian parents that were mad demanding.'

Kelly pouts thoughtfully. 'Well, what do your parents want you to be?'

'Me? Nothing. But it's sorta cultural to want your kids to become doctors or engineers or go into business. Anything else is considered a fail.'

'Because they want their kids to become high earners?'

'You do not understand. My lot *love* to brag. Telling every random on the planet how successful their kids are. It's a massive badge of honour.'

She narrows an eye. 'So how comes *your* parents aren't like that?'

I sigh and shake my head. Don't want to get into it. Don't want to tell this privileged white girl about my #BrownPeopleProblems so she can just have a laugh about it with her mates later.

'Well I think my mum wins the prize for Most Dictatorial Mother Ever. She wants me to be a –' her fingers twitch in the air like animated quotes – '*fierce, feminist prime minister with egalitarian values and conservative morals.*'

The thing is, I can totally imagine Kelly killing it at Prime Minister's Question Time. She practically owned Gilchrist before he weaponized her mum. 'That what you want?'

'Nooooo,' she says, curls bouncing like rings of flame. 'I want to write fantasy—'

The door slams shut. We jerk our heads in the direction of a very cross-looking Mr Gilchrist. Kelly scrambles back to her seat as he stomps over like he's going to rip our heads off.

He snatches up our pages, ignoring our protests. 'I asked for a single letter of apology, and what do I get? A story about a space princess and a picture of a ninja!'

'She's not a space princess!' Kelly says.

'He's not a ninja!' I say.

Mr Gilchrist blinks. 'I'm sorry. Have I just entered the Twilight Zone? Your brief was completely clear. Lucky for you, we have four more sessions to get your letters sorted out. It just so happens I've run into a bit of an emergency at home, so we'll have to try this again tomorrow. Off you go!'

He doesn't need to tell us twice. We grab our bags and bolt for the door.

'Same time, same place!' he booms after us.

Out in the corridor, we glance at each other. Without the four walls of a classroom imprisoning us, awkwardness sets in like rot. Kelly opens her mouth to say something.

'Laters,' I say, hurrying in the opposite direction.

CHAPTER 17

'Miss, did you hear about Muzna Saleem?' Kara says the next day as we're working through exam-style questions on quadratic equations.

Maths ain't happening for me today. A tiny mistake early on bloomed into a full-blown disaster. Two whole pages of it. FML.

Ms Mughal stares at the ceiling, tapping her chin. 'Is that the girl who foiled the terror attack last year?'

'That girl is goals!' Nawal says, slamming her hand against her wheelchair. 'She liked one of my selfies on Insta!'

Kara nods. 'Basically my cousin Sade went to the same school as her. She said that girl has the best luck.'

'How'd you figure that out?' Ray asks, turning round in disbelief. 'Poor girl nearly got killed by ISIS, and you're sat there saying she's lucky?!'

'Yeah, but she's, like, only seventeen, and in the *Metro* today, it said she's won a book deal,' Kara says excitedly.

Ms Mughal smiles broadly. 'Good for her. It'll be great to hear her side of the story.'

'What kind of book is she writing?' I ask on the off chance it's a graphic novel.

Kara shrugs. 'Didn't get to read the rest of the article. My phone pinged, so I put the newspaper down for a second, and some bare nasty tramp picked it up! When he realized I wasn't done, he tried to give it back. Dude got me, like –' She does an excellent impression of the vomiting emoji. 'As if I'm gonna be touching that paper now you covered it in your STIs!'

'Don't be so rude, Kara,' Ms Mughal says gently. 'Just because you can't afford to take a shower, doesn't stop you from being a human.'

Kara blushes, covering her face. 'Miss, now you're making me feel bad!'

'Miss gives us maths lessons and life lessons,' Ray says. 'Buy one, get one free.'

Ms Mughal laughs, reminding us that there are people working next door, so we shut up and get back to work.

'Are you OK?' she asks, her green eyes rising above my desk.

I nod before looking down at my book, which is a mess of scratched-out answers.

'Are you worried about Imran?' she whispers so quietly, I barely hear it.

I'm a deer caught in the headlights, and for one horrifying moment, her eyes turn yellow and wolfish, fangs trailing over her lips, before I realize she's triggered my imagination. She takes my stunned reaction as an answer.

'Don't be. As a school, we're looking out for you. It doesn't matter how successful a student might be on the pitch, there's no room for intimidation here.'

'Miss . . .' I start, wanting to offload and tell her how scared I am that Imran is going to kill me, or that his cousin belongs to one of the UK's worst gangs, and I'm worried they're going to come after my family. Then I think better of it – involving her will make her a target too. 'Can you start me off, please?'

She smiles, clicking her pen.

'Sorry I'm late, sir,' I say, lumbering into F10 at the end of the day.

Kelly is already seated, limbering up her fingers as if preparing for a rock-paper-scissors death match. She smiles at me, while Mr Gilchrist glares.

'Feels like déjà vu, doesn't it?' Gilchrist says. 'Grab a seat and get ready to spin a Pulitzer Prize-winner of an apology, since neither of you managed to finish yesterday.'

'Yes, sir,' I say, rooting through my bag for a pen.

Something pokes me in the side, and I see Kelly is offering me one. *No freaking way.* It's a floaty Superman one, like I used to own when I was small.

'Just to make things explicitly clear, I want you to start your letters "Dear Imran" and "Dear Melanie", followed by the opening words . . .' He grabs a brown pen and scrawls on the whiteboard behind. 'I am writing to you to offer my sincere apologies for . . .'

Sighing heavily, I copy down his words. Only I start to think that this is all lies, cos I'm *not* sorry. Imran is a prick and had it coming.

'Sir, I can't do this,' I announce.

'Can't or won't?' Gilchrist says, cocking an eyebrow at me.

'Both. Look, Imran Akhtar has a reputation, right?'

'Yes, he's captain of both the school basketball and football teams and has brought several trophies to Stanley Park,' he says curtly.

'Plus everyone thinks he's really hot,' Kelly adds.

I shake my head. 'He's bullied enough kids, and you know it. Even my dad says Imran's twice my size. I couldn't beat up the guy even if he was blindfolded and had both arms tied behind his back. So you gotta ask yourself – how'd he end up in hospital? Answer: it was an Act of God. And if Allah decides to teach Imran a lesson for whatever reason, who am I, or you, to mess with that?'

'He's got a point,' Kelly chips in. 'Maybe Allah made my fist fly and knock Melanie out too?'

'Silence, both of you! I've never heard such far-fetched nonsense.'

'Are you calling his religion "far-fetched"?' Kelly asks with a dramatic gasp.

Gilchrist falters. 'Don't be ridiculous. There are school rules here, Ilyas. You and Kelly broke them, and there's a price to be paid.' His phone goes off, and he snarls at it.

'Whoa, you OK, sir?'

His face goes bright red.

'Oh my days! Red Hulk!' I whisper.

'Thunderbolt Ross,' Kelly agrees.

'Right, you two. Not a peep out of you. I want your first draft letters ready in the next thirty-five minutes, or else!' He starts speaking into his phone, apologizing profusely to the caller as he retreats into the corridor.

I turn round in my chair to face Kelly with newfound respect. 'Thunderbolt Ross, huh?'

'Told you I like speculative fiction,' she says, smiling.

'That some posh word for *comics*?'

'Sort of. Superheroes is like a sub-genre.'

I realize I'm staring, swallow, and turn around to get on with my stupid letter.

'So, what have you written?' Kelly asks about twenty minutes later.

'Huh? Oh, just crap,' I say, clicking her Superman pen nervously.

'Want to hear mine?'

I shrug. It's all the encouragement she needs.

'Dearest Melanie,' she begins, perching on my table, and swinging her legs like a little kid. 'You are the most obnoxious, self-centred Melania Trump-wannabe that ever lived. I am well jel of all the people who never met you. In spite of that, I'm truly sorry. Sorry that I didn't knock your damn donkey teeth out! I don't care if your dad is a government minister who "might be able to get me an internship at the House of Commons". He's probably one of those sex pests they're trying to root out. Any day now, they're going to throw the book at him, and your whole family will have to jet off to some tax haven to hide out. Good riddance. Yours affectedly, Kelly Matthews.'

I howl with laughter, flapping my hand in the air. She tells me not to laugh before her own giggles give way to peals of laughter. When we finally stop, we look at each other, and we're off again. Man, I haven't laughed this hard since primary school.

'Frame it!' I suggest. 'You're a wicked writer, girl.' I take the letter, and read over it again, chuckling. 'Hey,' I add. 'What does "affectedly" mean?'

'Faking it.'

'Boom!' I say, laughing again. 'Man, I wish I could write like you.'

Her smile slowly fades. She opens her mouth, then shuts it, giving a little shake of her head.

'What?' I say.

'Ilyas, are you in a gang called DedManz?'

And just like that, the tentative bond between us melts like a bridge of ice, plunging us into choppy waters. Guess I was sort of hoping Kelly would see me for who I am instead of the people I hang with. She watches me closely, eyes more curious than judgemental.

'When I was younger,' I begin, 'Dad kept saying I should hang around with jack-the-lad types. Reckoned I took after my mum and sis a bit too much.'

'And that's a problem because . . . ?'

'Cos I liked drawing and colouring instead of football.'

She shakes her head, like she still doesn't get it.

'And . . . playing with my sister's fluffy white rabbit.' I flush deeply, wondering why I'm revealing stuff I've managed to keep hidden forever to someone I hardly know.

She perks up. 'Aw! Photographic evidence, please!'

Frowning, I hold up my phone. 'This is Spar —' my jaw muscles grind like malfunctioning gears '— tacus. *Spartacus.*' I nod twice, as if this makes it any truer.

'Oh my God, he's perf!' she says, clutching my phone, zooming in on Sparkle's cute bunny face. In the pic, Sparks is busy chewing a dandelion that, only seconds before, she'd been wearing between her ears like a Hawaiian girl.

'Not according to my dad,' I say darkly. 'He recruited this group of proper alphas to fix me. I'm not gonna lie: sometimes we have fun. But sometimes they do stuff that makes me feel *bare* uncomfortable.'

Jasmine's humiliation springs to mind, and I squeeze my eyes shut, trying to erase the horrible memory. 'So at the start of Year Eleven, Imran decides we're gonna be a legit gang.'

'DedManz, right?' Kelly says.

I take another moment to decide whether she's judging me before continuing. 'I'm scared at first, cos gangs are violent and that. But before you know it, bullies are backing off, and I feel like I have an actual superpower. Then when Imran wanted us to have a gang tag, it was *my moment*. A chance to share this side of myself I normally get slated for.'

I lick my lips, focusing on Kelly's gentle blue eyes.

'The truth is, Kelly, being in a gang when you're the guy at the bottom is proper stressful. You're forever trying to match up.'

'Tell me about it,' she says, propping her chin on a fist.

I give her a sceptical look. How does this bougie white girl's life compare?

'Your gang is about being manly,' she explains, drawing her hair back. 'Mine's about being the "right kind of girl". I have to get my nails done, buy crap on Oxford Street that I don't even want, and go to stupid parties where Jade and Melanie and Nicole pop pills and get off with preppy boys.' Frowning, she traces a swear word etched into the table. 'I'm the least cute one who needs to stop being kooky and watch her BMI.'

So here's the thing: I'm a don't-wannabe-gangsta, and Kelly's a poor-little-rich-girl, yet here we are having the realest talk of my life. And man, does it feel good.

'I like your kooky,' I say hesitantly. 'And your weight ain't nobody's business but your own. I'm so skinny, the bio teacher keeps using me as a prop.'

She gives me a playful shove, speaking in a southern drawl. 'Fooler!'

'Why do you hang with those mean girls anyway?'

'I'm a stuck-up white girl,' she says bitterly. 'Do you think anybody else wants to have me around?'

Her bluntness has me blushing. 'Well, you're definitely white, but I don't think you're stuck-up.'

She laughs.

'By the way, I lied.' My eyes wander off. 'Bunny's name is Sparkle. And I love her to bits.'

Kelly raises her chin. 'Way cuter. Spartacus sounded like a skin condition.'

The pips ring out, killing the moment.

'You going before Gilchrist gets back?' I ask.

'Yep,' she says, wrapping a big scarf round her neck and pulling on a pink woolly hat.

I hand her pen back. 'See you tomorrow,' I say.

CHAPTER 18

I'm walking through the corridor after break on Wednesday, minding my own business, when I trip and dive into a locker.

'What the hell?' My anger goes up in a puff of smoke when I see Noah standing over me, his freckles like an army of red ants preparing to attack.

'Paigon!' he says, spitting in my face.

I silently wipe the spit off with my blazer sleeve, scrabble to my feet, and start to head towards my maths class.

'Oi! You don't get off that easy,' he says, driving his shoulder into mine, forcing me to clang against the lockers again.

'Allow it,' I say, holding back tears that have no business existing. 'Man's already paying for what Imran started. Got it on my permanent record.'

He scrunches up his face. 'Who gives a shit about school records?'

'Er, colleges?'

'Don't be coming at me with yo sarcasm, you little fag.'

I see a flash of metal in his waistband, then it's gone, hidden beneath the curtain of his shirt. Suddenly it all comes flooding back: the day Zaman pulled a knife on Dad back at the shop. Is DedManz graduating into Dingoes?

'Ah, excuse me!' says Ms Mughal, planting fists on her hips. 'Your homophobic language has no place in school. Neither does your bullying. Apologize to Ilyas right now.' A beam of sunlight makes her eyes glow like Green Lantern's. Ms Mughal is powering up.

Noah looks her up and down, lip curling. 'Mind yo own bidness, woman.'

'Oh dear . . .' she says, smiling confidently. 'Let's try that again, shall we, *Noah Andrews*?'

He baulks like he just got tasered. 'How you know my name?!'

Her neck gyrates with the assuredness of a cobra. 'Must've picked it up in the staffroom.'

Noah's lips twitch nervously, too proud to say sorry, but too cowardly to cross Ms Mughal. 'This ain't over, fam!' he tells me, miming a hand pistol held sideways before vanishing.

Ms Mughal shakes her head and ushers me into her classroom while directing onlookers off to theirs.

'What was *that* about?' Kara asks as I slide into my chair.

I shake my head. 'Nuttin.'

'Didn't look like nuttin.' She grins. 'Hey, do DedManz make gangsta raps? If you need a girl with rhythm in your videos, I'm available!'

'OK, people!' Ms Mughal calls, clapping her hands for attention. 'Today we're going to assess whether you've actually understood all the algebra-cadabra I've been drip-feeding you, or whether you were faking it.' She raises a tray of scissors in one hand and a stack of white card in the other. 'Who wants to help me give these out?'

'Me, me, me!' Like someone hit the emergency ejection button on her seat, Kara jumps up and grabs the tray, beaming with pride.

'Dude, it's only scissors!' Ray says.

'Bruv, you do not want to be disrespecting a woman with that many pairs of scissors,' I tell him.

'Innit!' Kara says, bumping fists with me.

Once the activity has made its way into our hands, Ms Mughal tells us we need to cut out the equilateral triangles printed on the card and rearrange them to make a giant hexagon, so the questions and answers match up.

'And then,' she says, rubbing her hands together, 'you are going to show me your artistic side. Using colouring pencils or felt tips, I want you to transform your Tarsia hexagon into a beautiful picture or a lovely pattern. I don't mind which, so long as it means something special to *you*.'

Kara returns to her seat. 'Can we help each other with the maths part?'

'Try to do it yourself. I have faith in you!' Ms Mughal cries melodramatically, placing a fist over her heart.

Turning to the back of my exercise book, I start working out the answers.

'Oi, if you work out half, and I work out half, we'll have more time for the fun part. You in?' says Kara.

'Yaass!' I reply.

Me and Kara breeze through the questions, and in under twelve minutes we have the puzzle pieces arranged correctly. Ray asks Ms Mughal if we can have some music, and she reluctantly agrees to some 'quiet, clean' tracks.

Gluing my hexagon on to a larger piece of sugar paper, I whip out my art pencils and start sketching PakCore. In my head, I imagine the hexagon as his torso, and I sketch the rest of him on the sugar paper around it.

'Miss,' says Kara, settling into the chill atmosphere of the lesson. 'Are you married?'

'No, Kara,' Ms Mughal says, without looking up from her marking. She takes out an ink stamper and presses it to a page leaving a bright blue impression of a happy bee.

'My newly divorced uncle Leroy is gonna be so happy to hear that. He saw you at parents' evening one time.'

'Let the lady mark her books in peace,' Ray says.

'I'm calling it: that girl's gonna be a wedding planner when she's older,' Nawal says darkly.

Ray laughs, and Nawal smiles at him.

'Get on with your work, please,' Ms Mughal reminds us.

'My mum told me she doesn't mind who I marry so long as he's a light-skinned man,' Kara confides in me.

'Why?' I ask, surprised.

'Cos she's got dark skin, innit? And her family used to take the piss. She doesn't want her grandkids going through the same thing.'

'That is messed up!' I say, shaking my head. 'Go Pakistan, yeah – bleach creams *everywhere*. My sister always comes back with a shopful of Fair & Lovely stuffed in her suitcase.'

'Dude, that ain't nothing!' Kara says, like it's become a competition. 'In Kenya, they do these illegal injections to kill your melanin.'

'Whoa!' I shake my head and sigh. 'My sis hates me cos of my lighter skin and eyes. But I'd trade for her brains any day. She started up a YouTube channel when she was in Year Ten. Three years later, she's got twenty-three thousand subs. The girl is making serious Ps! Plus, companies are always sending her free stuff to review.'

'What's her channel about?'

'Hair, make-up. Sometimes Bollywood.'

'Does she have a skin-whitening tutorial?'

'It's like her most viewed! Just after "The Ninety-Nine Pee Glow Up".'

We both burst out laughing.

'Less skin-whitening, more mathsing, you two,' Ms Mughal says sternly, drawing some snickers.

'But, miss, don't you think dark skin is butters?' Kara says.

Ms Mughal blinks indignantly, putting her stamper down. 'No I don't, Kara – and neither should you. You and I can have a proper chat about it after the lesson.'

'Uh-oh . . .' says Kara.

I pat Kara on the back in solidarity and get back to my drawing. Twenty minutes later, I'm adding shadow effects to PakCore's eye mask, really making the vivid hazel of his eyes pop.

'Oh. My. Goodness,' Ms Mughal says, sneaking up behind me. 'That is *incredible*!'

Chairs are scraped back and people come rushing over to see my work.

'*That is lit!*'

'*Fire! Look at the quads on him.*'

'*You should draw comics for Marvel.*'

'*Marvel sucks. He should draw for DC.*'

My cheeks start to smoulder as the compliments come thick and fast. It's a small window into Imran's life whenever he shoots and scores or makes that perfect slam dunk. Getting rated by my whole class makes me feel alive. Suddenly I am visible.

Ms Mughal takes my Tarsia PakCore and hides it behind her jilbab. 'OK, everyone, back to your seats.' She shoos everyone away with a swish of her sleeve. 'I've seen plenty of amazing and innovative designs today. We'll have a mathsibition at the end, where we can walk around the room and check out each other's brilliant designs. OK?'

She waits till everyone gets back on task before returning my project to me.

'Well done!' she whispers. 'I grew up surrounded by comics because of my big brother. But I don't recognize this character. Is he new?'

'I, uh, sorta made him up . . .' My palms glisten with sweat, my pulse twanging in my throat.

Her eyes widen, and I notice little flecks of gold rimming her pupils. 'Is he Asian?'

I nod. 'British-Pakistani, like me. I call him PakCore.' In my head, his badass theme tune starts playing.

'Wow. May I take a picture?'

I nod, a bit thrown. Teachers are paid to encourage, right?

'You got skills, boy,' Kara says, nudging me. 'To be honest this peng ting looks a lot like . . .'

'Imran!' finishes Ray, leaning over. 'That is *so* Imran, down to the goatee.'

I flush, a hot mess of stuttered denials. 'T-t-total coincidence. This could be any Asian guy with a square jaw and good cheekbones.'

'Is this a peace offering so he doesn't kill you when he comes back to school?' Kara asks.

Stifling a gasp, I shake my head firmly. 'It was an accident. He's not going to kill me. Plus, this isn't him. Imran doesn't have hazel eyes.'

'Yeah, that's the *only* thing.' Kara nods, wisely.

I stuff my drawing into my rucksack before it invites any more speculation just as the pips go for break-time.

CHAPTER 19

The next morning, my alarm goes off at the usual time, and I pull back the duvet, shuffling to the bathroom as a yawn threatens to dislocate my jaw. I need to get myself ready for the dawn prayer. Amma and me are the only two who pray in my family, but Amma has trouble getting up in the mornings, so she prays *Fajr* late.

I move softly down the stairs, shrouded in darkness. My creative mind starts to wake up, turning the inky shadows into assassins, gathered at the bottom of the stairs, waiting in ambush. These are the Living Shadows – beings with mouths crammed full of purple fangs that crackle with electrical charge as they gnash their teeth. I imagine myself as PakCore, leaping over the side of the banisters in my pyjamas, my hands whipping out as I make the *Sign of Wahid*.

My body is a glow stick, searing through the darkness as my costume and powers answer the sacred call. The Living Shadows goggle as I make the Superhero Landing (cos why mess with a classic?). Fist pressed to the ground, shoulders rolled forward, I look up and give an almost maniacal grin. 'So you finally found out where I live?' I say. 'Thanks. Saves me the hassle of having to track down your creepy asses.' Enraged, the Living Shadows charge. We race towards each other in a head-on collision that will surely blow out every window in the house . . .

If making comics brings excitement to my boring little life, praying brings the peace. It's just about the only time I feel completely safe from all the crap going on around me. When I'm done, I fold up my prayer mat and head to the shed to feed Sparkle.

'Hey, Sparks!' I say, lifting up her thermal cover. She zooms out of her bedroom and bounces around with excitement. I open the door and stroke her fluffy head, my fingers sinking into her silky cap. She drops her ears and vibrates with contentment, making rhythmic chewing sounds.

'I met a girl,' I tell Sparkle thinking about how lonely Wednesday's detention was without Kelly. Guess she must've been off sick. Sparkle's blue eyes widen, then she winks. I chuckle softly. 'Nah, ain't like that, though. Her name's Kelly and she's really nice. Like funny and talented and stuff. Only she hangs out with this bougie group.' I add a scoopful of nuggets to her feeding bowl. She nudges my hand out of the way, plunging her entire head into the bowl, and starts chomping. 'I think she likes comics as much as I do.'

Rolling on my rubber gloves, I start mucking out Sparkle's tiny droppings.

'Good afternoon, sir,' I say cheerily, strolling into F10 for our next detention session that afternoon.

'Good afternoon, Ilyas,' Mr Gilchrist says in his bassoon voice, gesturing for me to sit down.

I glance over at Kelly, who gives me a little wave.

'It's Thursday, and neither one of you has managed to convince me you regret your violent actions.'

'Oh come off it!' I say. 'I wrote a letter using that example you gave yesterday!'

'He brought in an example?' Kelly asks with a laugh.

'Yeah, and I followed it to a tee.'

'Yes, mindless copying was never the point,' Gilchrist snaps. 'I told you right from the start that these sessions are about *reflection*. The letter is not the important element; the changed mindset is.'

'Then why are you making us do it over and over? You said

you weren't that Umbridge woman from Harry Potter, but you low-key are,' I say, rolling my eyes.

'Reprogramming,' Kelly says, narrowing her eyes. 'That's what this is really about. You're trying to deconstruct our identities until we think exactly like you. Isn't that illegal?'

'Oh my days!' I say. 'He's Illuminati!'

'Enough!' Gilchrist snaps, slamming a hand on his desk. 'Stop trying to find the joke in everything. Two members of this school sustained physical injuries because of your mindless actions. It is entirely possible that their parents will still seek legal action against the school.'

Yeah, right. Imran's mum doesn't speak English, and she's probably having the best time knowing Imran's stuck in hospital where he can't terrorize the world.

'If I can't even get you two to show remorse, how can I make a case before the governors to keep you on? You're both well into your final year. Exclusion at this point would have a hugely damaging effect on your results. When we took you on at Stanley Park, we promised to help you achieve your academic goals, and *you* promised to abide by school rules. I'm asking you to be mature about this, not just compliant. Help me get you back into the classroom without having this hanging over your heads.' He raps the table like he's trying to knock some sense into us. 'Write that letter of apology, please.'

I glance over at Kelly, and she raises her eyebrows, giving an almost imperceptible shrug. We both start writing.

Ten minutes later, Mr Gilchrist's phone goes off. 'Excuse me,' he says, going out into the corridor.

In silent agreement, Kelly and me rush over to the door to eavesdrop.

'What? You can't be serious!' Gilchrist says.

We poke our heads round the door frame and just catch the

back of his head sinking down into the stairwell.

'What do you reckon *that* was about?' I ask, wide-eyed.

'Well,' Kelly says, licking her lips. 'Clearly Mr Gilchrist is having an extra-marital affair with Lydia Pryce – the attending police liaison officer.'

I cover my mouth and choke with laughter. 'Omigosh, that is jokes! Wonder how that happened.'

'It started innocently enough,' Kelly says slipping easily into the role of Trashy Gossip Columnist, 'with the two of them discussing their miserable lives. Gilchrist's wife nags him for failing to make principal. Lydia says she's not been promoted to detective inspector because her colleagues can't handle the thought of a black woman in charge. "Oh I'd love you to take charge," Gilchrist says.'

I nod, butting in with my own salacious two-cents. '"Careful what you wish for!" she says, whipping out regulation handcuffs and her truncheon. Gilchrist gulps. Looking over their shoulders, they silently slip into an old broom cupboard and let their passions run wild.' I wave my fingers like a magician.

Kelly picks up the plot. 'They make out like the very teens they always complain about. Gilchrist has a moment of doubt because he's all middle-aged and hairy shoulders.'

I chuckle. 'And his mind's all like, *We shouldn't do this!* And his body's like, *We're totally doing this!*'

'Lydia puts his mind at ease,' Kelly says, her eyes sparkling with mischief, 'telling him that he needn't worry about the excess fur because *Beauty and the Beast* was always her favourite romance.'

'Aw man, that is grim!'

We both shriek with laughter.

'But seriously that was *dope*!' I say excitedly. 'Maybe we should collaborate on a story some day?' Too late, I sense the awkwardness and wish I'd kept my mouth shut.

'Do you want to hear one of my stories?' she asks suddenly.

'Sure!' I climb on to my table, folding my legs under me.

She pulls out a spiral-bound pad from her bag and flips through the pages. 'OK, here's a good one!'

'What's it about?'

'It's set in a dystopian future, where a mutant strain of flu is killing everyone.' She bites her lip.

'Go on . . .' I say, leaning forward.

'My main character is a girl called Cassie whose parents are top scientists tasked with finding a cure. Cassie hardly ever sees them, but when she does, they always look at her with this cold disappointment.'

I swallow, thinking of Dad.

'One day, shady government types break in and kill her parents, because the mum's found a cure, and they don't want the general population getting their hands on it. They don't find Cassie – she's hiding under the pool cover or something. With both parents dead, she has to piece together her parents' research and synthesize the vaccine. Then she's got to convince the authorities to vaccinate people with it, but they won't listen to a teenager—'

'Truth!' I interject.

'Cassie ends up having to get it to people through the water supply. And, well, I haven't figured this part out yet, but there'll be this group of rebels who she'll join up with, and they'll eventually let her try the vaccine out on one of them under pain of death if it goes wrong – cos *drama*!' She makes jazz hands. 'But the rebel is cured. Suitably impressed, they join her in her quest to get the vaccine into the water supply to save the world.'

'That is amazing!' I say, clapping. 'I could never come up with something that complicated.'

'Sure you could. I think it's actually kind of predictable.'

'No way! I mean . . . OK, maybe a tiny, tiny bit,' I say, holding my finger and thumb close together. 'But every story is, to an extent. I mean, I once heard there are only seven original stories that have been told since the beginning of time, and all the rest are recycling.'

'You know, I heard that too!' she says, looking more cheerful. 'So what's the story behind PakCore?'

'Oh, just some dumbness that happened to me in Year Five . . .' I laugh nervously.

Propping herself up on her elbows, she cups her cheeks expectantly. I falter, not wanting to get into it, but she doesn't look like she'll be giving up any time soon.

'OK, so I was like the biggest Superman stan since I was four . . .' I begin.

Kelly listens intently as I tell her about World Book Day six years ago, when Lee, Ryan and Alice got salty cos this brown boy dressed up as an icon. As I'm talking, she hangs on my every word, her eyes mirrors of sympathy as I shift about nervously.

'. . . So I came up with PakCore,' I continue, so engrossed that I forget to blink away the wetness in my eyes. '*Pak* from Pakistan, and *Core* from hardCore. Put 'em together and you get something sounding like *parkour*. That's his method of getting from A to B and making it look wicked.'

'That is *so* clever!'

'I just wanted a relatable superhero. Cool, handsome, strong. All that good stuff, but also brown.'

She nods. 'Even if your dad doesn't understand you, your mum has got to be proud, right?'

I smile. 'Amma thinks I'm the gifted one in the family, even though my brother's gone Harvard and my sister is a YouTube influencer. I know it sounds cheesy, but Amma means everything to me, especially since Dad thinks drawing is a total waste of time.'

'So good mum, bad dad? For me, it's the other way round, except Dad's almost always away on business, so I hardly ever see him.' She stares at her palms, rubbing a pen mark off. 'Mum forces me to go on these boring outings to museums and exhibitions, then makes me write about them.'

'For real?'

'That's not even the worst part. She *grades* my work. And if my grade isn't up to scratch, she makes me do rewrites.'

I'm worried my dreams will be crushed by family pressure and my body will be crushed by DedManz, and she's worried about her mum grading her extra work and her dad going on a grand tour of the world? But then I feel bad, cos problems are problems. It's not about what they are, but how they make you feel. And right now, Kelly looks exactly how I feel.

'Is your mum a teacher?' I ask.

She see-saws her hand. 'Mum's an education officer. She thinks she's doing the Lord's work because she works mostly with ethnic minorities, helping them on to courses to improve their job prospects.'

'*But?*'

'I don't believe in God, but if there was a supreme being, I'm pretty sure They wouldn't approve of closet racists like my mum.'

'That's a bit strong,' I say, reeling.

'Is it? What do you call someone who thinks immigrants should have the decency to leave their own culture behind if they want to be British? So many times, I've said, "Mum, you do realize that we borrow from other cultures too, right? Why should they have to give theirs up?" And she's like, "Well no one's forcing them to come here. Ours is the dominant culture for a reason." Mum believes racism only exists because certain people refuse to assimilate.'

'Wow,' I say, impressed by her brutal honesty.

'Yep, my mum's the fricking Borg Queen.'

I look at her, nonplussed.

'*Star Trek*?'

I shake my head.

'Call yourself a geek, Ilyas? Hang your head in shame.'

I do, making her chuckle.

'So back in the day, *Star Trek* had this scary alien race called the Borg. They were these half-organic, half-robot beings, all serving the hive mind. They'd go around sticking these IV tubes into any random species they fancied and turn them into part of the collective. The victim would completely lose their identity and only live to serve the Borg Queen.'

'That's a dope idea!' I say, clicking my fingers. 'Need me some *Star Trek*.'

'Just not the later stuff.' Kelly's face looks grim.

'Do your mates like *Star Trek*?'

She blushes, her confidence slipping. 'It's my dirty little secret. If they knew, I'd probably get unfriended.'

'So get better friends.'

'You mean like you did? Although . . . Imran's a total babe.'

I look at her in horror.

'Hey don't get all judgey; even Gilchrist stans him.'

'But aren't you supposed to be a *feminist*?' I can't believe what I'm hearing. 'Imran is the world's biggest woman abuser.'

'So he's a fixer-upper,' she says, smirking. 'All he needs is a smart girl to teach him how to be a better man.'

I snort. 'Good luck with that! Even his mum is scared of him.'

'I wish my mum were scared of me, then maybe she'd stop bullying me all the time.'

'Kelly, seriously — Imran is a bad man.'

'Can I see one of your comics?' she asks, abruptly changing the subject.

My eyes slide off to the right. 'OK, but I can't tell stories like you can. Plot-wise I'm completely shite.'

Kelly bats my reservations out of the air. 'Haters gonna hate. Personally I like to focus on what *does* work in a story. Makes you a happier person.'

'I got it on USB,' I tell her, grabbing my backpack.

'PakCore me!' she says, pointing at Mr Gilchrist's computer.

'OK, but I'm opening up a browser with an apology letter in case the dude finishes having emergency phone sex with Officer Pryce.'

Hovering over my file, I take a deep breath and double-click. Kelly stares at the screen, her eyes tracking from panel to panel as she follows the action. My heart unfolds like a deck chair and sits in my throat.

'This isn't a digital comic you downloaded off your Kindle, is it?' she asks when she's done reading.

I shake my head earnestly before realizing it's a compliment.

'Grade nine for drawing, you totes Da-Vinched it. Grade . . . seven maybe for story skills.'

I smile at her. 'Thanks!'

We start discussing plot holes and fixes. Kelly has so many dope suggestions, I actually start taking notes.

After a while, it dawns on me. 'Tomorrow's our last day together,' I say sadly.

Her lips begin to move, then suddenly we're plunged into darkness.

CHAPTER 20

'What the heck just happened?' Kelly asks.

I shrug. 'Power cut?'

'Oh shit! Do you know what time it is?'

I press the home button on my phone, bringing the screen to life. The first thing I see is a whole bunch of missed calls from Amma.

'It's half six!' I say, incapable of understanding how the sky went pitch black without us noticing. Guess time flies when you're geeking out.

'My mum's going to kill me . . .' Kelly says.

'She probably hasn't noticed, otherwise she'd've been blowing up your phone, innit?'

She shakes her head. 'My battery died at lunchtime, and Jade wouldn't lend me her power bar.'

'This is all Gilchrist's fault.' I scowl. 'Six whole hours of She-Hulk sex! Man, is *he* getting fired.'

Kelly gives a belly laugh. Soon we're both rolling, cos the whole situation is so mad.

I stop abruptly. 'Kelly, what if the caretaker locked us in?'

We stare at each other, the whites of our eyes almost iridescent in the darkness. Then we bolt for the door, heading downstairs in a flurry of flapping limbs and thundering feet.

The doors are sealed shut.

We bang on them, calling for help, punching the disabled door-activation button. Nothing happens.

'How comes the motion sensors aren't working?' Kelly asks,

waving her arms like she's trying to flag down a plane. 'If we spend the night here, we'll die of starvation or pneumonia. Whichever comes first.'

'That happens, I'm coming back as a zombie, and Gilchrist's brains will be on the menu.'

'I think I'll come back as a poltergeist and give all the bullies terminal wedgies.'

'Even Imran?'

She covers her mouth with both hands. 'Oh my God, you don't want to know the kinds of things I'd do to him!'

In spite of myself, I laugh.

Every fire escape in the building is locked, but luckily a few classrooms have been overlooked. Thank God for shabby cleaners. My phone holds the gloom at bay as we enter a science lab, but the power is fading fast.

A cool draught wafts under my eyes, drying my sweat. A second later, I see Kelly's silhouette in front of a partially open window, beckoning me over like a shadow puppet. Together we push open the window and toss our bags out. Then we climb on to cupboards lining the wall.

'Ladies first,' I offer.

'Forget it,' Kelly replies, pushing me forward. 'I may need your skinny corpse to break my fat fall.'

The spangled sky stretches across the world like a veil. A full moon glows among the constellation of stars, staring down like a gigantic eyeball.

In my mind, I'm PakCore, poised at the top of a skyscraper. Behind me lurk the Living Shadows; in front lies certain death. With only a slim chance of survival, I remake the *Sign of Wahid*, receiving a ferocious power upgrade that may very well consume me . . .

'Hurry up, or I'll push you!' Kelly snaps.

I bend my knees, muscles like cherry bombs, adrenalin lighting their fuses. Pushing off through my heels, I launch upwards, starting a mid-air rotation.

Oh my God, I think. *I'm actually going to do this!*

Suddenly the rotation reverses, gravity dragging me down. My stomach shrinks to the size of a pea, before I crash into the wet earth, crying out in pain.

'What the hell was that?' Kelly calls from the window.

'Kick the Moon?' I say weakly.

She sits on the window ledge and eases herself down gently, her DMs absorbing the worst of the impact. She pokes me with her boot. 'I think the moon kicked back.'

Reaching down, she pulls me to my feet. I'm shook by how strong she is. OK, so she never looked like Jade and the rest of those cookie-cutter Barbies, but I reckon Kelly could probably carry me home.

She shakes her head. 'What were you thinking?'

'Dunno,' I say, checking myself over for a dislocated limb. 'I just kinda saw the stars and wanted to reach for them. All that stuff you said about my drawings, kinda made me feel like I could . . .'

For a moment, Kelly is nothing but a bushy silhouette, breathing fiercely. Then without warning, she bear hugs me.

'I gotta go. See ya!' She takes off, flying out of the gates.

CHAPTER 21

Amma slams a bowl of porridge down in front of me. A splash of milky oats leaps on to the table cloth.

'You're a bad bitch,' Shais purrs under her breath, stirring her smoothie with a bendy straw. The thick pale liquid is her own revolting recipe. Slugs must've been harmed in the making.

Suppressing a shudder, I reach for the maple syrup. In the kitchen, Amma's tablet is broadcasting the local news. The reporter's going on about some shoot-out at a factory.

'Where were you *really*?' Shais probes.

I squirt the amber liquid over my steaming porridge. 'I told you: detention.'

'Till seven? You could at least try making your lies a bit believable.' She snatches the bottle and adds a squeeze to her own macrobiotic nightmare.

My eyes widen. '*Shais . . .*'

'Well it's true. You could've pretended you went round to a friend's house and got caught up playing PlayStation or whatever idiotic activity—'

'Listen!'

'Don't speak to me like . . .' She trails off, hearing the reporter on the tablet.

'. . . *as Andrés López and twenty-one-year-old Zaman Akhtar.*'

My sister lets out a little gasp, nails pressed to her lips like diamante shields.

'*Notorious gang DX Dingoes is suspected to be operating in at least six boroughs in south London, but the full scale of the picture is as yet unknown. For now, charges of drug trafficking, embezzlement and firearm possession are expected.'*

'That boy was working at our shop!' Amma says in disbelief. 'He was carrying on with my own daughter, and I didn't even know! I must call your father.'

Shaista gets up, mumbling incoherently, before stumbling into the corridor. Amma follows Shais, and soon I can hear her muffled sobs. My own heartbeats go staccato. Come Monday, Imran will be back at school, and now that I know he's the cousin of a convicted gangsta, murdering me doesn't seem so far-fetched.

'Today, you are going to gain some experience in answering exam-style questions under timed conditions,' drones my English teacher, Ms Pettigrew.

I glance round at Noah, who is glaring at me. He jabs a finger at his phone, instructing me to text him my answers, or else. Daevon seems to be texting under his table. A few seconds later, Denusha's phone vibrates, and she starts giggling.

'Hush!' Ms Pettigrew snaps.

'It's not my fault if someone keeps sending me inappropriate dick pix,' Denusha mutters sulkily.

I wonder what she thinks an *appropriate* dick pic is.

'Any questions? No? Best of luck. Your time starts now.' Mrs Pettigrew stretches a bony finger towards the virtual timer. The numbers roll back as the thirty-minute countdown begins.

Today, I decide, opening my exam booklet, will be the day I score top marks and free myself from the brotherhood of the damned. If I can do it in maths, I can totally do it in English.

Section A is about Shakespeare, and skimming through the choices, the name Ariel jumps out at me. *Disney questions!* my demented brain thinks happily, before realizing it's an extract from *The Tempest*. I try to read it, but Sebastian the crab has begun singing 'Under the Sea' in my head. Only halfway through, it becomes a mash-up of Jme's 'Man Don't Care'.

I'm caught between having a flat-out panic attack and laughing hysterically when there's a knock at the classroom door. Mrs Pettigrew puts a finger to her lips, indicating to the messenger that he shouldn't disturb us. The boy hands over a note, and Mrs Pettigrew looks at me.

I swallow.

'Ilyas, Mr Gilchrist wants to see you in his office. The rest of you remain silent and keep working.'

Grabbing my bag (just in case I'm being fast-tracked to an exclusion) and dodging a kick from Noah, I follow the kid out. 'What's Gilchrist want?' I ask him.

The kid shrugs.

Could Imran's brain have haemorrhaged, leaving him a vegetable? My stomach ties itself in knots.

I knock on the deputy principal's door and shuffle into his office. Seeing Kelly there fills me with relief. Then I notice Gilchrist is a mess. Hair like a swirl of ice cream, red-radish eyes and belly poking through a shirt that is buttoned all wrong. Gilchrist gestures for me to take a seat.

'I'm sorry to pull you out of class, but I had to see you both urgently. Yesterday I received some shocking news.'

Imran passed away. I am so going to Hell . . .

'My wife was admitted to hospital last night.' The final word comes out in an emotional squeak, which he covers up by coughing into a boulder-sized fist.

Kelly helps him out. 'Is that why you didn't come back for us yesterday?'

He sighs looking like a forlorn bear. 'I was in shock . . . Completely slipped my mind.'

I exchange a glance with Kelly. 'Look accidents happen, innit?

It's cool. I won't say nothing to my mum.'

Kelly nods. 'I already told my mum I went to the library and didn't realize my phone had died. She thinks I'm irresponsible. Nothing new there, then.'

'I'm so sorry . . .' Gilchrist says.

'Do we still have detention after school?' Kelly asks.

Gilchrist shakes his head, rubbing a creased hanky under his nose. 'Just give me your letters at the end of the day so I can hold on to them for Monday.'

We nod and get up to leave.

'Remember, Ilyas, Kelly – life's too short to hold grudges.'

Closing the door behind us, me and Kelly exchange worried looks.

'Reckon he's having a breakdown,' she says sagely.

'Having? Already had one, more like! His eye bags were like hammocks for dolphins.' I sigh. 'Anyway, better get back to my "exam style" English test, I suppose.'

'It's like these people don't realize it's nearly the Christmas holidays,' she says, making me realize the exam idea wasn't just Ms Pettigrew being extra. Instead of winding down for the end of term, they're winding us up.

I watch her plodding away. 'Hey, Kelz,' I call, making her whirl round. 'Gotta ask. Why do you wear them boots?'

She looks down and shrugs. 'Because I like them?'

Kelly's friends hate her boots, and they seem to pull all the strings. Something doesn't add up. 'No offence, but they sorta look like man boots.'

She goes very quiet. 'They belonged to my dead Uncle Fiz.'

I swallow the foot in my mouth. 'Hey, sorry man. I didn't mean to be disrespectful.'

She crouches down, rubbing at a scuff mark. 'Uncle Fiz was the only member of my family who ever thought it was great that I wanted to be an author. Mum hated him.'

'Cos he supported your dreams?'

'That also, but mainly because he was gay and proud. She wouldn't let me see him because she thought he was corrupting me.'

'That is cold!'

Kelly sighs, her eyes glistening, and I immediately realize how close she must have been to this Uncle Fiz.

'I guess it's not completely her fault – she's from a really strict religious family. She didn't even go to his funeral.'

'But you did?'

She nods, smirking. 'I was only ten. I caught a bus and turned up late. His funeral was fab-u-lous. So many weeping drag queens in one place! They played the 1974 Elton John-Bernie Taupin collaboration "The Bitch Is Back". Uncle Fiz totally believed in reincarnation.'

I smile sympathetically. 'So you wear his boots to show solidarity.'

'And to piss Mum off, obvs!'

We both crack up.

'When I'm wearing these boots, I feel I can do anything – hop on a bus or take a rocket to the moon. That's how Uncle Fiz lived his life.'

'I hope he comes back as a unicorn. One with a rainbow mane.'

'He'd *love* that!' She gives me a goofy grin, then clip-clops down the corridor.

CHAPTER 22

'Yo, bro! You got a mo?' Daevon calls.

I'm standing in the lunch queue, getting stressed cos Mrs Waldorf, as part of her Make-Stanley-Park-Outstanding campaign, has shortened the lunch hour to forty-five minutes and launched some messed-up system letting kids from different years in at different times. Basically she thinks us Year 11s are bullying the lower school. Like making us hangry is going to fix that.

I scowl at Daevon. 'What you want, *bredrin*?' I hope I injected enough sarcasm into the last word to show him that all this 'brother' stuff is bollocks.

'You been ghosting. Where you at?'

'Dude, we literally just had English together!'

'Oh yeah.'

'My life ain't changed except I have detention with Gilchrist on a regular basis cos *someone* got him involved.'

'That someone was trying to save your life. Look, hate me all you want. Imran's back in school on Monday. Facts.'

'And?' I act like I'm not bothered by the news I've been dreading.

'We need to settle this beef. Don't want to see you get hurt. You and me were tight – remember that?'

'Stop holding up the queue!' snarls a dinner lady, misting the stainless-steel food containers with spittle.

'Yeah, can I get one of them, that, and a Radnor – the red one, please,' I say, pointing.

'Ilyas, Noah's on a mission to stab you,' Daevon whispers in my ear. 'His idea of a welcome back for Imran. Just watch your back, OK?'

'You, uh, wanna join me?' I say, jerking my head towards a table. It's a peace offering because, truth be told, I've been raging against my boy Daevon, when this aggression belongs to Imran and Noah. If he's remembering the old days, then maybe he does care.

Daevon looks away. 'Gonna take a rain check till you smooth things over with the big guy. See you Monday. Hopefully.'

It's the end of the day, and I'm standing outside F10. This is it. The last time me and Kelly will ever be together.

A little digging revealed she's in Set 1 for everything. Hell, last year she was a ball girl for the Wimbledon women's semi-final. Whether Kelly decides she wants to be the prime minister or a best-selling sci-fi author, nothing in life will ever hold her back. We're from totally different worlds, and in spite of everyone always going on about 'breaking the rules being the coolest thing ever', no one wants to cross the border into Freakdom.

I take a deep breath, then knock on the door. Poking my head round, I see Mr Gilchrist sitting there with his hands pressed together.

'Hello, Ilyas. Had a good day?' he asks in a distant voice.

I shrug. 'School's school, innit?'

He nods. 'Indeed it is. Ah, here's Kelly!'

I watch Kelly hurry in and take her regular spot, just behind me.

'Well,' Mr Gilchrist says, clearing his throat and frowning. 'I hope you two have finally managed to produce sincere letters of apology. I think we're all a little tired of this rigmarole.'

Kelly and me hand over our letters. Gilchrist studies them carefully, breath whistling through his hairy nostrils. He glances up, blue eyes flicking back and forth between us. 'I'm impressed. I really hope you mean what you've put down here.'

'Absolutely,' Kelly says, zipping up her bag. 'How's Mrs Gilchrist?'

'Much better, thanks,' he says.

'That's a relief,' I say. 'Hospitals are spooky places.'

Kelly smiles sweetly. 'Can we go now?'

'In a minute. Right, so here's the plan for Monday. You will both arrive at 8 a.m.'

'That's like half an hour early!' I say in surprise.

'It is *exactly* half an hour early, yes. This will give you ample time to come to my office and meet with Imran, who will be returning to school. He has been discharged from hospital. Kelly, a similar arrangement will be set up for you and Melanie by Mrs Waldorf.'

Other than one swallow, Kelly's poker face holds up way better than mine.

'Once we're all ready,' Gilchrist says, 'your letters will be returned to you, and you will have a chance to read them out to your victim. With any luck, your apology will be accepted, at which point we'll be in a position to draw a line under this unpleasant situation. Do you understand?'

'Yes, sir,' we both say.

'Good. Believe me, the new GCSEs are hard enough without having all this hanging over you. I fully expect you to keep your noses clean for the rest of the academic year. Is that clear?'

'Crystal,' Kelly says, pulling on her coat. The pale grey fur is so long and thick that she looks like a yeti.

'Got it,' I agree, slipping on my jacket.

Gilchrist rolls his eyes, 'Off you go.'

Kelly zooms out the door. I stare open-mouthed. Would it have hurt to smile or at least say bye?

Five days of detentions. Five days of friendship. Now the detentions are over, so are me and Kelly.

'See ya, sir,' I say heading out.

I nearly well up when I see Kelly stood by the double doors. She taps her watch meaningfully, and I rush towards her, unable to suppress the grin splitting my face.

'I've told my mum I have detention, so I'm good for the next forty minutes. Wanna hang before my piano lesson?' She slings her backpack over a fluffy shoulder.

'Here for it!' I confirm.

Little bubbles of joy flood my chest as her arm slips neatly into the crook of mine and she drags me down the corridor.

'I picked up a cool new manga at the library today and I hear they're making it into a movie. Are you into anime?'

'Not really,' I confess.

She stops walking and points to a little furball hanging off her bag on a golden keychain. 'Do you know who this is?'

I squint at the ball of fluff with the crazy googly eyes and pointy ears. 'Bugs Bunny?'

For a moment I believe she's going to hit me as her cheeks balloon with frustration.

'You don't know Ghibli?'

'Is that an anime studio?'

'It's *the* anime studio.' She grasps my shoulder, 'We are going to have ourselves a little anime-fest tomorrow at my place. Your attendance is mandatory. What's your digits?'

My heart does a happy dance as we exchange phone numbers.

'What do you want to do now?' she asks, as we head out of school.

'Let's get coffee,' I say, mentally tasting gingerbread latte on my tongue. 'Did you say something about *piano*?'

'Ugh. Mum thinks piano lessons make me a shoo-in for

Cambridge.' She pinches her temples and shudders, making me laugh. 'Plans are afoot to move me to a grammar school for A levels.'

'Cambridge, huh?' I say, impressed. 'I'll be lucky if my dad even lets me go uni.'

'Why wouldn't he?' she asks as we approach the Starbucks knock-off.

A man in a trench coat comes sauntering out, then holds the door open for Kelly giving her a creepy wink. She smiles sweetly, then hugging my arm, drags me in. As we join the queue, I let the warm, syrupy smell flow over me, rubbing my frozen hands together.

We order lattes – me, a gingerbread; Kelly, a red velvet – then carry them over to a quiet spot near the window.

'So why do you think your dad won't let you go to uni?' she asks, picking up the thread I thought she'd lost interest in.

'He thinks it's my duty to continue the family business. When Great-Grandpa Mian came over here in the sixties, Asian food wasn't a thing. He saw a gap in the market and opened up a small grocery store selling all the stuff immigrants were missing from back home. You know, *bhindi*, *karela*, *fufu* and *ackee*. Dude was OG.'

'That must've been *so* popular.' Kelly swirls her latte with a straw, then licks the cream off the end.

'Nah. Tons of people had the same idea, innit? I'm not saying G-gramps didn't make money, but never enough to build the empire he was dreaming of. His son, my grandad Hamza, was wicked smart. Went to uni and everything, but it didn't do him any good.'

'Why not?'

'Cos racism?' I take a long drag on my straw, the sugar giving me a hit. 'It messed him up. He tore up his hard-earned degree and went to work at G-gramps's store. Years later, he had my dad, who eventually inherited the store. Since my bro Amir's gone America and disowned us, I'm next in line to carry on the family tradition.'

'Sorry, but that sucks,' Kelly says, examining her straw. 'You get it from both ends: tradition and racism. I know *I* couldn't handle it.'

'Not like I get a choice.'

She falls into a reflective silence. 'Mum helps people get qualifications to improve their job prospects. No offence, but nearly all of them are people of colour. She reckons it's because "certain communities don't value education".'

'What do you think?' I ask, studying her expression.

Kelly shakes her head, wild curls bouncing free of her hood. 'Well, based on what you've just told me about racism, she's guilty of victim blaming.'

I stare at her, barely able to believe my ears. 'You reckon?'

'Come on, you think I don't know my own privilege?'

I blush, because it had crossed my mind. Mostly because I once mentioned white privilege in a PSCHE lesson and ended up in detention with Mrs Waldorf who told me to 'stop seeing colour'.

Something suddenly occurs to me.

'The Afrobeats in that Morocco-trip assembly. That was you, wasn't it?'

She covers her mouth and giggles. 'Oh my God, Jade got so pissed! I love me some Swift, just as much as the next girl, and I know Afrobeats doesn't cover all of Africa, but I couldn't resist.'

We fist bump.

Salivating, I gaze at the counter like a meerkat. 'How do waffles sound?'

'At 4.20 in the afternoon? Sounds like yum.'

I hop over to the counter, returning with a platter of delicious waffles and four different syrups.

'I was thinking,' I say. 'How comes Melanie got a week off school? All you did was punch her in the mouth.'

'Apparently she was in therapy. Hashtag *first-world problems*.' She gives me an ironic grin before slathering her waffle in chocolate syrup. 'Soooo, does Imran have a girlfriend?'

'New one every day!' I say with a chuckle. 'Man's a regular thirst trap.'

'What sort of girls does he go for?'

'Hot, stacked, braindead!' My laughter falls flat when I catch a flicker of disappointment on her face. 'Hey, Kelly, you do *not* want to be taken in by that fool. Trust.'

She pokes holes through her waffle. 'Jade hates him because she's classist. Melanie, because she's racist. Nicole absolutely loathes him because he turned her down. Why do you hate him enough to mess with him?' she asks curiously.

I frown, stubbing my toe on the base of the table. 'Cussed my mum,' I say in a quiet voice, all those feelings threatening to overwhelm me again.

'Ugh! Why do boys always get so triggered when someone insults their mum? Do you think your mum even cares what some teenager she doesn't even know thinks of her?'

I shake my head. 'It's ain't that. Amma – my mum, yeah – she's like the sweetest person ever. She's the type to love you before she even knows you. Cuts me up to hear Imran saying sexual stuff about her.'

Her eyes widen at the mention of 'sexual stuff'. 'Well, you know what? He's a dick, and karma came calling.'

Hearing her diss Imran makes me feel unbelievably happy, and I hurriedly cram three forkfuls of waffle in my mouth to hide my smile.

'Do you think Melanie will forgive you or . . . ?' I want to add, *can we be friends instead?*

'It could go either way, I guess. But hey – what I can't control isn't worth worrying about.'

Solid advice, but she doesn't look like she entirely believes it herself. The truth is I can't help worrying about Imran. But with final exams not that far away, at least there's an end in sight.

'Can I ask why you hit your girl Melanie?'

She sighs, putting down her fork. 'She kept harping on about Uncle Fiz's boots being ugly and embarrassing. She was pressing all my buttons, and I let slip why I wear them. "Newsflash!" she said. "Wearing dead gay boots is so not cool. What did he die of anyway – AIDs?" I lost control.'

My eyes widen, then I shake my head. 'That was low. Know what's funny, Kelz? You and me both got suspended for standing up to bullies. We shoulda got medals.'

'I know, right? What's up with the world?'

CHAPTER 23

'Amma, can I talk to you, please?' I ask, with Sparkle nestled in the crook of my arm, pink nose twitching.

It's Saturday morning, and Amma's monthly weekend shift at the library.

'Later, *beyta*,' she says, adjusting her hijab in the mirror. 'We've got a tai chi instructor coming in, and Chantelle's just texted to say she can't make it.'

'Just while you're doing your hijab then?' Sparkle's ears perk up, hearing the tension in my voice. I tickle her fluffy cheek till she settles down again. 'I just wanted to let you know, I wrote that letter of apology to Imran, and Mr Gilchrist is making me read it out to him on Monday so we can put it all behind us.'

Amma nods. 'Mr Gilchrist called me yesterday asking me to accompany you.'

'I'm really trying, Amma.'

'I know. I just wish you were sorry in your *heart*.'

I frown, looking down at Sparkle. 'He said stuff about you, Amma. Proper filthy stuff.' My cheeks burn with shame recalling Imran's crude words.

She looks at me. 'You silly, silly boy. Do you think you've "saved my honour" by hitting that boy? Do you have any idea how embarrassing it is to have other mothers offer me sympathy for raising my son wrong?' The tears lining her eyes are like acid in my throat. 'This is all Osman's fault.'

'What is?' Dad says, emerging from the sitting room with the sports section of the newspaper in his hand.

Amma waves her hijab pin at him. 'The reason your son got suspended was because of this stupid code, this masculinity, that you are so desperate to instil in him.'

'Our son finally shows some balls, and you want to castrate him?' he asks in horror.

'I don't have time for this!' Amma grabs her bag and storms out the front door, slamming it behind her.

'Oi,' Dad says, making a whistling sound. 'You putting me in the dog house with your Amma, lad?'

I shake my head.

'Real men don't grass.' He gives me a warning look. 'Next time you wanna shoot your mouth off, remember that.'

I nod.

'And why are you carrying that rabbit around like a bloody handbag?'

'Her claws need trimming . . .'

'You gonna be painting its nails too?'

I shake my head, flushing.

'Go on – give it to Shaista.'

'I can't. She doesn't want Sparkle any more, remember?'

Dad clucks his tongue looking from me to Sparkle, making me feel like a deviant.

'Um, I'm gonna be over at Daevon's for most of the day. Studying.'

'Studying made Amir into a selfish git. Careful it doesn't happen to you.' He thumps my back and heads to the kitchen to grab the blood-pressure-reducing cocktail Shais cooked up in her cauldron for him.

Kelly lives in a detached house on the south side of town, somewhere I've never been before. The pavements are so clean, they practically sparkle. The Matthews' property is three Tudorish buildings whacked together – all shingled white walls with dark half-timbering. There's a massive tall one with a steeply pitched gabled roof, a thinner one to the left with its own wooden porch, and a much smaller, single-floor building beside it. I gently close the front gate behind me and walk up the long stone drive. Two cars are parked outside – a turquoise Mini and a four by four. Off to the side, I spot a garage, where I reckon her mum keeps the silver hybrid, though there's probably room for a couple in there.

Approaching the front door, I catch sight of myself in the large bay windows: black-and-gold-foil adidas hoody paired with ripped skinny jeans from Primark. I suddenly feel too ghetto for this place, and the instinct to bail bubbles to the surface. Pulling back my hood, I give my scalp a good rub. Fluff from the fabric lining has caught on my head stubble, and I'm suddenly worried her mum might think I have nits.

I ring the doorbell, telling myself my shakes are down to the cold weather. Somewhere inside the house, someone is listening to Radio 4.

Just as I'm about to ring the doorbell again, it swings open, and standing before me is a thin blonde lady in a beige silk blouse and black leather trousers.

'Yes? Can I help you?' she asks, eyes travelling all over me like she's trying to work out what I'm selling.

'Hey, er, *hello*. You must be Kelly's mum. I'm Ilyas Mian.' I stick my hand out, trying to be a gentleman.

Mrs Matthews visibly flinches, so I stuff my hand back inside my kangaroo pocket.

'Is Kelly in?'

'Oh, you're one of Kelly's friends. Yes, she mentioned you were coming, I just hadn't realized . . . Do come in after you've wiped your feet on the mat.'

I scrub my already-clean trainers on the mat. 'Shall I take them off?' I ask, making sure I sound friendly, not sarcastic.

She blinks in surprise. 'Good heavens, no. There's no Axminster here, and we're not *that* house-proud.'

I laugh along with her, though I have no clue what an Axminster is. In my head, I'm imagining the prime minister swinging an axe at the leader of the opposition.

She brings me into the entrance hall, and I kid you not, there is an honest-to-God chandelier dripping with more bling than the pimpest of pimp daddies. Double doors with golden handles and frosted glass panes stand to the right, and it's virtually impossible not to imagine a gigantic ballroom lurking behind it. A mirror the size of a dinner table is up on the wall, encased in an ornate cream frame. Etched into it are words from some poem I don't recognize. To my left, stairs sweep skyward, laid with plush grey carpet, guarded by two polished newel posts.

'What did you say your name was?' she asks.

'Ilyaaaaaaas,' I say, nearly dislocating my jaw.

'Well, hello, *Elias*.'

Somehow she still manages to pronounce it wrong. I suppress the urge to facepalm.

Kelly comes tumbling down the stairs in a furry pink onesie. Her mother's face is priceless.

'What on *earth* are you wearing?!'

'It's a *kigurumi* onesie, and it's super comfortable, thanks,' Kelly replies. 'Me and Ilz are going to be chilling out to a Studio Ghibli marathon, so I think you'll agree, it's the perfect wear. Come on!' She grips my hand and whisks me up the stairs.

'Sorry about her,' Kelly whispers. 'Borg Queen. Remember?'

She throws open her bedroom door, and I stumble in. I think I actually turn in a full circle, mouth hanging open like a dead fish. It's *beautiful*. 'Kelly, man, your house is a *palace*.'

She wrinkles her face as if the compliment embarrasses her. 'You should see Jade's place. They have *nine* bedrooms and a boat house.'

But I'm not interested in Jade or anybody else.

'I totally forgot to send the memo telling you to bring a onesie,' she says, poking around in her wardrobe. She whips out a plush yellow Pikachu number and shakes it at me.

'Nah, I'm good,' I say, physically backing away.

'You wouldn't stretch it or anything. You're definitely smaller than I am, anyway.'

She drapes the onesie around my neck like a scarf, then practically wheels me through a door. I gawp cos the girl's got her own bathroom. Shais would kill for an en suite.

'Don't be long!' she calls rapping on the bathroom door. '*My Neighbour Totoro* starts in T minus three.'

Kelly's counting down the last twenty seconds when I reluctantly emerge.

'Check you out!' she says, wolf-whistling. 'Gotta catch 'em all.'

'Man looks like a banana,' I say miserably.

She pulls my hood up. 'There, now you're definitely twenty-five per cent more Pokémon.'

We sit together on her bean bag – shaped like a giant world globe – and she grabs the remote. The door flies open. Kelly's mum brings in a tray with snacks and drinks. She gives me a plastic smile, her eyes taking in my onesie, lingering over my crotch.

'Er, Kelly insisted I wear it for the cartoons . . .' I say, hoping she doesn't think anything dirty is going on here.

'That's fine. Just keep the door open, please,' she says, stiffly giving her daughter a meaningful look.

'Mum!' Kelly snaps. 'It's the middle of winter. Doors were invented to conserve heat.'

Her mother turns her disapproval up to a solid ten. The door situation is not up for debate.

'I hope you realize you're contributing to global warming,' Kelly says reproachfully.

'It's a risk I'll have to take. You know the rules. Door open or Elias will have to go home.'

'Sorry, Mrs Matthews,' I call, cringing as she leaves.

Mopping her eyes with a bundle of tissues, I see that Kelly's wet face is flushed pink.

'You were right,' I say, clearing my throat as the credits roll. 'That was *intense*.'

She sniffles into her tissue before blinking at me in disappointment. 'Why aren't you crying?'

'I am,' I say, hitting my chest. 'Man's tears are internal.'

There's a quick rap of knuckles on wood, and Kelly's mum reappears in the doorway. Even the woman's knocks sound sarcastic.

'What is it, Mum?' Kelly calls from the other side of the bean bag. At some point during the movie, we must have slid off it and ended up on the floor without realizing.

Mrs Matthews's plastic smile returns. 'Elias, would you mind if I have a quick word with my daughter?' she says, motioning for Kelly to get up.

'Course not . . . I really love your house, by the way.'

She ignores the compliment, muttering to Kelly, who has joined her at the threshold.

'He's staying for lunch,' I hear Kelly state.

An uncomfortable silence follows, during which her mother's lips twitch.

'Er, maybe I should be getting back?' I say, getting up. 'Ms Mughal set us a ton of homework . . .'

'Don't bail on me now, bestie,' Kelly says, wagging a finger. 'We still have Lunch and Story Time to cross off my bucket list, and *then* you can go home.'

Bestie? The only thing I can do is nod.

The Matthews' kitchen and dining room is open plan. The kitchen section is like a showroom with about a billion different cupboards, a double oven and *two* massive fridges. I squeeze my eyes shut and pray some day I can buy a kitchen like this for Amma. Shaking away my daydream, I try to impress Kelly's mum by pulling a chair out for her at the dining table, but she shoos me away, telling me not to be so old-fashioned.

'We're all feminists in this house,' she says reprovingly. 'Hand me your plate, dear.'

A slice of pink mystery meat is placed on it, followed by baby roast potatoes and perspiring asparagus. She's reaching for the gravy boat before I find my voice.

'Er, Mrs Matthews, I can't eat meat. Sorry.'

She freezes, staring at the piece of meat as if it just insulted her. The woman is not happy.

'Mum, I told you Ilyas is Muslim,' Kelly says crossly.

'Well Muslims eat meat too, so long as it doesn't come from a pig,' her mother replies. 'Isn't that right, Elias?'

I meet her steely gaze and feel my knees tremble. 'Only if it's halal . . .'

'I have a Muslim student who happily snacks on sausage rolls at social gatherings. He even indulges in the odd glass of wine. Are you not like that?'

'I . . . uh . . .' I shake my head.

'Mum, stop making him feel uncomfortable,' Kelly snaps, striking the table with the handle of her fork.

'Kelly, it's OK. Really,' I say, not wanting to cause tension. 'I'll just have some of the veggies, please.'

'That's very reasonable of you, Elias. Sorry, but you *do* need to tell me if you have special dietary requirements.' She places an assortment of steamed vegetables on my plate. 'I'm many things, but sadly "mind reader" isn't one of them.'

A toxic silence fills the room. For a while, the only sounds are the scraping of knives on plates and my chewing, which is way too loud. I'm so embarrassed by it, I hardly eat a thing.

'So,' Kelly's mum pipes up finally, pushing a slice of folded flesh inside her mouth. 'What do your parents do?'

'My mum's a librarian, and my dad runs his own business.'

'How lovely. Do you have any ambitions?' She fills a fluted glass with red wine.

'Not really,' I say quietly.

'He does, actually,' Kelly interjects. 'He's going to be an amazing comic book artist. He has a brilliant idea for a superhero. Something that's never been done before.'

'Superhero?' Mrs Matthews says, like she doesn't know whether to laugh or despair. 'I would've thought you were too old for that sort of thing.'

'Do you think babies write their own books?' Kelly is slaying with the comebacks, burning like the brightest beacon. Man, in that moment, not only can I see her as prime minister, but the best one that ever lived.

'So what does this superhero do that's so very different from the rest?' Mrs Matthews asks.

'He's British Pakistani and Muslim. And he has a whole unique origin story,' I babble.

'I would've thought bringing religion and nationalism into comics was anathema. How does it differ from propaganda? As you can see, Elias, we like to have stimulating discussions over our meals.'

I struggle to put my thoughts into words cos this woman is terrifying. Plus she's speaking a language I barely understand.

'It's about representation,' Kelly says, rolling her eyes at me. 'All this time, we've had a bunch of white dudes saving the world. Same old, same old is boring.'

Mrs M titters against the back of a delicate hand, weighed down by a rock nearly as big as the chandelier. 'Good heavens, how seriously you young people take your entertainment!'

'Mrs Matthews, don't you think there should be more female superheroes so young girls can look up to them?' I say.

Kelly's mum dabs at the corners of her mouth with a napkin. 'No, I don't. Women have always been more sensible and practical than men. All this superhero worship just demonstrates delusion. As I've told Kelly, I believe that fantasy – or "speculative fiction", if you want to be grandiose about it – is the opium of the people. It distracts people from the real issues. No wonder there's so much political upheaval in the world.'

'The world's in trouble because of an orange troll named Trump,' Kelly snaps.

'Come, come, you can't blame all the world's ills on one individual,' her mum says easily. 'Most of the world's leaders are – surprise, surprise – men. Until this is addressed, the decline will continue.'

'But that's just it,' I say, finally finding my rhythm. 'Equality comes from people power. So how do you motivate them? Since comics are so hot right now, why not use them to inspire the youth? All the best ideas start out as dreams.'

Mrs Matthews gives me a superior smile as she swirls her glass. 'If you say so. Personally I think they arise from a sound education. It's why I spend my life helping less fortunate people gain access to it.'

Kelly puts her knife and fork down. 'And how does that make

you feel, Mum? Hmm? Like a great white saviour?'

'Kelly, please don't . . .' I mutter.

'Not everybody does things for fame and fortune,' Mrs Matthews says, bristling. 'Isn't that right, Elias? You're happy to pursue a career in comic books even though you know it will never pay the bills. But what it will give you is personal satisfaction.'

'Oh it'll pay, all right,' Kelly says, her chin jutting proudly. 'Ilyas and I are going to collaborate on his brilliant comic. Better strap in, Mum, because it's going to rock this world.'

CHAPTER 24

On Monday morning, I have seriously mixed feelings about going to school. On the one hand, I am dreading facing Imran. On the other, I am hype for Kelly. I carefully pack new pages of my PakCore comic into my bag for her to take a look at.

Amma is waiting for me outside in the car. I feel like a little kid again, being driven to school, but Gilchrist expects her to be part of this 'reconciliation' thing just to emphasize how important it is.

'Don't forget this,' she says, wrapping a scarf round my neck. 'We don't want you ending up with a cold this close to the end of term.'

'Thanks, Amma.'

'You made a mistake, Ilyas. I'm proud of you for owning up to it. I'll be even prouder when you apologize to Imran.'

I sigh, a protest rising up my throat. Amma watches me closely. I press my lips together and nod.

Driving to school this early in the morning is surreal. The place is a ghost town with a funny little milk float buzzing along like an apparition from the past. As we drive further into town, I see dog-walkers and joggers with smartwatches strapped to their wrists. One of these joggers is fricking hot. It's, like, minus two degrees out there, but she's rocking her shorts.

Amma clears her throat. 'Hijab isn't just about this, young man,' she says, indicating her scarf. 'It's also about *these*.' She gestures at her eyes, making me blush, and I lower my gaze.

Once Amma has parked her car, we head over to reception. Most of the desks are still empty, collages of bright Post-its covering computer screens like shutters. The lady at the main desk looks up and smiles at Amma.

'Ilyas or Imran?' she asks me.

'Ilyas.'

She starts to make small talk with Amma, having a go at me for dragging my mum down to school on such a cold morning. Then she starts talking about her own son being a 'little terror' who bit his nursery teacher's arm. She has no idea where that sort of behaviour comes from, but she's taking him to see a child psychologist next week. Amma sighs sympathetically, quoting research about the positive effects of green spaces. I yawn, lamenting the extra half-hour I could've had in bed.

The receptionist takes us over to Gilchrist's office.

'Good morning, good morning!' Mr Gilchrist says, standing up to shake Amma's hand.

'Good morning, Mr Gilchrist,' Amma replies. 'Sorry, I don't shake hands.'

'Oh, of course not! Won't you sit down?' he says, a little flustered. 'I must say, you're very prompt.'

'Ilyas was eager to get this off his chest as soon as possible,' Amma says simply.

I glance nervously across at the other seat, imagining Imran sitting there, glaring at me. Discreetly I shove it a few centimetres away with my toe while Gilchrist is rooting around in his top drawer for my letter.

'Nervous?' he asks, cocking a shaggy eyebrow at me.

'No. Yes. I dunno, sir. I just want this beef to be over with . . .' My voice breaks, and I blush.

'I'm here to make sure that's exactly what happens.'

'Sir, I'm scared he's going to—' I hold back the words 'kill me' and shake my head.

'Take revenge? Let me put your mind at ease. The whole point of this meeting is to end this feud and prevent repercussions. The school will support both of you. You have my word.' He glances up as there is a knock at the door. My heart skips a beat.

The receptionist pokes her head round. 'The other student is here with his mum.'

'Perfect. Send them in,' Gilchrist says.

Imran strolls in and crashes on a chair, manspreading like he owns the place. I notice he's got a nose stud that sparkles like a tiny star. There is absolutely no sign of him ever having been injured. His tiny, frail-looking mother flashes me a death look, then perches on the far side of Imran, muttering as she adjusts her turquoise *dupatta*, bracelets rattling like shackles.

'*Assalaamu alaykum*,' Amma says.

'*Vaa salaam!*' Mrs Akhtar shoots back, shading Amma by refusing to even look at her.

'OK – first of all, thank you all for coming,' Mr Gilchrist says, pressing the wooden veneer of his desk so hard it crackles beneath his fingers. 'I'm especially grateful to Mrs Akhtar and Mrs Mian, who have taken time out to attend this important meeting.'

Imran smirks because his mum spends all day watching Urdu dramas on TV or on the phone to Pakistan.

'You're welcome,' Amma says. 'We both want things to be resolved quickly so our sons can get on with their studies.'

Imran's mum asks him in Punjabi what Amma just said. He tells her to shut up. Gilchrist raises eyebrows.

'My mum don't speak English, innit,' Imran says, folding his arms across his broad chest, thrusting hands into his armpits.

I study him again, scanning for the head wound. I decide he must have Wolverine's mutant Healing Factor because there isn't a scratch on him. Even his nose piercing looks healed.

'Oh, well, please do translate for her, Imran,' says Gilchrist, smiling at his mum.

'Calm.' Imran nods, not bothering to translate a word.

'So, I just want to preface this meeting by stating the facts,' Gilchrist continues, consulting a printout. 'There was some name-calling in the boy's changing room at the end of a PE lesson, which resulted in a physical altercation between your sons. Ilyas sustained injuries to his nose and mouth, while Imran fell back and cracked his head open.'

'No, no,' interjects Imran's mum. She points at me. 'He have knife! He kill him, you know?' She makes stabbing motions in the air.

Mr Gilchrist shakes his head. 'No, Mrs Akhtar. There were witnesses, and we checked the boys' bags. No weapons of any sort were involved.'

When Imran doesn't say anything, Amma speaks up, translating Gilchrist's words into Punjabi for his mother.

'*Leh!*' his mum says, thrusting her palm out in exasperation. It's clear that in her mind, everything is a conspiracy against Imran, and I'm the spawn of Satan.

'Consequently, and as per school guidelines, Ilyas was suspended for a week. Following on from that, a week's worth of detentions was set. I am satisfied he has had time to reflect on the error of his ways. During this time, he penned a letter of apology to you, Imran, which he will now read aloud.'

Imran turns his chair round to face me, a cocky smirk spreading across his face.

Amma pats my back, letting me know she's here for me. I swallow twice, then start to read.

'Dear Imran,' I begin.

'Sorry, didn't catch that,' Imran says, bending forward and cupping his ear. 'Think the head injury might've made me a little deaf.'

Gilchrist glares at him. 'Don't be silly.'

'Dear Imran,' I repeat, my feet itching. 'I would like to apologize to you for causing your head injury. I never meant for it to happen. You called my mum names, and I responded with violence, which I now know was a stupid thing to do. I want you to know I acted in the heat of the moment, and my judgement was i-i-i—'

'Impaired,' Amma says gently.

'Impaired,' I get out. 'I shouldn't have hit you, and I am really sorry. I would also like to apologize to your mum for all the stress I have caused her. Finally I would like to apologize for bringing the school into disrepute. I hope you can forgive me. Yours faithfully, Ilyas Mian.'

Amma squeezes my shoulder and nods her head. I sigh, the tension finally slipping from my shoulders.

Gilchrist prompts Imran with raised eyebrows. 'Well, I'm sure you'll agree that was an admirable apology. It takes a great man or woman to admit their mistakes. Would you like to say anything to Ilyas in return?'

Imran shrugs, scratching his nose. I now spot some redness around his stud, which makes him more human.

'You let me down, fam. I treated you like a brother and protected you from bullies. And you went and stabbed me in the back. But it's calm. I'mma be the bigger man and let things slide. But you try something dumb like this again, even *I* won't be able to stop my mum from going straight to the feds. You feel me?'

His mother glares over his shoulder at me. '*They'll lock you up in prison. The inmates will see a Pakistani boy and think you're a terrorist. They'll rip you into pieces!*' she hisses in Punjabi.

My eyes widen in fear.

'Don't say anything back,' Amma says. With those gentle words, she's informed Gilchrist of Mrs Akhtar baiting me.

'OK, well let's wrap this up with a little handshake in the spirit of good sportsmanship, shall we?' he says.

Imran looks at me and smiles. I cautiously hold my hand out, and it's gobbled up by his giant one. For one horrible moment, I know exactly what he's going to do. Crush every bone in my drawing hand so the only talent I have is lost forever. But instead he yanks me towards him and gives me a proper bro-hug.

'I own you,' he whispers.

CHAPTER 25

I'm jamming stuff in my locker at break, when multiple shadows fall over me like nets. I whip round to see Imran flanked by Noah and Daevon. My stomach bungee jumps itself into knots.

'You took out your cornrows,' I say to Daevon, distracting myself and everyone else from my impending death. Daevon's hair is a puffy globe with a wooden afro comb poking out like a side parting. I wish I had hair like Daevon. 'Man looks peng!'

Daevon gives the ghost of a smile, twisting his curly beard hairs pensively. 'Thanks, blud.'

'You done it yet?' Imran asks abruptly. 'Got jiggy with a girl?'

My insides shrivel. I assumed putting him in hospital was my ticket out of this gang. 'Look, maybe it's best if I don't hang with you guys any more . . .'

'DedManz for life, bro. We got each other's backs till death do us. You feel me?'

The threat is clear as he makes the DedManz hand signal. Four seconds is the extent of my great protest before responding with the same sign of loyalty.

'We cool then?' I ask, with disbelief.

Imran chuckles, rubbing his knuckles over my skull like a scouring pad. 'Yeah, course. We're basically wolves. We growl, we fight, we lick our wounds, then carry on.'

Grabbing my shoulder, he leads me out into the chill air of the playground. Surrounded by DedManz, I feel like a ball being dribbled to the edge of a cliff.

'Anyway,' he says, blowing on his hands. 'Noah here tells me he saw you hanging with a Becky. Which one is it?'

I swallow. 'Noah's full of it. Man's so high, he'd hump a tree and swear down it was Ariana Grande.'

Daevon laughs as Noah jabs me in the stomach. My breakfast rises in a sizzling sauce of gastric acid. I glare at Noah.

'Leave him,' Imran tells Noah. 'Ilyas is nails. Little shit put me in hospital, innit?'

He booms with laughter, and Noah and Daevon join in. I giggle like the wuss I am.

'How long was man in for?' Noah asks.

Imran shrugs. 'Just overnight. Pretended it was longer cos I didn't wanna come back to this dump, innit?'

DedManz roar with laughter just as Kelly rounds the corner of the school building into the playground.

Jade and Melanie step into view, laughing, their clones Nicole and Victoria bringing up the rear. A flash of anger flares in my mind. How dare Kelly sell out so quickly? Then I remember I'm doing exactly the same. We're just a couple of kids who wish we were braver than we are.

'You like that girl, don't you?' Imran says so close to my ear, it sounds like he's inside my head.

I jolt, quickly looking away and shaking my head.

'Sure you do,' he persists. 'Her name's Jade. Check out all that gorgeous blonde hair and her rack.'

The fact that he's not talking about Kelly comes as a huge relief.

'I see you checking me out,' he continues as if speaking to Jade. 'But every time man gets close, you back off.'

'Gal's racist!' Noah suggests, hocking up some phlegm and shooting it inches from my foot.

'Nah, just scared. Scared she'll like it a bit too much.'

Noah grins, his eyes strangely dull and lifeless. 'Let's find out after school. Your mans will hold her down for you.'

'Noah, man,' Daevon says squeezing the bridge of his nose. 'You always take it too far.'

I look at Daevon with newfound respect.

'Look, I gotta go,' I say, hoping to get away before the conversation turns uglier.

Imran snags my skinny wrist. 'Yo! DedManz is leaving the building. A whole week without tagging? Fools gonna start claiming our turf.'

Once again, I find myself scooped up in a tidal wave of bodies and marched along to the school gate.

'Lunch passes?' demands the dinner lady at the gate, her dry face barely visible between a thick scarf and a woolly hat.

Imran flashes his forged pass, while Noah and Daevon bundle me into the street.

Outside, Imran ignites his vape pen and blows a big ball of smoke into the air.

'You nuts?' I say to Imran. 'Gilchrist's gonna be keeping an extra close eye on you and me. We go bunking, we're dead meat.'

Imran whirls round and backhands me. I feel the tiny capillaries burst in my cheek bringing tears to my eyes. The fierce wind amplifies the pain.

'Gimme status, fam!' He thrusts the drawstring bag of paint cans into my shaking hand. 'Hold on to these and do your ting when you're told. Otherwise keep your mouth shut.'

I catch Daevon's eye. He silently plucks out his afro comb and teases the fluffy ends of his hair.

'Come on!' Imran calls, jogging up the Crompton bridge.

A truck roars under it, filling the air with the beefy stench of horse manure.

'Daev, I can't do this no more . . .' I whisper.

He looks at me and shrugs. 'Up to you, mate. It's one tag

or a whole lotta hassle. You decide.'

Struggling with my own conscience, I ball my fists. 'I just wanna be free to do my own thing.'

'Shoulda thought of that before you took the DedManz pledge.'

'Oi! Where's my mans at?' Imran hollers, leaning over the bridge. In a fluid motion, he leaps up on to the edge.

'Look at dem slow bitches!' Noah's scathing face rises into view.

Imran closes his eyes and throws his arms wide. 'I'm king of the world!' he shouts. He tips backwards, where Noah sacrifices himself as a crash mat. They both tumble out of sight, hooting with laughter.

'They were just *joking* about rape, man?' I say to Daevon, trying to keep my hysterical voice down.

'Locker room bantz, innit?' he says stiffly.

Tears prick my eyes and make my voice wobble. 'I made a mistake, Daev. But I know what I want now.'

'Yeah? And what's that?'

'I want out.' I touch his arm. 'Help me, bro. *Please.*'

Daevon studies the desperation in my eyes before glancing up to Imran on the bridge. 'You try leaving, Imran's gonna stab you.'

'Then I'll do a runner. I'll grab my shit and take off.'

Daevon cough-laughs. 'You think Auntie Foz's gonna be cool with that? Not to mention you'd be leaving your family as collateral.'

My eyes widen in horror. 'Imran wouldn't go that far . . .'

He turns to face me. 'You seen the news lately? London's become the capital city of stabbings. Don't forget who his cousin is, neither.'

I punch the rail in frustration, grazing my knuckles. 'So you're saying the only way out of DedManz is to become an actual dead man?'

'Pretty much,' he says, starting to climb the steps. He clicks his fingers and points. 'Or it's just one tag.'

I drag my feet up the concrete stairs, peering over the side, wishing I could switch places with one of those lorry drivers, spend all day on the road, running away from relationships, arguments and problems.

'You lot wanna see something cool?' Imran asks when we finally make it to the top.

'Here for it, bruv,' Daevon wheezes, hands on knees.

'Get ready to have your minds blown.' Imran yanks his tie down and over his head, tossing it aside and ripping open his shirt.

A pair of black-and-blue angel's wings unfurl under Imran's collar bones. The edges are pink and raw, but fine shading and diluted inks make it look 3D.

'How on earth did man get a tattoo?' Noah asks. 'Last time I went, I got told not to come back till I'm eighteen.'

'What's the matter, Ilyas? Don't like man's tattoo?' Imran asks, seeing my face.

I catch a glimpse of another mark, just above his waistband. It reminds me of something, but he quickly hitches up his trousers before I can make out what it is.

'Dope,' I lie. 'But what you gonna do when you're old and wrinkly?'

He laughs. 'If the feds don't get me, I'm staying young *forever*.'

'Me too,' Noah agrees.

'Some day, we're all getting tagged,' Imran says, slapping a palm over his heart solemnly.

I sigh, scratching my sideburn, realizing that my art is all about somebody I don't even like; realizing that when people see me, they actually see Imran, or at best one of his lackeys. Daevon might say it's 'just one tag', but that's till the next one. And the one after that . . . 'Where do you want it?'

'What colour do you normally start with?' Imran asks, glancing into the drawstring bag of paint cans. 'Yellow?'

'No, brown.'

He grabs the brown and pushes it into my hand, tucking a zip-seal bag of special nozzles into my pocket.

'Best hold tight, fam,' he advises solemnly.

There's time to blink before Imran lifts me and flips me over the side of the bridge. Suddenly the world is upside down, and I'm swinging like a pendulum above noisy traffic.

'What you doing?!' I cry, hissing and spitting like a feral cat. From between my feet, I see Imran's grimacing face. He's holding tightly on to my ankles, a vein throbbing on his forehead from the effort.

'Stop squirming, you idiot, or you're gonna die!' Noah says.

He and Daevon have grabbed on too, flanking Imran.

'Please!' I beg, going rigid. 'Pull me up! I ain't ready!'

'Naw, you ready, fam,' Imran says, feigning sympathy.

'Please! Daev!'

Daevon meets my eyes, and I see the conflict in them. 'Just shut up and spray the damn tag!' he shouts. 'Quicker you do it, quicker we can pull you back up.' He cusses, spitting over the side.

Blood rushes into the bowl of my skull, drowning my brain. '*Please* . . . I can't breathe . . .'

'Do it or we'll drop you!' Noah shrieks, giving my left leg a terrible shake.

Imran's after a Heaven: a tag in a place so difficult to access, it immediately boosts your gang's rep. I shake the can, whimpering as it sets me off swinging again. The rattle of the glass bead is the sound of my teeth.

'You're doing great!' Daevon shouts, even though I haven't even started yet.

A fine mist peppers the air as I push down on the cap. My shirt takes some serious blow back, but the majority lands on the bland grey concrete, building up to a glossy coat. A suicidal determination uncoils in my chest. If I'm checking out, my final piece is going to be INCREDIBLE.

'Red!' I bark.

A disembodied hand lowers the red paint can, and soon I'm working like a pro in an art studio and never mind that I'm upside down. Each fresh puff of paint breathes new life into the DedManz tag. Imran's tattoo has given me ideas . . .

Lens flares and starbursts are my final tricks. Even with my nose practically brushing up against it, the tag appears to float a good three feet *in front* of the bridge. I am stoked to view the illusion at street level – and the right way up.

'OK, man is done. Pull me back up,' I call.

Nothing happens.

I look up and see Imran staring at me with disassociated calmness. To his right, Noah is holding up his phone, filming me with the evilest grin on his face.

'What's going on?' I ask with growing trepidation.

'You disrespected the boss, fam,' Imran says glibly. 'And there's a price to pay.'

CHAPTER 26

A black hole of despair swallows my gut. All that separates me from a massive drop and solid tarmac is Imran's vengeful hands wrapped round my ankles. Twenty-five feet below, a stream of potential witnesses whizz by. Won't do me any good if I'm a broken body lying dead in the middle of a busy road.

'Imran, please!' I beg. 'It was an accident! You know this . . .'

'Shut up!' he roars, giving my ankles a violent shake.

Bile floods my mouth, overflowing into my nostrils. I choke, then start to scream.

'What you doing, man?' Daevon asks in horror, trying to haul me back up.

Noah's fist crashes into the side of his face. Daevon tumbles out of sight.

'You people need to learn to put some respeck on my name!' Imran spits, a shudder of rage coursing through his body. Meanwhile, I'm dangling from his psychotic grasp, praying to God for a miracle.

'Look – he pissed himself!' Noah sniggers, aiming his phone at my damp crotch.

'OK, you guys got me. Now let me up, man. Please!' I beg.

'You don't seem to understand how gangs work,' Imran says. 'I'm the Don. If my own mans disrespect me, gangstas start believing they can pull the same shit, and DedManz dies. That ain't happening. I got a lot riding on this.'

Has he been at the crack again? DedManz is just some stupid game we play to make ourselves feel important. Then I make a horrible leap. The tip of a tattoo I glimpsed earlier was the pointed ear of a dingo – a DX Dingo. Imran must have gone big time, and my death is probably his initiation. A way for him to prove himself, and for Zaman to have revenge on Dad for ending his relationship with Shais.

I beg for my life without shame, but Imran's already shaking his head. 'You brought this on yourself, fam.'

And then he lets go.

I scream before realizing he has only let go of one ankle. He yanks on the other one, tossing me back on to the bridge like a leg of lamb.

'Con-grat-u-lations!' Imran says, squatting down and lifting my head so I look into his eyes. 'You get to live. Now go home and wash the pee-pee out of your pants. And remember who da boss.' He rises up. 'Come on, lads.'

CHAPTER 27

The rest of the week passes in a blur. Several times, I see Kelly in the playground, but she keeps her distance. Today she gives me a sad smile on the way into assembly. There's a video going round of me on the bridge. She obviously thinks I'm a total coward. Still, I wish with all my heart she'd reach out to me.

But it's never gonna happen. Why should she be the one to make the first move? And after Imran owned me, I'm just too scared to do it myself. The best thing I can do for Kelly is to keep Imran the hell away from her.

'Today we're celebrating Movember at Stanley Park!' Mrs Waldorf announces into the microphone at assembly, once Mr Gilchrist has got us to behave for her.

She's wearing a false moustache, which unfortunately draws attention to the fact that she's a dead ringer for Hitler. 'Today's assembly will be taken by Year Eleven!' she trills.

Jade appears onstage, radiant as a Snapchat filter. But ever since Kelly gave me the deets on her, it's difficult to be impressed. Lurking behind the glamorous curtain isn't the Wizard of Oz; it's the Wicked Witch herself.

A guy called Chris steps up to the microphone. He's one of those popular kids who gets involved in everything. He's proudly wearing his thick brown moustache and ginger beard. Man looks like a regular Viking.

'Prostate cancer is a serious matter,' he tells us gravely, while Jade nods, giving Serious Face. 'Us men aren't very good at talking about our health. A trip to the doctor is the stuff of nightmares for most of us. Sometimes we're met with ridicule if we finally do say something to friends.'

'Feeling sick again, dear? Must be man flu!' Jade says theatrically.

The lower school laps it up, giggling like an army of chipmunks.

'One in eight men will be diagnosed with prostate cancer in their lifetime. The number doubles for black men,' Chris says.

'What's he saying that for, though?' Daevon complains.

'To raise awareness?' I suggest.

He looks at me. 'Yeah, well put an actual black man up there then, innit?'

Next up is a pre-recorded video. Jade and her friends' backs are to us, but I recognize Kelly straight away because of her bright red bushy hair. The five strut away from the camera, their arms interlinked, then spin round dramatically. They reveal themselves to be wearing different-shaped moustaches, pulling surprised faces for effect. Each girl takes it in turn to talk about the particular moustache she is wearing and drop grim factoids about prostate cancer.

Last up is Kelly. 'This is the Rock Star,' she tells us, pointing at the classic Movember tache, twitching it for effect.

The video cuts to her wearing a leather jacket, holding a bright red electric guitar in the shape of a cartoon explosion. She rocks out, bouncing up and down on one foot, giving a guitar solo, which has got to be from a backing track. I laugh and clap my hands.

Imran glances over at me, a mocking look in his eyes. 'Trust you to get excited by the DUFF.'

'What? She's funny. Plus, she ain't fat,' I say loyally.

'Open your eyes, fam. That's some nasty lard arse that Becky be twerking. And she's got hair like a witch,' Imran says, chuckling.

'Definite DUFF, bro,' Noah says. 'Watch dat bitch jiggle.'

I want to punch Noah in the face, breaking every tooth in his stupid caged mouth. How dare these fools shade Kelly. She's ten times braver and smarter and cooler than any of them.

Too late, I notice Imran studying me. 'Oh my days, y'all. Ilyas be a chubby chaser. Go on then.'

I blink, trying to contain my emotions. 'Huh?'

Up onstage, Chris is telling everyone that he will be shaving off his beard and moustache at break-time and that buckets will be coming round to classrooms to collect donations.

'Look at that tramp,' Imran says, distracted as he scowls at Chris up onstage. 'Break-time, mate.'

Good, I think. *I've got no clue what your beef is with Chris, but knock yourself out. Just leave me and Kelly the hell alone.*

But Imran has a memory like an elephant. He gestures at Kelly with his goatee.

'That's your target, Ilyas. She's the lucky girl you get to strip. And don't forget to film it.'

I shake my head. 'I told you—'

'What do you reckon Gilchrist would do if I cut myself and tell him you did it?' Imran says casually.

My eyes widen. 'Bro, you wouldn't do that though.'

'I reckon your mum might top herself if that happened, especially after all the trouble with your sister and the shop . . .'

Everything Daevon warned me about is coming true. This isn't just about me any more. It's about my family too. My face says it all.

Imran winks. 'Now you get it.'

In the background, I vaguely hear Mrs Waldorf telling everyone to support Jade and her mates at break-time as they sell fake moustaches or paint them on under the archway.

'But you said DedManz means bros for life,' I plead. 'Looking out for each other no matter what.'

Imran nods. 'Exactly. Man needs to take care of his mans. Haven't you been listening to the assembly? You gonna get prostate cancer if you stay virgin.'

'Leave him,' Daevon says.

Imran gives him the finger, and, just like that, Daevon is defeated. He's as scared as I am.

'But it's haram,' I persist.

'So? Pray for forgiveness later, innit?'

The air becomes humid, and the bitter taste of bile coats my tongue.

'You gonna do it, like a Don?' Imran asks, eyebrow raised like a sword.

This isn't a mandem; it's a slavedom. Somewhere along the line, Daevon, Noah and me forgot how to survive alone and made Imran our master.

My head nods like it belongs to someone else. Someone I really don't like.

CHAPTER 28

'You all right, Ilyas?' Ms Mughal asks, squatting beside my table.

I come back down to earth with a bump and am startled by the fresh fabric-softener scent of her – as if she just breezed out of a washing machine. It triggers a forgotten memory of when me, Amma and Shaista went to the local laundrette six years ago. Amma gave us four pounds each to spend at the newsagent next door. Shaista bought a copy of *Seventeen* (even though she wouldn't be seventeen for another five years) while I got a pad and pencil. I spent the afternoon in a wide beam of sunlight, leaning against Amma's side as she read from her Kindle, sketching PakCore doing amazing things. Back in those days, he was nothing more than a desi Superman rip-off, but he meant the world to me.

Now my world is filled with gangs and violence.

I blink at Ms Mughal, surfacing from my thoughts. 'Sorry, miss. I was daydreaming.'

She pulls a face. 'This isn't like you. You've been my star student since you joined this class.'

Kara leans in so close, I can smell the fruity Maoam on her breath. 'I thought *I* was your favourite. You cheatin' on me with this boy?'

Ms Mughal laughs. 'You're all my favourites. Now if you don't mind . . .'

Kara takes one look at my dazed face, then gets back to work.

'So.' Ms Mughal turns back to me. 'Anything you'd like to tell me?'

Suddenly I want to tell her *everything*. She seems so much like a fairy godmother with her beautiful smile and her kind eyes.

Slowly I shake my head. 'I'm good.'

'What did you do for work experience last year?'

The randomness of this question finally wrenches me from my stupor. 'Er, worked for my dad at his shop.'

'Any career plans for after you smash your GCSEs and A levels?'

'Uh . . . probably working for Dad.' I am so low-key depressed right now, I can't even hide it.

She adjusts her jewelled hijab pin: a shiny amethyst surrounded by spiky golden stakes. 'I was talking to my brother about you. He works in advertising, producing graphics and special effects. But he's also a huge comics fan – he has an entire basement dedicated to countless issues sealed in plastic wallets.'

'Plastic wallets? That is next level,' I say, grinning in spite of myself.

'And don't get me started on his cabinet full of Funko Pop! and Hot Toys figures,' she says, shaking her head in dismay.

'A whole cabinet of sixth scales?! Man must be minted.' I know that even one of those figures costs well over a hundred quid.

She sighs. 'And possibly *crazy*, but don't tell him I told you.' She winks conspiratorially. 'He's very sensitive about it. So, Idris said there's going to be an open call for comics creators in December. There's a twenty-five-thousand-pound prize for the best entry and a chance to have someone in the industry develop your idea.'

'Seriously?' I say, perking up.

'He's picking me up from school today. Come back at ten past three if you want to have a chat with him. I promise he's not in the least bit intimidating.'

I gawk.

'You're a very good teacher,' Kara whispers, having listened to our entire conversation.

'Even though I'm a serial cheater who tells you all that you're my favourite?' Ms Mughal asks. 'Appreciate the feedback, Kara.' She winks, gathers her midnight jilbab, and goes to help Nawal.

At break-time, I spot Kelly under the arches with her gurls. They've set up a stall with a row of plastic chairs. Some of the chairs are occupied by kids having moustaches painted on, most of them lower school.

'Come on,' Daevon says, slapping my shoulder. He's carrying a large plastic bucket for some reason. 'Let's watch Chris get owned.'

I look at him in surprise. 'What's Chris ever done to you?'

He smirks. 'Come on – *everybody* hates Chris.'

'Don't you ever feel bad about all the evil stuff Imran makes us do?' I sigh.

'It's called *life*, Ilyas. If I'm not the man with the whip, I'm the man getting whipped.'

'Or you could be the man who chucks the whip away. No whip, no one gets hurt.'

'You talking about being a hero? Martin Luther King was a hero. Malcolm X was a hero. They ended up dead. You still wanna be a hero?'

'Nah, I'm all right.' I know I'm a lightweight. Now if I was PakCore, things would be way different. Realization dawns on me that me and Daevon are never going to be able to open up to each other.

I watch Kelly painting a moustache on a ticklish Year 7's finger.

Daevon follows my eyes. 'You gonna put the tip in?'

'Dude!' I say, mortified. 'When did everything become about sex?'

'You kidding?' he says, laughing. 'We're teenagers. Sex is all I ever think about. Even in Gordon's class, which is the unsexiest place on the planet!'

I shake my head, but now he's got me curious. 'You done it, then?'

He nods, smirking in a self-satisfied sort of way. 'Denusha. That girl, bro! She into some nasty . . .'

I tune him out. Right now he could be Imran or Noah, because the thing that makes Daevon unique, and my friend, has slipped away. I'm left with this sexist DedManz drone.

A Year 7 screws up her face as Kelly uses a make-up wipe to scrub away a moustache that went badly. When I'm with Kelly, I always feel like I'm my best self: spreading positivity and art and stories into the world.

Suddenly an amazing sensation has me mooing like a cow. Daevon is running his afro comb over my scalp, firing nerve endings with every stroke.

'Just sprucin' up my boy,' Daevon says, sticking the comb back in his own hair. 'Now stop checking her out like a creep and go get her, tiger. Before someone else does.'

When is he going to realize this is about being mates, not hormones or urges or whatever?

He wheels me towards the arches just as Kelly finishes drawing the outline of a moustache on a girl's finger. The girl holds it under her nose and pulls a face. Her little friends giggle and take selfies with her.

When I look back, Daevon is heading off to the field where a crowd has gathered to witness Chris getting a shave. Two teachers are on duty: the head of RS and a trainee.

Standing in line under the arches, self-consciousness sets in as I realize I'm the only boy queuing up.

'Yes?' Jade asks.

My tongue swells like a sponge dropped in water. This Poison Ivy's beauty can paralyse.

'You already have a moustache! Of sorts.' She laughs.

'Wait . . .' says Melanie, flexing her fingers for what I can only assume will be malicious air quotes. 'Isn't this "gangsta mans" from the bridge meme?'

Jade does a double-take, recognition registering in her eyes.

'No, it's not,' Kelly says, stepping in their way. She curtsies like a RADA-trained actress. 'Hail, fellow well met. Taketh thou a seat, sir, and I shall upon thy fair cheek moustache maketh.'

I sit down, grinning like a fool, rummaging in my pocket for change. 'How much?'

'A pound,' says Jade. 'More if you're feeling generous, since all proceeds do go to charity.'

The twenty-five-thousand-pound comic book prize springs to mind. With that sort of cash, I could go uni, help my family out, *and* make an Angelina Jolie-style donation to charity. But I'm getting ahead of myself. Does PakCore – this idea I've been obsessed with since Year 5 – even have what it takes to win a competition?

'Which cheek?' Kelly asks, blackened paintbrush poised like a quill.

'Up to you, so long as it ain't a bum cheek!'

We both crack up. I feel a deep admiration for Kelly. She's being nice to me in front of her mates who so obviously hate me. Could I return the favour? But here's the thing: Kelly's mates don't want to sexually humiliate me. This is why I have to keep DedManz away from my friend.

While Kelly inks up my right cheek, I wonder if I should drop in news of the competition. Fifty-fifty – twelve and a half grand each. Not that someone like her would need the cash, but fair is fair. Meeting Ms Mughal's brother is probably a good first step. If the competition is legit, I'll bring Kelly up to speed tomorrow, I decide.

She straightens up abruptly, rising on to tip-toes. 'What's that about?'

Melanie glances across to the field, shielding her eyes from the harsh winter sun. 'A ghetto fight over some fried chicken. Hot wings, probably.'

Clearly Kelly's punch to the face failed to knock any sense into her. I twist round in my seat. Kids are surging on to the field, congregating round someone wearing a scarlet-and-gold Cavaliers hoody.

'Is that Imran?' Kelly asks.

'I think so . . .' I murmur, watching the crowd around Chris flock to Imran instead.

'Hey, I haven't finished painting your mo on!' yells Jade after a Year 8 girl escaping to the field. 'You're not getting a refund!'

'Aren't you curious?' Kelly asks.

Gotta admit I actually am. Kelly pulls me up and, for better or worse, we're suddenly part of the mass migration.

'Kelly! Don't you dare!' shouts Melanie. But her voice is drowned out by the playground-wide commotion.

By the time me and Kelly manage to push through, Noah, Daevon and a couple of guys from the basketball team are working the crowd, collecting donations in plastic buckets, which look nicked from the caretaker's cupboard. Imran poses on his throne, gripping his chin pensively, cheekbones more on fleek than ever. He is a *GQ* cover brought to life.

'OK, fans!' he growls in a sexy-tiger voice. A hallowed silence falls over the gathering. 'See this peng topknot? I'mma shave it off in the name of charity. Man's head gonna be bare-arse *naked*. So donate generously, yeah?'

'Y'all need to dig deep!' bellows Daevon, electing himself hype man.

'This be a once-in-a-lifetime event, fam!' Noah yells, making weird hand signals, which he probably thinks are cool.

'Shut up and take my money!' squeals Kara fanning herself with a fiver.

'Excuse me!' shrieks the RS teacher who had been supervising Chris's event before it flopped. 'This event wasn't authorized by senior staff.'

Imran kisses his teeth at her. Taking their cue from the unofficial Fresh Prince of Stanley Park, the crowd starts booing her in an epic show of solidarity.

'I'm doing it for charity, though!' Imran explains. 'Think man wants to walk around looking like some *pendu* with no hair? I'm doing it for poor people in Pakistan.'

'The school is raising money for *prostate cancer*!' snaps the teacher.

He goggles at her like he can't believe she just said that. 'What, you think we ain't got prostates in Pakistan?'

'*Ooooooooh!*' the crowd jeers in unison.

The teacher glances nervously at the sea of angry faces. The Cult of Imran has converted them into a mob. The student teacher babbles something about calling senior teachers for help as she bails. From the look on her face, I reckon she's out to save her own skin.

Chris bustles into the fray, looking like he lost a fight with a lawnmower. He's sporting exactly half a beard and one-quarter of a mo. 'Do you have any idea how long it took me to grow this beard? You're spoiling weeks of planning just because you want to hog the limelight!'

Imran stands up, and they face off, like a poster for some testosterone-fuelled versus movie. Suddenly the corners of

Imran's mouth curl up. Chris's whole face twitches in confusion.

'Let the people decide,' Imran says, acting like a benevolent king. 'You wanna see man shave all this off?' He pulls out his hairband, letting his luscious locks fall about his face like Don Juan. 'Or you wanna see *this* –' he gestures with his chin at Chris – 'shave his ginger pubes?'

'*Imran! Imran! Imran!*'

Imran's fandom is legion. If this fool ever ran for prime minister, I'd hate to think what might happen. Chris goes bright red, and I feel for the guy. He has a reputation for being a try-hard, but does not deserve this.

'*Wooo!* Imran!' cries a girl to my left.

I turn my head and see it's Kelly. A pang of jealousy, as hot and fiery as the tip of a soldering iron, punctures my gut. How can she be impressed by Imran? He's EVIL.

'Come on my Gs!' Imran roars. 'Dig deep and gimme them Ps. And I will shave it all off for you. Down to the bone.' He runs a hand through his long hair.

I feel like I'm on a ship about to capsize as the pushing and shoving intensifies, the frenzy for Imran to entertain us blowing up. So much cash changes hands that within minutes the collection buckets are overflowing. These people have to know not a penny of it will make it to charity.

Jade and Melanie come jostling to the front. They give Imran both barrels with glares straight from the bowels of Hell. He winks at them, and though Melanie gives him the finger, I notice colour rising to Jade's cheeks. That's when I realize how truly powerful Imran has become.

Daevon holds up an electric clipper for the audience to see. God knows where he got it. Unless . . .

It suddenly occurs to me that Imran must have been planning to sabotage Chris's event for days. I remember the comment he made in assembly: *Look at that tramp. Break-time, mate.*

I wonder what their beef is about. A dirty look? A misunderstood comment? Will Chris end up as the next Stanley Park meme?

'Listen up!' Imran bellows, commanding the crowd more effectively than at least half the teachers could. 'Whoever donates a twenty, I'mma let *you* do the honours.'

The crowd reacts with delight to this news.

'Brave man!' I say, having been on the receiving end of enough nicks and yanks with Dad's monthly buzz cuts. I wonder what Imran will look like bald.

'Don't be tight!' Imran goads the crowd. 'Man is starting to look like a loser.' He pouts with flirtatious cuteness. He's turned manipulation into an art form.

'Here!' Like the Lady of the Lake wielding Excalibur, a hand shoots into the air brandishing a crisp new twenty.

Heads turn to see who it is. The girl steps into the ring, and my heart drops.

It's Kelly Matthews.

CHAPTER 29

The crowd goes quiet as Daevon ceremoniously hands the clippers over to Kelly. He proceeds to give her a crash course in hairdressing. Imran takes his shirt off to a wild cacophony of wolf whistles and appreciation for his angel-wings tattoo. He grins devilishly, flexing for the fans. Then he goes dead serious, bouncing on the balls of his feet, throwing quick punches like he'll be getting in the ring with Anthony Joshua.

'Ugh! Look at her,' Jade says snarkily, shaking her head.

Melanie nods. 'Acting like a ghetto hoe. Tell me she's being ironic now.'

I want to tell them to shut up, but I'm too busy battling my own corrosive mixture of jealousy and horror.

The clippers buzz to life in Kelly's hand. 'I don't want to hurt you,' she says, giggling foolishly, unsure where to start.

Nearly two thousand people have flocked to the field, yet Imran's eyes still manage to find me. He glances at Kelly then back at me and winks. It's the moment I realize he's not done with humiliating me yet.

'Do me,' he says, making fists, legs jackhammering.

Daevon flaps his arms to get the crowd excited – anticipation levels now going through the roof.

Kelly runs her fingers through Imran's beautiful hair, blushing profusely, covering her mouth, backing away, grimacing, then finally moving in for the kill. Imran screws up his face, and the crowd is loving it. Me? I want her to act like the feminist she's supposed to be and lop that bastard's head off. The clippers devour his hair with electric fury. Handfuls of thick hair fall on to his shoulders like raven's feathers.

'I don't think I can do any more!' Kelly says, fanning her cheeks.

'I'll do it!' shouts Kara, pulling off Zumba moves in her excitement.

A flock of hands fly into the air; desperate fans wanting to touch Imran's head. For a split second, I wonder if he could be the Antichrist.

Imran ignores them all. He grabs Kelly's hand, gently manoeuvring the clippers back to his scalp. I grind my teeth as the seconds stretch into minutes. The whole thing feels way too intimate. The crowd laps it up.

Minutes later, Kelly is done. Imran stands up and poses like a wrestler. Even without his hair, he is still perfection. His chiselled skull looks like a Michelangelo carving. The only imperfection is a small pink scar at the back of his head. This, I realize, is where I accidentally brained the bastard. Phones rise into the air, and flashes strobe like lightning, the moment instantly uploaded to Snapchat, Instagram, Twitter and YouTube. Imran's star power has now gone viral.

'One of me and the girl!' Imran roars, pulling Kelly on to his lap. She clutches on to him tightly in surprise, and they both laugh, their mouths uncomfortably close as more pictures are snapped.

'You lost your chance, bro,' Daevon whispers in my ear. 'She's Imran's now.'

I barrel through the masses, fighting my way out. I get cussed for pushing, and I cuss right back. My head is a mess of betrayal and disgust. A couple of senior teachers are on their way down, and suddenly everyone's hightailing it.

Kelly said I was her bestie. I did everything I could to protect her from Imran and would never have betrayed my friend, not even if it meant getting thrown off another bridge. Thought she was smart; thought she was different.

CHAPTER 30

It's the end of the school day, and I'm nervously pacing up and down the corridor in the maths building. I'm about to take another peek through Ms Mughal's window when the door flies open and Year 7 kids come pouring out, saying bye to her and chattering excitedly about their lesson.

'Miss, I made a card for you,' a girl announces, and honestly, she's the cutest thing. She's dwarfed by a giant *kawaii* backpack shaped like a cupcake. *Fun Hong* is written on it in marker so neatly, it's practically font.

'For me?' Ms Mughal asks her, acknowledging me with a nod.

The girl turns to look at me, alarmed. 'Um . . . I'm *embarrassed*.' She tips her head forward to hide her flushing cheeks.

'You don't have anything to be embarrassed about. This is Ilyas, and he's a fellow artist. Just like you, Fun,' Ms Mughal says.

Fun peers at me suspiciously, and I nod. 'Yeah, yeah. I'm all about the creative arts.'

'OK, but if anyone laughs, I'm gonna cry,' she says matter-of-factly, unzipping her backpack and pulling out the handmade card.

Fun has drawn a *chibi*-style picture of Ms Mughal teaching a class full of cute little animals. *To my favourite teacher* is proudly written across the top in lavender glitter glue.

Poor Ms Mughal looks like she's going to cry.

'This is literally the cutest thing ever, Fun!'

'You got talent,' I chime in, cos I know how good it feels to hear it.

Fun hugs her bag. I can almost see happy stars popping above her head like an animated filter.

'Oh!' she says, placing a hand over her mouth. 'I wanted to tell you something else too, but I'll tell you tomorrow instead. Can I come at break-time?'

'Of course you can. And thank you so much for this card. It's going on my wall, and every time I feel down, looking at it will cheer me right up,' Ms Mughal says.

Fun giggles, then scampers down the corridor, pausing only to wave, before vanishing down the stairwell.

'Smart kid,' Ms Mughal says with a dewy-eyed expression. 'Come in, Ilyas, and take a seat.' She kicks off her shoes and slips into a pair of bright orange Nikes. 'Just going to zip off to collect my brother from reception. Back in five. OK?'

'Sure . . . Miss? Can I open my comic on your computer? To show your brother, I mean?'

She gives me an affirmative thumbs-up, before zooming into the corridor, her jilbab flapping in the slipstream.

I log in to her computer, slot in my memory stick, and open up my file. Up on the interactive whiteboard, my comic suddenly looks different. Nausea grips my stomach. It's like my comic has mutated since I last saw it. A billion rookie mistakes fly out at me like ninja stars. Proportion, expression, perspective – it's all wrong.

I close my eyes, trying to slow down my jacked-up heart. 'You're imagining things. It was fine last week when you showed Kelly. Not that she cares anyway,' I mutter to myself.

'Imagining things is good practice for a comic book artist,' comes a new voice from behind me. 'I'm Idris, Ms Mughal's brother. Nice to meet you.'

He has the same bee-stung lips as Ms Mughal. But there the similarity ends. His eyes are chocolate brown, a unibrow hovers above thick glasses, and he is big – tall and very wide.

'This talent-in-the-wings is Ilyas,' Ms Mughal tells him, walking into the room behind her brother.

I shake Idris's hand, feeling like a dork for having been caught giving myself a pep talk.

'Whoa!' he says, glancing up at the board. 'Is this your own work?'

'Yeah,' I say, smiling shyly before switching gears. 'Why – is it bad?'

Both he and Ms Mughal look at me like surprised geese.

'Are you being modest or do you seriously not know how talented you are?' Idris asks.

I cover my mouth with both hands. If Dad could see me right now, he'd give me a smack for being so girly. But I am so overcome with emotions, my hands are shaking.

'D-d-do you think I have an actual shot at winning?' *Boom* – it's out: the thought that's been plaguing my mind ever since Ms Mughal mentioned the competition.

Idris smiles thinly, sitting down on a table, his legs spreading in his beige trousers. 'Tell me more about this character. Does he have an origin story? Who are the bad guys? Where is it set?'

'Take your time,' Ms Mughal says gently, gliding over to a table at the back. 'I'll just be over here marking some tests.'

I tell Idris all about PakCore. He nods encouragingly, but doesn't let on whether he thinks it's great or if he thinks it sucks.

'Do you reckon I have a chance?' I ask again.

He deflects the question. 'How much do you want to win?'

'Oh man!' I say, shaking my head deliriously. 'More than Lois Lane wants Superman. More than T'Challa wishes the Vibranium in Wakanda had stayed in Wakanda. More than—'

'OK – I can see you're committed,' Idris says, chuckling. 'The Kablamo! Kon IV competition takes place just before Christmas.

That's not a lot of time, so I'm going to be blunt with you.'

Ms Mughal looks up from her marking. 'Not *too* blunt, please.'

'Psh! I'm never too blunt,' he says.

'Ha! You used to call me Stick Insect Gal and say my superpower was getting blown away in the wind.'

'Only because society told me to be jealous. But thankfully I'm BoPo now.' He pats his stomach.

This is a guy Daevon should meet.

'So, Ilyas, can you handle the truth?'

I nod, gulping.

'Your artwork is incredible, the Living Shadows make seriously creepy villains, and I love that you came up with a British Pakistani hero. A move that's long overdue.'

'OK,' I say uncertainly, waiting for the sting in the tail.

His unibrow curves like a rainbow. 'But the actual character of PakCore seems too familiar.'

I blush, wringing my hands. 'But I made him up! He's a mash-up of loads of different characters. Something old to make something new.'

'That's the problem, my friend. It's really easy to identify your individual inspirations.' He ticks them off on his fingers. 'Superman, Spider-Man, Ghost Rider.'

All that effort drawing those pictures, scanning the images, and digitally enhancing them. Literally hours and hours of hard graft. And all this time, I've been polishing a turd. A *stolen* turd. Who does that?

'How can he fix it?' Ms Mughal interjects quickly.

Idris shrugs his round shoulders. 'It has to come from inside you, Ilyas. Producing original ideas to order is bread and butter for any comic book artist. And with this genre at saturation point – thank you, Hollywood! – it has become almost impossible to come up with something that hasn't been done before.'

I nod gloomily. 'There's probably tons of people entering the competition anyway. Like, adults and that.'

'But –' Ms Mughal waves her pen like a magic wand – 'your drawings are already on a par with those of adults, so that's one hurdle down. Just need to fine tune those brilliant ideas of yours. Please help him, Idris. Can't you see how much he wants this?'

Her brother shakes his head. 'Come from you, it must,' he says in a nasalized voice, pushing his ears out in imitation of Yoda. 'But what I *can* do is show you a promotional video I made for a small comics company called Diamond Chain. Maybe it'll inspire you, and your ideas will build from there.'

He puts the smallest USB I have ever seen into the port and double-clicks on a video file. My mouth falls open. The stylish cartoon images shift and pan and *breathe* – a noir comic book brought to life. A creative big bang happens inside me, and a million possibilities shimmer before my eyes.

'It's called a motion comic,' he explains. 'Lots of movies use them in the opening credits nowadays. I made this one in After Effects, manipulating the original artist's drawings.'

'How?' I whisper, my eyes like hubcaps, my heart rate spiking.

'I'll show you.'

CHAPTER 31

Saturday morning, my phone pings. A text from Kelly.

Yo, Ilz! Where my bestie at?

Doing homework.

Can you come round? We can order pizza
with mac and cheese croquettes and ice cream.

Soz. Need to finish history.

Screw history! Let's work on PakCore.

I flash back to her working on PakCore's life model, giggling
nervously while stroking his stupid sexy scalp.

PakCore is dead.

OMG The Death of PakCore!!!
The fans will go crazy. Expecting you in T minus 5
or I'm sending the Black Order after you. xo

A traitorous smirk breaches my defences. I miss Kelly. Besides,
with a genocidal order of alien mercenaries on your back, well,
who could say no to that?

*

I gaze up at the Matthews' large, picturesque house. Hearing that Mrs M is enjoying a spa weekend in Swansea swung it for me.

Kelly throws open the door before I even ring the bell. She's wearing a beige robe with a green hood pulled low over her eyes. Massive pointy ears poke out on either side.

'Come early, you have,' she says, hands folded in front of her, making that familiar nasalized voice.

'You know, you're the second person to go Yoda on me this week,' I say.

'Really?' She rips off the hood, revealing a ballerina bun sitting on the crown of her head. Without her waves spilling everywhere, she almost looks like a different person. 'Who was the first?'

So I go inside and tell her all about Idris and the Kablamo! Kon IV competition.

'Oh my God!' she says. 'This is totally a sign. Place your hands upon the scared bun of prosperity.' She pitches her head forward so my nose is virtually nesting in her hair, the fresh apple scent of it filling my nostrils.

She glances up at me. 'Is that a thing? Can we make it a thing?'

'Let's not,' I suggest.

'OK. But at least tell me you see this is a sign.'

'Not really . . .' I admit, scratching an arm.

'We were talking about collaborating, right? And then *this* drops. There aren't any coincidences, Ilz. Just psychic engineering.' She taps her head. 'And prosperity-activating buns, obvs.'

'So you're still up for collabing?' I ask, raising a doubtful eyebrow.

'Did you hit your head on the way over? Of course I am!'

I shake my head. 'Look, don't take this the wrong way, yeah, but I like doing things on my own. All my life, I've had people tell me what to do, how to act, what to say. And I'm a loser, so I do it.'

'You're not a loser . . .' She gently pushes my chin with her fist.

'Don't lie, fam. You know I'm at the bottom of the food chain. If I didn't have Imran and DedManz, I'd be in a full body cast by now.'

She drops her eyes because she knows it's true.

I scratch my neck, gearing up to poke the elephant in the room. 'Why'd you pay twenty quid to shave Imran's head?'

Silence.

'It was for charity,' she eventually says, twisting an ear on her bathrobe. 'Plus, he was being really funny.'

'He's not a nice guy . . .'

'Nobody's perfect.'

'But he looks it. That's the problem. I've seen so many girls get burned cos they got too close.'

'Well I'm not "so many girls". Besides, it was nice to get one up on Jade and Mels. They always have to be at the centre of everything. And for once it was *me*.' She grins impishly. 'Anyway . . . I believe we were talking about entering this competition?'

I swallow, trying to arrange my thoughts. 'Comics is the one place I get to call the shots. The one place I cannot be controlled.'

Kelly's eyes sparkle. 'You can still have ownership, silly. I'll be Jack Kirby to your Stan Lee. Look, *you* came up with the character, and *you* found out about the competition. This dream belongs to you. I'll just figure out how to make your ideas gel.'

'But it's your dream too . . .'

She shakes her head. 'My dream is to be the author of the sassiest, smartest, science fictioniest novel ever. I'll settle for nothing less than a ten-book deal thankyouverymuch! But I'm pretty sure I need to work more on my writing before that can happen. So for me, your comic will be like an internship.'

'Thanks, Kel,' I say, smiling. 'Swear down you're the best

thing that ever happened to me.'

'C'mere, you li'l scamp!' She draws me into a hug and rubs my back.

'Check me out getting hugs off a Jedi Master! Right now, a whole fandom of nerds must be snapping their plastic lightsabers in protest.'

'Grope you naughty, I must,' Kelly says, making grabby hands.

'Oh my days!' I yelp, skipping away, then breaking into a full pelt.

She chases me round the house, both of us giggling like little kids, careening round corners, sliding down banisters, rolling under tables. I realize that Imran hasn't stolen Kelly away from me after all. The Hair Shaving Incident was nothing more than a blip: normal service has resumed.

I skid into the kitchen, only the floor has recently been waxed, and my feet fly out from under me. Kelly follows too closely, and we both end up in a heap just in front of the oven. We howl with laughter, tears streaming from our eyes.

I suddenly sit up straight. Kelly stops laughing when she sees the expression on my face.

'What's up?' she asks, panting for breath.

I turn to look at her, my eyes wider than Sparkle's after she's smelt food. The big bang that began after watching Idris's video has finally reached critical mass.

'Kelz, I got it!' I announce. 'I know how to make PakCore stand out from the crowd!'

My wild pencil marks streak and mesh across Kelly's A3 pad. With a final zigzag and a couple of curlicues, I push the finished drawing towards her.

She stares at it with reverence. 'This looks like Ms Mughal.'

I nod. 'Don't you get it? She makes the *perfect* superhero. High school teacher by day; defender of the oppressed by night. I honest to God saw Ms Mughal pull off a kung fu move one time when she kicked a door shut. Just imagine what seeing someone like her saving the world would do to a hater's mind.'

Kelly makes hand explosions beside her head. 'Ooh I could have fun writing her lines. Just think of the clapback potential!'

'Make 'em savage,' I reply, making fists.

'I'm sold. So what are we calling this avenging angel?'

I scratch behind an ear, lower lip protruding. 'Dunno yet. I reckon she'll tell me her name when she's ready.'

'Makes sense. I'm calling my flu story *Project X* until it's finished. That's when you know what the heart of the story is, then the name just pops out at you.' She narrows her eyes, scrutinizing my drawing. 'Hmm!'

'That don't sound like a good *hmm* . . .'

'Something else just popped out at me. Two somethings, in fact. You're definitely going to have to modify the design.'

I glance at my drawing. Poised like a lioness on the hunt, my superhero's jilbab ebbs and flows around her like liquid silk, green eyes flashing with formidable vengeance. The Living Shadows have gathered round in a circle of doom, creeping forwards, electrical fangs bared. But the smirk on her full lips makes it clear they don't know who they're dealing with.

I look up at Kel. 'Why, what's wrong with it?'

'Tits and ass.'

'But I didn't!' I yammer.

'You most definitely diddo, kiddo,' Kelly says, placing a hand on her hip. 'And look at that micro waist! How's a girl to kick bad-guy arse on an invisible stomach? Try mansplaining your way out of that!'

I'm roasting so bad right now, you could have me with gravy.

'If you want this character to be unique, Ilz, we have to give her realistic proportions so our fans won't end up aspiring anorexics.'

'I dunno how it happened!' I say, sweating a river – I don't want Kelly thinking I'm a perv. That's Imran's job. Amma taught me better.

'Relax – you're just a victim of everyday sexism.' She sighs affectedly. 'Women have been objectified to the point we've almost stopped noticing it.' Kelly gestures to the picture. 'Why do some Muslim women wear a gown anyway?'

I take a moment to consider all the women in my family who wear jilbabs. 'I guess so you have to listen to what they're saying instead of checking them out.'

Kelly drums her fingers along her jawline. 'Like an objectification shield?'

I shrug.

'That actually makes a whole lot more sense than the oppression angle we hear so much about.'

'Yeah, the media loves its daily dose of shit-stirring,' I say. 'My sister's a beauty vlogger. On World Hijab Day, she posted a video special in which she interviewed some of her mates about why they wear the hijab.'

'I'd like to see that,' Kelly says, beaming. 'I think all women should wear whatever they want without being judged or banned or assaulted.'

In her Yoda robe, she looks so totally comfortable; so unapologetically Kelly. Does Jade even know this side of her exists?

'OK, Lieutenant Mian – stand by to improve the character design on my mark,' Kelly says, raising a finger in the air before bringing it down sharply. 'Engage objectification shielding!'

'Aye aye, cap'n.' I flip the page and start over, sketching a less sexualized version of my character, this time bursting through a stained-glass window in an explosion of coloured glass and smoke. A flickering in my peripherals distracts me. For a moment, as if it was really there, I see the vape jellyfish Imran blew back at the abandoned park over half-term coursing through the air.

I blink, and it's gone.

'Oh my days!' I practically scream as an idea replaces the jellyfish. 'I know what her superpower is: *Phantom Breath*!'

'Explanation, please?'

Over the years, I've watched Imran smoke everything from shisha and spliffs to bongs. This is my opportunity to turn something evil into something good. 'She has mystical lungs, which produce Phantom Rings. These rings can shift between gas and solid.'

'Deposition to sublimation, eh?' Kelly mutters, tenting her fingers.

'They can also change size. So she can blow one at an enemy and, depending on what she's looking for, can bind them like a straitjacket. Or strangle them into unconsciousness with a shrinking ring round the throat.'

'Gruesome. I like!' Kelly says, nodding like a bobblehead.

'Or she can blow acidic vapour, which can eat straight through metal. You know – to melt guns and that.'

Kelly waves her hand in the air as if she's in class. 'Ooh! Ooh! How about this? She can blow an entire cloud of acid rain and melt enemies in a torrential downpour!'

I consider it. 'Or if she concentrates hard enough, she can blow a cloud that envelops enemies before switching to thundercloud mode and frying the fools in an electrical storm!'

Kelly claps her hands excitedly. 'Any thoughts on a name yet?'

In my imagination, fresh from cuffing enemies' hands behind their backs with frisbee-like Phantom Rings, the character glances over her shoulder. A cop is asking her who to thank. She starts telling him thanks aren't necessary, then thinks better of it. Going anonymous gives the press a free pass to pick a name for her. *Muslim Maiden* or *Burka Bae*. She tries not to retch, then announces her name as clear as a bell.

'Big Bad Wafiyyah,' I announce. 'But we'll shorten it to Big Bad Waf.'

'As in the Big Bad Wolf?'

'Think about it! The wolf goes around terrorizing the three little pigs by doing what?'

Kelly looks baffled, then a smile creeps across her lips. 'Huffing and puffing!'

'Exactly.'

'Swear to God, you're a creative genius, Ilz! I can practically see your brain throbbing!'

'Team effort,' I say sheepishly.

'We're totally making Waf's eyes hazel though, because yours are really pretty.'

'You think?' I say, wrinkling my brow.

She prods me in the centre of my chest. 'Don't milk it, mate, or Yoda will have to get handsy with you again.'

We burst out laughing.

Kelly and me spend the rest of the morning coming up with ideas for Big Bad Waf, feeding off each other's energy and excitement. Our minds form an almost telepathic link. I'll start out describing something, and she'll finish off, somehow knowing exactly what I was going to say. Kelly reins in my craziest ideas and plays Sexism Police. The fact that DedManz has rubbed off on me in little ways I hadn't even realized is actually pretty disturbing.

When the pizza guy arrives, Kelly insists on talking to him in Yoda-speak. I try not to laugh.

'The crazy is strong with this one,' he says, winking as he takes his tip.

Kelly has ordered us a feast, which we spread out across the dinner table. Starting at opposite ends, we wolf down the insanely delicious food followed by illegal amounts of ice cream – the kind made with clotted cream.

With full bellies, we return to our creative brainstorming. By the end of the day, we have enough material for an entire series of comics. I don't say it out loud – don't want to jinx it – but I'm starting to believe me and Kelly have a very good crack at taking home the big prize.

CHAPTER 32

Sunday at Chez Mian is bliss. With Zaman in custody, and DX Dingoes at war with the Bloo Bludz, our family is finally out of the heat. Following a large lunch, calorie-rich dessert and family bantz, us Mians go upstairs to indulge in one of our famous super-long siestas.

As I'm rolling about in my bed, trying to find that perfect spot that will trigger sleep, an overwhelming sense of foreboding suddenly attacks. It grips my throat like an invisible assassin, squeezing a gasp out of me.

I shoot up ramrod straight, listening to the ambient sounds of the house. Difficult when your blood is thunder, and your ears are acting like amplifiers. Closing my eyes, I try to hone in on the cause of the psychic disturbance. A false alarm. As I'm settling back down, I suddenly catch the tiniest sob.

It's enough to rouse me from my bed.

I leap up, slip on my sliders and scramble into the corridor. Everyone's bedroom door is closed. Dad's peaceful snores punctuate the hollow silence, but my Spidey sense is pinging.

Curling my hands round the cold banisters, I peer down into the entrance hall. Another sob; this one as clear as breaking glass. I scurry down the stairs and push open the sitting-room door. Amma is curled up in the armchair, covering her face. Her shoulders quake with silent sobs, the telephone receiver lying at her feet.

'Amma, what's wrong?' I ask, kneeling beside her, squeezing her shoulder.

Amma looks up. Her puffy wet face scares me because Amma

is the most together person I know. She clings to me, crying into my bony chest, our roles reversed.

'Don't cry, Amma. We'll sort it, whatever it is,' I say, grabbing the discarded phone and whacking it back on the cradle.

'This isn't the type of thing that can be sorted, *beyta*,' she finally says, drawing away and blowing her nose like a bugle horn. 'Your auntie Ambreen is losing her mind.'

I am shook. Mum's sister is only five years older than her. 'W-w-what?'

'She's very sick.'

'Well, can't she come back here and get treatment?'

Twenty-five years ago, my auntie Ambreen baffled my grandparents by wanting to up sticks and move to Pakistan. She eventually got her way, got hitched to my rich uncle Sohail and began enjoying the Swag Life. Pakistan isn't the place people think it is. If you have money, like my uncle Sohail does, life can be pretty sweet.

Amma is staring into the middle distance, no longer in the sitting room with me, but four thousand miles away in Lahore, holding her sister's hand. I suddenly feel very lonely.

'She has early-onset dementia,' Amma says, almost to herself. 'It's very rare in people under sixty-five. None of us knew what it was. She'd always got bad grades at school, and she was so forgetful. Called herself a "Beverly Hills Bimbo". Made us laugh. Oh how she made us laugh! We never thought for a moment it could be a disease. Her poor kids!' Amma starts to cry again.

Feeling beyond inadequate, I stare at my feet. A series of flashbacks fills my mind. All the times Auntie Ambreen came to visit, and how excited me and Shais and Amir would get knowing she never came empty-handed. Dad complaining cos the sweets she'd bring weren't Desi. Auntie telling Dad Asian sweets are 'diabetes in a box'. I consider reminding Amma about this, but worry it might make her even sadder.

'Amma, can't she pull through? Like, if we pray really hard?'

Amma frowns, rallying to answer my question. 'There's no coming back from this, *beyta*. She's deteriorating quickly. Soon she won't be able to remember any of us.' She says a prayer in Arabic. It's the one you say when disaster strikes, and you tell Allah you trust Him even though your heart is breaking.

'I'll go mosque, yeah, and pray for her. I'll stick a twenty in the collection box,' I babble, wanting so desperately to make it better. I can't see Amma like this. She's too nice to have to suffer any more disasters.

Amma pats my head sadly, clearly appreciating the thought. 'Will you be OK without me for a while?'

My heart implodes. The thought of Amma gone is unbearable. But how can I be selfish at a time like this?

'Yeah, course,' I say, like it's no big deal. 'Take all the time you need. I could come with?'

She shakes her head promptly. 'Absolutely not. You've got your GCSEs round the corner. Osman might want you to take over the store, but I know you've got your heart set on university. Without idiots like Imran getting in your way, I know you'll flourish and make us proud.'

Now my own eyes are filling with tears.

'I'll tell everyone how much you wanted to be there.' Amma wipes her eyes, the armchair creaking as she gets up. 'Suppose I'd better talk to your father . . .' Her eyes cut back to me, whirlpools of worry. Placing her hands on the sides of my head, she tilts my face up. 'Promise me . . .'

'Anything,' I say.

'Promise me you'll try to get on with your dad and Shaista. We don't get to choose our family, but trust me, blood *is* thicker than water.'

A week without Amma passes by feeling like an entire month. Everyone at home pitches in to make it run smoothly, but we're all wearing our game faces. I take over cooking responsibilities after Shais cremates beans on toast and tries to pass it off as something she saw on *The Great British Bake Off*. Sometimes Dad orders takeaways, but they're too expensive and never match up to Amma's cooking. The only silver lining is not having to see Imran at school as I'm too busy getting my homework done in the library so I can get on with the housework when I get home.

The following week, I see DedManz in hysterics, passing Imran's phone around at lunchtime. I wonder if Chris's shaving fail got the full meme treatment.

'What's good?' I say, making with the daps.

'My Becky's been busy with the Thot Filter,' Imran says, grinning from ear to ear.

I glance at the screen and see a girl morphed into doll-like cuteness by a filter. The pouting girl is Kelly.

'I don't get it,' I say, sweat beading my brow. 'How does that make her a thot, though? Everyone uses that filter.'

'My *yute*,' Imran says haughtily. 'That filter makes ugly girls look buff. Only thots do shit like that.'

I shake my head, my cheeks buzzing. 'Why you stalking her Insta anyway?'

'Cos man's going to get jiggy with this piggy!' Imran laughs loudly.

Daevon sees my expression and taps Imran. 'Stop it, fam.'

Imran glares at him. 'Why? What's it to you?'

'Come on, man. You know the girl is Ilyas's mate . . .'

'Bros before hoes,' Imran intones, pounding the table with knuckles of stone. 'Number one rule of DedManz.'

Noah looks at me with disgust. 'Why you making friends with dumbass girls anyway?'

'Kelly's not dumb,' I reply, my lip curling. 'She gets nines for everything, and she's going Cambridge, innit? And anyway, girls always get better exam resul—'

'Bitch, you gay?!' says Noah, slapping my face.

Imran turns to look at me with amusement. 'What is it with you and Becky-with-the-bad-hair, anyway?'

'Her name's Kelly.' Naming my friend gives her back her dignity. 'She gives me a hand with my writing.'

'Yeah? Well she's gonna give me two hands with my wanking.'

Noah and Imran boom with laughter. Daevon shakes his head and mouths, *Go*.

I take my cue and leave, my heart thudding in my chest.

At the end of the day, I'm about to ride out of the school gates when I hear a sound like a shire horse galloping behind me. I glance over my shoulder and see it's Kelly.

'Ilyas!' she says, puffing to a halt as I squeeze the brakes. 'Wanna go down the cafe and talk Big Bad Waf?'

I should say no, that I have to get on with the *tarka daal* and make the *roti*. But, honestly, I miss being fifteen instead of fifty.

'Sure!' I say, hopping off my bike so we can walk together.

'So I've got a script,' she tells me, trying to catch her breath.

'I thought you were writing the prologue.'

'I was. My ideas snowballed, and I couldn't stop! I tried to stay faithful to your vision of her, but I've added a few feminist touches. Let's have a read through and see how we feel.'

'Cool!' I say. 'Then I can get on with the layouts and panels and that.'

Once we reach the front of the queue, Kelly orders us hot-spiced apple drinks, popcorn cookies and a lemon tart each.

'Penny for your thoughts!' she says, spreading the goodies on the table between us. 'Ugh! I sound like Mum.'

'Ain't nothing wrong with that,' I say, grabbing a cookie.

'You've met my mother. You know this is not true.' She cuts her tart with a fork, flavouring the air with the zest of lemons. 'She found the pizza boxes in the bin and asked me if I had you over while she was out. So I said yes, and she went very quiet.'

'Does she hate me?'

She pauses to look at her phone and sniggers at a message.

I can't help but wonder who it's from.

'I think she preferred it when you were Jade or Melanie or even Chris.' She pulls a face, and it's so unselfconscious, it makes me laugh. 'I haven't even met *your* mum yet. Hint, hint!'

'Amma's gone Pakistan,' I say glumly. 'She went to be with her sister before she loses her memory. You know – from dementia.'

Kelly pauses, trying to figure out whether I'm being serious or if this is just a very bad joke. 'Sorry. Why didn't you tell me this before? Wait – doesn't dementia only happen to really old people?'

'I can't right now,' I say, feeling my throat sealing up like an allergic reaction.

She studies me, and I drop my eyes. They're playing a song on the radio that I thought was going to have a good beat but is lacking. A woman is telling her giggling mate that she's going to dump her boyfriend if he buys her any more 'old lady' perfume for Christmas. Outside, a Scottish terrier is yapping at a surprised bull mastiff, while its owner stares through the window, licking his lips.

'When life gives you lemons,' Kelly says, pushing my plate towards me, 'eat lemon tarts.'

I smile and take a bite.

She grins. 'So here's what I was thinking about Big Bad Waf . . .'

CHAPTER 34

> Yo, Kelz. got the place to myself this weekend. Wanna come round do comics?

After a week that has dragged on forever, saved only by my time hanging out with Kelly, I can't think of a better way to spend my Saturday. A minute passes with no reply. I stare at my phone screen, checking to see if the message failed to send.

Ten minutes later, my phone vibrates, and I pounce on it.

> Sorry, busy x

That's a downer. I look at the Kelly's text one more time, then push my phone away.

Cheering up is what I need, and nothing on God's green earth cheers up a comic book fan greater than a variant cover. The thought gets me hype. Considering my options, I eventually settle on the traditional portrait route for the debut issue. Getting my hands dirty feels good, using pastels and chalk on matt black paper; dipping into a pot of water every now and then, for eye-popping colour boosts. Pretty soon, I have Big Bad Waf staring back at me, rendered in lines as vicious as knife slashes, layered with smudged tones for the illusion of volume. Metallic gold and neon pastels play off each other, bringing her hazel eyes to mesmerizing life.

Turning the paper first one way then the other, I make sure I haven't subconsciously given her a boob job or a Brazilian Butt

Lift. That's when a major design flaw hits me like a ton of bricks: *How does she keep her identity secret*? For a moment, I consider giving her a niqab, but realize this would interfere with blowing Phantom Rings. I run a hand across my mouth, absent-mindedly smearing neon colours into my beard. 'Wait, what if . . .'

Throwing down another sheet of black paper, I make a second drawing very similar to the first, but under her hijab, I sketch PakCore's eye mask. Definitely better, but still no wow factor. Picturing Ms Mughal in my mind's eye, I zero in on her hijab pin, that halo of golden spikes surrounding an amethyst crystal. Snapping open my eyes, I quickly sketch a golden crown on top of her hijab – making each tine an ornate sword or dagger.

Now for the moment of truth. Mentally severing all ties with my work, I take a step back and open my eyes.

I scream with joy. 'Ladies and gentlemen, take a knee, cos my queen Big Bad Waf has finally arrived!'

Big Bad Waf is everything PakCore was and more. Athletic and fierce; powerful and mystical. The final colour palette is simple: glittering bronze skin, hazel eyes and the vast blackness of a rippling jilbab. Red lips? Forget it. Catwalk heels? Nope – think Uncle Fiz's boots. But my favourite part has to be that fierce crown.

Comic book world, I think, *you are so not prepared for what's about to hit you.*

CHAPTER 35

Monday morning, I'm late to first period – I had to hand-wash the plates cos the dishwasher wouldn't start. Mr Welch, my geography teacher, is not happy.

'Don't just slink in and sit down. Why are you late?' he snaps.

'Sorry, sir. I didn't hear my alarm this morning.'

He gives an indignant snort and turns back to the board.

'What we doing?' I ask Ray, quickly getting my books and pens out.

'Dunno,' he says, looking how I feel. 'Something about rivers and levees, I think.'

I skim-read the text.

'Ilyas, you're Muslim, right?' mutters Ray out of the blue.

I nod, writing the date and title in my book.

'So I was wondering . . .' He shifts uncomfortably, his cheeks going pink for some reason. 'Are you guys allowed to date people from other religions?'

'Muslims aren't down to date unless the end goal is marriage. But people do whatever they want, innit?'

Ray processes this. 'Do you reckon . . . Nah, forget it.'

Just as I'm writing down the answer to the first question, he changes his mind.

'Do you reckon Nawal would go out with me?' He looks like a chameleon dropped in a bowl of strawberries.

'Bro, you need to ask her that.' His depressed face gets me in the feels. 'But for what it's worth, she seems pretty into you.'

'For real?' he says, with hopeful eyes.

I give him a confidence-boosting back slap, then turn my attention back to the textbook. Unfortunately the words don't make any sense, even after reading through twice. The late shift I worked at Dad's shop yesterday is taking its toll . . . Then Shais threatened to make dinner, and I didn't want to die of food poisoning . . . Just need to close my eyes for a moment, give them a short rest . . .

'*How dare you turn up late and fall asleep in my class!*'

Sitting up so fast, I nearly somersault backwards off my chair. A chain of drool stretches from my lips to the table.

'I see!' Mr Welch continues, trembling like a self-contained earthquake. 'Instead of doing the set task, you've been drawing *queens*.'

At some point between arriving late and falling properly asleep, I've drawn Big Bad Waf winking and tipping her crown, a boot placed squarely in the middle of a felled enemy's chest. The pose is so sassy, I can't not be impressed.

'He is a queen!' someone says, getting some laughs.

Then Welch goes off on one, blasting me for being tired. Why do teachers think shouting at someone has the same effect as a can of Red Bull? It's mad demotivating, not to mention humiliating. Then to top it off, he sets me a detention, forcing me to stay awake for an extra forty minutes after school. Madness. Whoever bullied Welch as a kid knocked the logic straight out of his head. This is why scientists need to develop a vaccine against bullying.

I sigh, propping my head firmly on my hands. Gonna need to stay awake for the rest of class before I get myself into any more trouble.

The rest of the week at school drags on in a predictably boring way, until the weather that's had reporters and my mate Kara whipped into a frenzy all week finally arrives on Friday as I'm on my way home.

Snowflakes like ostrich feathers tumble out of a colourless sky, coating south London in a blanket of whiteness. Squeals of delight fill the air as kids try catching snowflakes on steaming tongues. Kara and her cousin are belting out a gospel version of 'Let it Go' while a trio of Year 7s on the opposite side of the street are competing with 'Do You Want to Build a Snowman?'

I bury my hands deeper inside my pockets, seeking refuge from the blistering cold. Out of the corner of my eye, I see a black Volvo slow down, and the passenger window lowering. *DX Dingoes!* my paranoid mind screams. Instinct kicks in, and I dive to the other side of the pavement, ready to roll over someone's wall at first sight of the barrel of a gun.

'Hello, Elias! Hope I didn't give you a fright?' It's Kelly's mum, who is just about as far away from DX Dingoes as you can get. 'Can I offer you a lift? Such inclement weather!' She flings open the door, spilling toasty warmth into the street.

'Aw thanks, Mrs Matthews!' I say, climbing in, making sure to mind my manners. Even if I'm not middle class, rude is rude, and I don't want her making assumptions about Amma. I glance into the back. 'Where's Kelly?'

'Oh, she won't be joining us,' she says, giving the indicator a flick and pulling out. 'She's getting extra help from her maths teacher, which is actually why I wanted to speak to you.'

'Me?' I ask in a small voice, starting to feel like a caged mouse.

She cranes her neck, eyes like chips of ice. 'What do your parents do?'

'Uh, you asked me this before . . .'

'So I did! You said your father was a taxi driver.'

I blink.

'Or a security guard? I forget which.'

'My dad is a businessman,' I say, trying not to sound annoyed.

'Specifically what kind of business?'

'Produce. Dad owns a shop on the high street.'

'Ah, a greengrocer.'

Somehow she makes it sound like Dad sells copies of the *Big Issue* outside Quindom station.

'You see, Elias,' Mrs M continues, cutting through the snowflakes with a jet of screenwash, 'our families are really quite different. Kelly comes from a long line of proud academics. For the first time in her life, my daughter is struggling with her studies. She's been distracted for weeks.'

'Yeah, I heard they're making the exams harder every year.'

She gives me a look. 'No, I don't think that's the case at all. Kelly used to be friends with girls like Jade and Melanie and Victoria. Serious girls, all academically motivated. Ever since the incident with Melanie, she just hasn't been quite as focused.'

'For what it's worth, Mrs M, Melanie is a nasty piece of work.'

'It's worth *nothing*,' she says, slamming on the brakes, practically giving me whiplash. 'High school politics get left behind. I know what girls are! At loggerheads one minute, bosom buddies the next. Exam results are what you carry forward. Now I know Kelly is very talented and can apply her mind to nearly anything, but her father and I want her to focus on academic pursuits. I understand it must be very exciting for you to have someone like my daughter helping you with your story books. I respect your choice, I absolutely do.' She nods like she's proud of how liberal she can be. 'You are passionate about becoming a graphic novelist. But you both stand at opposite ends of the talent pool. Therefore I am going to have to ask you for a favour I know I have no right to.'

She turns to face me.

When I was younger, I saw a cartoon version of *A Christmas*

Carol on YouTube. There was this one scene I will never forgot: Jacob Marley – Scrooge's dead partner – untying his head bandage so his jaw popped open like an overhead bin on a plane, letting out an otherworldly wail. Scared me shitless. This is what Mrs M's face is doing to me now, although without the wailing bit.

'I want you to leave Kelly alone.'

'You can't ask me that!'

'No, perhaps not, but I am anyway. Deep down, I think you want what's best for Kelly too. Please, *please* leave her alone.'

Shame crawls inside my chest, hot and spiky. Mrs M thinks I'm a parasite out to drain Kelly of all her talent. Floundering out of the car – which incidentally is nowhere near where I live – I want to slam the door so hard, the window shatters.

But I won't. I'm not who this woman thinks I am, and she doesn't get to change me.

As soon as I get indoors, I go to feed Sparkle some apple crunch treats.

'Hey, Spark-fu,' I say, stroking from silken head to cotton-ball tail. A cloud of fluff, almost like a ghost Sparkle, rises up and drifts away. 'What you moulting for, girl? It's like the North Pole outside.'

Sparkle cocks her head at me quizzically, then begins licking my hand.

'Mrs M thinks I'm leeching Kelly's talents. It ain't like that, Sparks! We're a team. Put us together and magic happens.' I furrow my brow. 'Only now she's ghosting. Do you think Kelly still likes me?'

Sparkle sidesteps this question by hiding her face in the nook of my fingers. That ain't good. I rack my brains, trying to figure out what I did wrong. Is she pissed at me cos I took so long to invite her over? Does she think I'm a freeloader cos I let her pay for me back at the coffee shop? Did her mum finally get to her? By the time I'm done analysing, my ego is confetti. As I pull out my phone, Sparkle chitters.

'Yeah, yeah, I know – Mrs M told me to get lost. But screw her, innit?'

Sparkle executes a bunny ear flick making me laugh.

> Hey, Kelzebub!

> Hey, Ilz-ifer Morningstar! Sorry about earlier. What did you want?

> I've been working really hard on the comic.
> I want to show you all the cool stuff I made. ☺

> I heart your comic but I'm with my boyfriend right now.

My heart drops three floors, landing in a dumpster. Don't get me wrong: Kelly is my best mate, and I'm not jealous in *that* way. My problem is *who* that boyfriend might be. I pause, before typing again.

> Is your boyfriend Imran?

Part of me is still holding out, praying that the answer is no. But as the seconds balloon into minutes, hope fades.

> Fill you in on Monday. Luv ya! X

Whoomf! The dumpster catches fire. Seven words, one symbol. A lethal combination I will spend my entire weekend obsessing over, wondering whether Kelly has outgrown me. Just like Daevon did. Mrs M's all up in my grill when it's Imran she should be worried about. He's the real danger here.

Having chewed a hole through her willow ball, Sparkle looks at me with defiant pride, then hurls it out of her window.

I think about hopping on my bike and riding up to Kelly's place to warn her that she's making a terrible mistake. Or even just giving her a regular call. No good can come of her dating Imran. Literally everybody knows the man's sleaze all over. But all the bastard has to do is bat those thick eyelashes at you, stroke that angular jaw, and you forgive and forget.

No one is safe from his charms.

CHAPTER 36

'Ilz!' It's Monday lunchtime, and Kelly has come over to sit next to me on the memorial bench.

'Hey!' I say, my heart twinkling like the Bifröst rainbow bridge of Asgard. We're hanging together in school, and she doesn't seem to care who sees. 'How was your weekend?'

'We went to an incredibly sketchy club, and they thought we were over eighteen and let us in. It was brilliant!'

She's happy, but it won't last. I have to protect her. 'Kelly . . .'

'Thanks for giving me space, Ilz. You're the best. Which is why I feel like I can tell you everything now.'

Bracing myself for the worst, I hold on to my knees for support.

'You're right. I'm dating Imran. Wait, don't hate me!'

I shake my head. 'Never. But . . .' Static crackles as I rub my scalp. 'I think you're making a big mistake. A *huge* mistake. Everybody knows Imran is a sexist pig.'

'I know he can be difficult, but that's just his tough-guy persona. He has this whole other side that's really sweet. We've been talking for ages, he asked me for my number after the Movember thing, but I didn't want to tell you before. You seem so down on him every time he's mentioned. He asks about my writing, and he bought me *this*.'

She thrusts her hand out like a new bride. On her finger is a giant Medusa Hip Hop ring: a black and gold centre encircled by cubic zirconia. I don't mention that they cost a fiver at Brixton market.

'Look, Kelz, the other day he was showing his mates your Insta page, and they were taking the piss.'

The hurt in her eyes is like one of Big Bad Waf's vape rings squeezing my throat.

'Hey, Kelly! Wanna watch man shoot some hoops?'

Suddenly Imran is towering over us, spinning a basketball on his finger. My cheeks prickle, afraid he might've heard me bad-mouthing him.

He grins at her, and though her lips twitch, the seed of doubt I've sown is starting to take root. It surfaces as a whorl on her forehead.

'Have you been showing your friends my Instagram page?'

He shoots me a death stare. 'That what my boy told you?'

Kelly raises her eyebrows, waiting for an answer. I am so happy right now, even though I may pay for it in broken teeth later. Imran is about to be served a big slice of comeuppance.

'Yeah, I did,' he finally admits, bouncing the ball. 'Course I'mma show my boys the lovely girl my heart belongs to.'

WTF?!

I'm sick in my mouth, but certain a smart girl like Kelly will be able to see through his fakeness. Glancing at her face ends that hope. She's making goo-goo eyes. He reaches out, and she readily places her hand – the one with the tacky ring – inside his. The urge to grab her other hand and pull her away is overwhelming.

'See you around, fam,' Imran says making a clicking sound and winking. Then he leads Kelly away, Pied Piper style.

I don't see Kelly again till a couple of days later at school. I walk up behind her and tap her on the shoulder.

'Kelly, man, we need to talk.'

She looks up and down the science corridor, then nods. 'Yep, guess we do.'

'People are laughing behind your back. *Imran* is laughing

behind your back. You need to dump this player. You're too good for him.'

Her eyes shift between mine, in a detached sort of way that has me worried. 'You're pretty convincing.'

'Huh?'

'I know what this is really about. You're angry with me because I haven't been spending time with *you*.'

'Oh my God – I swear on my life, people are chatting shit about you!'

'I know, OK?' she snaps back. 'This school is a mean place where people get off on criticizing others. How dare a fat chick date a hot boy? It's hard enough ignoring them without you reminding me every five minutes.'

'But I'm trying to *protect* you.'

'I don't need protecting. God! Just because I'm a girl, doesn't automatically make me a damsel in distress.'

'Does Imran know this?' I shoot back.

'I'm helping him become a better man. It's not his fault he hasn't had any strong female role models.'

'So you're basically saying all the girls he's treated like shit deserved it?'

'No, that's not what I'm saying at all. I'm just saying that if you don't respect yourself, than you can't expect anyone else to either. Nobody's challenged Imran before. People assume he's a sexy thug, then blame him when he plays up to that stupid stereotype.'

'You've only known him five minutes, and you think you have him all figured out? He's not some loveable rogue, and you're not some mystical feminist goddess with the power to fix him. Did you hear about the guy from DX Dingoes who got arrested for firearm possession? He's Imran's *cousin*.'

'So because my mum's a bitch, that makes me one too?' She

stands up, her eyes brimming with hot accusation.

'No, Kelly, that's not what I meant.'

'I know exactly what you meant. Thanks a lot.'

She turns on her heel and walks away.

CHAPTER 37

'Hey, man, really appreciate this,' I say as we walk through the shopping centre.

It's a late Saturday afternoon, when there are slightly fewer shoppers about. Zayn Malik's new song is playing, and a flash mob wearing clown wigs has gathered by the fountain. A middle-aged bloke with a big red nose is barking orders, handing out banners.

Daevon looks at me and smiles. 'No problem. You been through a lot lately. Plus, Mum's stuck me on some low-cal diet, but man needs his carbs, right? Gotta boost them muscle gains.'

'Auntie Candice ain't making patties no more?' I ask in horror. His mum's patties are legendary. One bite, and you're hooked for life.

'Worse. She's making healthy ones with quinoa and adzuki beans and kale. Taste like shit.'

I notice a couple of girls checking Daev out. With his hair tied back and his slick goatee, my boy is looking damn fine. It makes all this dieting business even more messed up. He should embrace the extra pounds.

The merry-go-round with bright flashing lights and loud carnival music is up ahead. We stop, watching cartoonish cars spinning round and round. Most of them are empty. I glance up at the sign. Five pounds a ride. No wonder there are so few takers.

'Brah, you ain't thinking of riding, are you?' Daveon asks with concern.

I chuckle. 'Nah.'

'Auntie Foz used to bring us here back in the day. Remember that?'

'Back when they weren't trying to fleece you. You seen them prices?'

Daevon glances at the kids on the ride. Their well-dressed parents stand around taking pictures and shouting things like 'Weeeeee!' and 'Don't go too fast!'

'Your mum let us ride bare times! Then she'd buy us candyfloss on a stick or them spiral lollies. Oh man, remember those giant lollies? Like something outta Wonka's factory!'

Daev's reliving the good times, not realizing that what made them so good was the fact that we never worried about what we looked like or what anybody else thought. We were living our best lives.

'Say, where is Auntie Foz at, anyway?' he asks.

I stick my hands in my pockets, kicking my scuffed trainers. 'Pakistan. My auntie's badly sick.'

Daevon lets out a low whistle. 'That sucks.'

We're quiet for a while, lost in our own thoughts.

'Hey, they replaced the sweet shop with a health food shop!' he says, pointing indignantly. 'Bet you any money it's a government thing. Stupid prime minister sugar-taxing my life!'

'You remembered it wrong, fam. The shop's on the other side of the food court, behind the escalators. Remember all them import sweets? Sour Patch Kids, Mike and Ikes, Tootsie Rolls.'

'That's some memory,' Daevon says, looking impressed. 'No wonder you got moved up to Ms Mughal's set. I wish I was smart . . .'

'You *are*, though. Imran and Noah are holding you back, and it pisses me off!'

His eyes widen in apparent surprise at my bluntness. 'Nah, it's the system. They want to oppress us. Besides, even if you're right, it's too late now anyway.'

I shake my head. 'Not really. Bet your parents would sort you out a private tutor if you asked. You'd be *breezing* the exams, fam. End up going some posh uni and wearing a suit.'

But Daevon isn't listening any more. He's licking his lips, dimpling. 'You reckon the American candy store is still here?'

'Only one way to find out.'

We turn around, and I nearly jump out of my skin when I see Imran. He's wearing a brown leather jacket and black jeans that are so ripped, he probably popped them in a blender instead of the washing machine. His arm hangs round the shoulders of a tall girl shoehorned into a patterned minidress. Other than the smile, it's a whole different Kelly. This one has straightened hair, parted in the middle and glittering like it's been sprayed with crushed rubies. Her large blue eyes are framed by what Shais calls 'feline flick' eyeliner. Thick buttery lip gloss clings to her mouth in a suggestive sheen.

I look away, embarrassed. What is she doing? Swapping the persona Jade's crew created for her to become the girl Imran wants her to be isn't an upgrade. I'm heartbroken cos she is so much better than this.

'Bro!' Daevon gets Imran's attention just as I'm figuring out a stealthy exit strategy.

We DedManz dap, but my eyes are on Kelly. She smiles watching the kids on the merry-go-round. The smile is all glass. She's clearly latched on to the kids so she doesn't have to look at *me*.

'What you guys doing here?' Daev asks.

Imran slides an arm around Kelly's waist, surprising a squeal out of her as he draws her into a kiss. He grins at us, eyes lingering on mine, while Kelly looks flustered. 'Treating my woman, innit?'

Kelly is not your woman! I want to scream. *She belongs to no one but herself. And right now, she's making a big mistake, and even though she's blanking me, I still care. I hate you, Imran.*

'Hey, Kelly . . .' I say instead, hoping she'll at least make eye contact so I can transmit a last-ditch warning. A flash of my eyes would do it. But her face goes stiffer than burned toast, brushing crystallized hair away from her jaw.

'We're going to miss the start of the movie.' She gives Imran a meaningful look.

'What movie you guys watching?' Daevon asks.

Imran laughs. 'Some superhero shit, but gotta please the lady, innit?'

Jealousy blooms in my chest. Superheroes was *our* thing. How could Kelly betray me like this? Especially with Imran dismissing it as 'shit'.

Kelly has the decency to blush, but yanks Imran's arm with enough force to get him moving.

'See you boys later,' he calls as they walk off together, his left hand cupping her butt.

I cuss, punching my fists together. Daev places a hand on my shoulder.

'Easy. She isn't putting out, anyway. Imran'll get bored soon enough.'

Hearing that makes me feel a little better. Kelly hasn't betrayed herself. But I'm still worried cos Imran is going to see her as some sort of a posh-girl challenge. Can anyone defy the evil powers of Imran Akhtar?

'Sugar is what my boy needs.' Daevon slings an arm across my shoulders and, singing 'I Want Candy', walks me to the American sweet shop.

Sunday afternoon, I'm busy making a revision timetable on my laptop, trying not to get depressed by the amount of hard work and cramming that is looming over me, when my phone rings. It's a welcome distraction . . . until I see that it's Kelly. I pick up anyway.

'Hey,' she says.

'Hey,' I reply, matching her aloof tone.

A sigh. 'I don't want us to be like this.'

'Dump Imran. Simples.'

'Why can't you be happy for me? He's your friend too.'

'He's not my friend. He's just a guy I hang with cos I'm too scared to walk away. You saw the meme, right? That was Imran dangling me off a bridge till I pissed myself. That's who you're dating.'

'I'm sorry Imran was a bastard to you. There's really no excuse. But, well, we don't choose who we love. It just sort of happens.'

I sigh too. 'You taught me about power imbalances. You said you were gonna make Imran a better man. But the only person I see changing is *you*.'

'I'm fifteen years old, trying to figure things out just like everyone else. Sometimes you have to compromise your ideals a bit.'

'You're feeding his ego . . .'

'It's not like he isn't making an effort for me too. He sat through a two-hour movie he hated. If that isn't love, then what is?'

I'm so done with talking about Imran. 'Can I tell you some amazing ideas I've had for Big Bad Waf?'

'Sure.'

Just like that, I change the subject, telling her about some cool new plot twists, getting myself more and more worked up before realizing this isn't a conversation. It's a monologue.

'Kelz?'

Silence.

'Earth-One to Kelly?'

'Yes, I'm here! Sorry.'

'Were you listening?' I ask, my cheeks burning.

'Absolutely.'

'So, you're coming over tomorrow to help?'

'Oh, um, sorry, Ilz. I'm sorta busy tomorrow.'

'But Kablamo! Kon IV is only weeks away!'

'You'll manage. I'd only get in the way . . .'

'You could never get in the way. Not ever.'

'That's really sweet and all, but . . .'

She lets out a long sigh, and I brace myself for impact. You can change the subject, but you can't change someone's mind.

'I can't live in stories any more, Ilz.'

'Oh,' I say. Knew it was coming, could feel it suffocating me like Living Shadows, but I wasn't prepared for how much it was going to hurt.

'All my life, Mum has made decisions for me: trips to museums and galleries, dissertations and piano lessons, Latin classes and chamber choir. I thought I loved making stories as much as you do. See, your love is pure. Mine was only ever about escapism.' She swallows, clearing her throat. 'Imran is exciting, Ilyas! He's more into me than any guy I've ever dated. I'm usually just a way for boys to get closer to Jade or Mels.'

I open my mouth to beg her not to be so dumb. Imran is more evil than Thanos and Darkseid combined. What she sees as attention is just him wearing her down. But if I speak up, Kelly is going to think I only care about my comic, and I'll lose her. Maybe Mrs M was right, and I am a parasite . . .

'Then be with him,' I say, emotionally drained, finally defeated. 'I mean, if it's what you want.'

'Oh my God! I knew you'd get it eventually. You're the *best*.'

If I'm the best, then why do I feel like the absolute worst?

CHAPTER 38

'Grrrr! Miss, I can't do this!'

Ms Mughal glances up from Ray's book. 'Of course you can, Kara. It's essentially just drawing bits of circles – something you've been doing since Year Seven.'

'But I was rubbish at it back then as well,' Kara moans.

'You're doing it right,' I tell her, glancing over at her diagram. 'Your dodgy compass is the problem.'

'Can I borrow yours then?'

'Sure, lemme just finish mine.' I measure the gap between the compass point and the attached pencil, then whirl an arc across my worksheet, trying to represent the locus of a water sprinkler. 'Why did the examiners have to mess up an already difficult topic by bringing in Inequalities, anyway? It's like sticking you in a cage with scorpions *and* snakes. Overkill.'

'Preach!' Kara says, then leans in closer to share some gossip. 'You know that girl who paid twenty quid to shave Imran's hair off the other day?'

I try not to flinch. One slip, and I'll have to start over, which is too much for a Monday.

'Well apparently she's dating him now! Dunno what he sees in her.'

'Dunno what she sees in *him*,' I counter.

Kara swots my arm. 'Salty bish!' My pencil tip slips, marking a squiggle in the middle of my diagram. 'Oops . . .'

Sighing, I rub it out and start again.

'What's with the shade, though?' She looks at me expectantly.

'I thought you boys were mates again.'

'Imran's a thug, and the thug life ain't for me.'

'Girls love a bad boy. I'm thirsty for it.' She cackles.

'You do realize he's been putting it around. Like, a *lot*.'

'Well then he must be great in bed!' she says, flicking her tongue and making randy cat noises. 'Don't look at me like that! Boy's fine as hell.'

'She's not bad either.'

Her eyes nearly pop out of her head. 'Have you not noticed how much make-up that hoe's been wearing? It's like she's taking lessons offa Mrs Waldorf.'

I finally snap. 'Imran screws around, and he's a *stud*. The girl wears make-up, and she's a *hoe*. Do you not see the double standards here?'

'Yeah – but everyone, like, idolizes Imran.'

'So why have you got these then?' I ask, holding up her bag, pointing at the assortment of badges with feisty slogans: *Riots not diets! Feminist & Proud! Cuterous.*

'Savage!' Nawal says, clapping her hands. 'The boy is a better feminist than you, Kara.'

Kara sticks her nose up in the air. 'It's not a competition.'

'What's a cuterous?' asks a Alfie.

'Some place you came out of,' says Nawal, making everyone laugh.

'Can I have you all looking at the board, please!' calls Ms Mughal. 'I'm going to demonstrate how to answer questions one through four, since quite a few of us are struggling.'

At 3.10 p.m. I see Kelly coming out of her languages class and hurry over.

'Hey, I know you don't want to help me with my comic any more, but could I ask you a coupla questions about your notes?'

I pull them out of my rucksack.

'There's an inter-school football match on in ten minutes . . .' She sees me deflate and touches my shoulder. 'But you should totally come.'

I scowl. 'Since when do you care about sports?'

'Um, since the captain became my boyfriend?'

'So you're spending time going to Imran's games, which you hate. Does he listen to your stories?'

'Do you?'

Her question throws me.

'Project X,' she reminds me pointedly. 'You haven't asked me about it even once since those detentions with Gilchrist. All you care about is *your* comic.'

A fine mist of acid coats my tongue. 'You said you weren't gonna work on Project X till uni, otherwise of course I would've asked. I think it's badass!'

'Oh really? So what's it about then?' She folds her arms.

'World epidemic of the flu. Cassie finds a cure and joins a group of rebels to get it to the people, but sinister forces are afoot. See? I *do* care about your dreams. And I care about you, which is why I don't want to see you get hurt.'

'But I'm not going to get hurt. Why do you keep saying that? It's like you want it to happen. Anyway, I'm just not into stories any more.'

'Imran's changing you. I miss your curly hair.' I glance down at her kitten heels. 'You've even stopped wearing uncle Fiz's boots.'

Her cheeks colour. 'Well maybe change isn't such a bad thing? We're all growing up. Having a boyfriend is important to me right now. I shouldn't have to apologize for it.' She grips my arm, eyes twinkling. 'Try it! Find yourself a cute girlfriend.'

Suddenly I feel like everything hangs on my next words –

screw 'em up, and I've lost her forever. If it was a picture, I could draw what I need to explain. But words? I've been lazy, looking to Kelly for those.

'Yeah, well you concentrate on *growing* up. I'm going to go win twenty-five grand! Never needed you in the first place, fam.'

I walk off, my lies ringing in my ears.

CHAPTER 39

With my hands in my pockets, I meander into the shop after school. '*Aagaya munda, tere!*' One of Dad's workers announces my arrival, signing an autograph in the air with cigarette smoke.

Dad tells him off for smoking inside, then turns to me. 'I really hope you haven't come asking for pocket money, because you're getting zilch from me.'

I shake my head, gesturing with my hands still inside my jacket pockets. 'Er, can we talk over there?'

Dad looks puzzled, but nods. Ever since Amma left, he's given up shaving and grown a beard that looks like Rocket Raccoon's butt glued to his face. Some of the regulars think Dad's gone religious, which he likes to play up to, quoting sayings of the Prophet, which I think he made up. The truth is he's lost without Amma. He leans against a shelf of dessert mixes, their colourful packets promising results that never happen in real life.

'I thought about what you said,' I begin. 'I wanna start working for you now.'

'What about school?'

'Forget school,' I say, unable to make eye contact.

His shaggy eyebrows rise. 'You in trouble again?'

I shake my head. 'All that studying and homework and exams – it's just not me.'

'Look, son, I appreciate the offer, but it's against the law. Come back when you're eighteen, then we'll talk.'

'But it's doing my head in!' I yell.

Dad's workers give me some side eye.

'You missing your mum?'

I look at Dad in surprise. Not because of what he said, but how he said it. His voice was softer than I've heard in a long time. Maybe Dad isn't the Neanderthal he pretends to be. Maybe no one is. Only, it's like trying to be cool: you do it cos you think other people expect it.

With a tiny shake of my head, I shrug. 'Amma's busy, innit?'

'I'm sure she wouldn't mind you skyping her.' He takes a long drag on his e-cigarette, then registers my look of surprise. 'Your old man's trying to quit.'

'Since when?' Amma's been trying to get the man to quit for *time*.

'Since your Amma's been gone,' he admits, rubbing his forehead. 'I was a chain-smoker when I met your mum. Fifteen bloody cancer sticks a day!' He strokes his scalp, looking crestfallen. 'Had hair on my head back then, instead of me shoulders. You was never short of a stick of gum whenever Foz was around, I can tell you! But gum will only take you so far.' He takes another drag on his e-cig, then smiles. '*I'm not marrying someone who smells like the backseat of a school bus*!' He smiles, recalling her words, tapping off non-existent ash. 'God she was cute . . .'

'Did you quit?'

'Cold turkey,' he confirms grimly. 'Oh your Amma was worth it, mate. Prettiest Pakistani girl in all of London. Even the *goras* were begging her for the time of day. She never did understand all the attention. Not stuck up like the rest of them la-dee-da girls.'

'You really love her, don't you, Dad?' I say.

His eyes narrow to ellipses, taking a longer puff. 'Best thing that ever happened to me, mate. Then you lot came along and spoilt everything.' He gives me a wink. 'And your old man slipped back into old habits.' He looks at the e-cig regretfully.

'Say "Shava Shava"' blares out from someone's phone, startling us. One of Dad's workers is performing the classic Bollywood dance, right there in the middle of the shop floor, busting out moves like a regular Amitabh Bachchan.

Dad chuckles and shakes his head. 'What a knob.'

'Dad, when you were a kid, did anyone ever bully you?'

'Course they did, you numpty! Tell you what: prepared me for life, didn't it? I got smart and starting hanging out with the *goondas*. We were right terrors – nicking stuff and smoking pot. And don't you go spilling your guts to Amma about any of this!'

I shake my head, promising. 'So you hung out with the rude boys for protection?'

For a moment his face darkens, then he sighs and slouches. 'Sad truth is, you're either a bully or you get bullied. And no one likes a grass.'

Real talk. I wish he wasn't wrong, but I still want to hug him. But that's not us – never has been. So I offer him a smile instead. 'Thanks, Dad.'

He nods, taking another drag on his e-cigarette. 'Any time, kid.'

CHAPTER 40

I ride to school on Friday morning, harsh wind slashing at my eyes. Yesterday the heavens opened, and the rain came pouring down, dissolving the snow, and with it everyone's dreams of building snowmen.

Aquaplaning across slippery roads is hard enough without my phone going off like a mini rocket. *Ping, ping, ping!* When did I get so popular? Seeing Gilchrist at the gate, I hop off my bike and sombrely walk into school.

'OMG! Have you seen the video?' some random asks.

'What video?' I ask.

'WhatsApp, mate. Some hoe giving uckers badders!'

I frown wondering what's so exciting about that. Cyberspace is full of worse. In fact, if aliens exist, some day they're going to intercept all the porn floating around out there, think human beings are a race of perverts, and blow up the planet. Shame.

Jade and Melanie are standing by the lockers huddled together in front of a phone.

'Oh my God!' Jade says, hamming it up. 'That girl is *never* coming back from this.'

'She's going to contract at least three different kinds of STIs from that big brown monster!' Melanie says excitedly, before pretending to vomit.

'Shall we watch it again?' Jade asks, her lower lids curving into crescents.

'Yah!' Melanie says, giggling. 'Such a greedy slut.'

A sinking feeling starts in the pit of my stomach. I crawl into the dark space under the stairs and pull out my phone. Sure enough, I've been sent a video too entitled *Dis White Thot*. With growing trepidation, I press play. To the left of the screen is a girl with cascading red curls hanging over her face. To the right of the shot are the slim hips of an Asian guy, the v-cut of his abdominal muscles partially visible above unbuttoned jeans.

'I don't feel comfortable,' says a nervous voice from under the curtain of hair; a voice I wish so badly I didn't recognize.

The guy's voice has been edited out. Of course it has. His hand cups the roundness of her cheek, parting her lips with his thumb. She stares up into his face, and I realize he must be saying something, because she's nodding in response.

'OK,' she says, hooking her fingertips over the waistband of his black Calvin Kleins. 'But don't—' Once again, the sound cuts out.

The rest of the video will haunt me for life. My chest shrinks with every second, each lung compressed to a small flesh brick, breathing no longer possible. Oinking, grunting, squealing pig sounds have been dubbed over the video. **SLUT!** and **#ThotPatrol** flash across the screen as a siren wails.

I don't realize I'm crying till a tear splashes on to my screen. Then my hand starts shaking so hard, I drop my phone. *She's stronger than this!* I tell myself desperately. *She can handle anyone and anything!* But even plastic explosives placed at a weak spot can bring a bridge tumbling down. Imran is sly, hiding the camera like a prankster so Kelly didn't even notice it. And even though the whole school will know it's him – you can't actually tell.

How does a girl with off-the-scale smarts end up in a sex tape filmed by a dumbass like Imran? The tears leak faster now, cutting streams across my cheeks. I clamp a hand over my mouth, silencing a wail trying to escape, racking my brains for a way to save her from the tsunami of bullying that's headed her way. Why couldn't

I have gone round her place the first time she'd texted me about her mystery boyfriend? I knew Imran would hurt her. Some bestie I am.

Unable to change the past, I focus on fixing the future. Could I contact WhatsApp and make them delete the video? Should I set off the fire alarm to cause a distraction? Is there a hack that can make everybody's phones fry within a one-mile radius?

In the end, I do the only thing I think will work.

KELZ, DO NOT COME TO SCHOOL TODAY!

There is cheering and applause in the corridor. Wiping away snot and tears, I peer out from the shadows as on-trend caged heels patter up the corridor. The shoes are unfamiliar, but the walk is not. I'm too late, and straight away the roasting begins.

I want to leap out of my hidey-hole, machine-gunning disses, throwing punches, sending teeth scattering like rice at a wedding. Hopelessly outnumbered, sooner or later I'd fall and get my head kicked in. But I'd go down fighting for my best mate Kelly, cos that's what friends are for. Except that's only the Ilyas in my *head*. Real World Me is gripped by terror, ashamed that I'm afraid the dirt will stick to me too. I'm powerless to do anything but watch.

The Dark Ages are back at Stanley Park when public executions were a thing. Kids from all years have gathered round to yell abuse at Kelly. Phones and tablets are held up like mirrors, looping the embarrassing video so the moment can never end. Oinking and sex noises echo from multiple speakers. The air grows moist with the stink of hate and malice. This lot are baying for blood.

Kelly's head whips left and right, stunned by the ferocious hostility of the crowd. The girls call her 'slut', the boys ask her 'how much?'

'Imran!' Kelly snarls in angry desperation.

Surely *now* she realizes her mistake in trusting the scumbag with the face of a movie star?

Imran's eyes are half-lidded and sly, a smile playing on his lips. The signs are all there. While I'm stuck playing musical statues, Imran is about to destroy Kelly.

'Sorry, do I know you?' he says, getting a generous round of laughs.

Someone pushes a phone in Kelly's face, filming this new interaction. Kelly bats the phone away with a powerful backhand. It strikes the wall with a loud crack.

'Oh yeah,' Imran says, pointing at her, his eyes glittering demonically. 'You're the fatty from that video going round. Gyal, you is ratchet.'

'What are you talking about?' she says, her voice leaking strength like a bullet-riddled tyre. 'You said you loved me. You said I could trust you.'

'Are you high?' He pulls up his collar, looking at his adoring fans instead of her. 'Why would man get uckers badders offa you? No offence, but I got better options.'

'Stop lying!' she yells, frustration making her voice crack. 'Everyone knows it's you.'

'You wish. I only date girls that respect themselves, innit? Oh yeah, and they gotta be pretty.'

The laughter becomes a mini earthquake; the vibrations restarting my engines. Storming towards Kelly, I shove the onlookers aside. I throw my arms around her, hiding her from the world. She looks at me, and I get scared. Her eyes are as wild as a hunted animal, the kind who'll readily gnaw off a limb just to escape. She pushes me off so roughly, I nearly lose my feet. People howl with laughter. Kelly breaks into a run, heading straight for the exit.

Imran catches my eye and winks. It's the spark that ignites my fury and finally loosens my tongue.

'You're a piece of shit, Imran,' I say, in a voice that is so loud, I barely recognize it as my own.

'You say something?' he says, bristling. His cropped scalp appears to brush against the ceiling, his wide shoulders stretching the full width of the corridor.

I glance nervously at the crowd of hungry onlookers, then back over my shoulder as the exit door bangs shut. 'Yeah,' I say, turning back. 'Clean your ears out, cos there's more.'

The audience laps it up, telling Imran to end me.

'Everyone knows that's you on that video,' I snarl.

'And?'

'Kelly loved you. God knows why, but she actually loved you. And this is how you treat her?'

'Ain't my fault Fatty got slutty.'

More gasps and hysterical laughter.

'She ain't no slut, fam. What she did, she did for love.' I shake my head, exasperated by his attitude. 'You got your dick out to hurt her. You secretly filmed a private moment without her permission. There's only one thot here, and it's you!'

'*Oooh. You gonna take that, Imran?*'

'You calling me thot, boy?' Imran asks, rounding on me.

'You're worse!' I bare my teeth, my nostrils stretching across my cheeks like they're going to split, and I don't even care.

'What, you think just cos we hang together, you can shoot yo mouth off? You're gonna get bodied, mate.'

'You forget I cracked your head open and put you in hospital?' I shriek, vibrating with rage. 'I'm a crazy-arse piece of shit with nothing to lose! Come at me, bro. I'll kill us both.'

'Ilyas got balls!' someone shouts.

Everyone, including Imran, glances round to see who it was.

I'm positive it was Daevon, though he's looking over his shoulder too. It gives me a massive boost, so that when Imran turns back, I'm ready for anything.

Imran stares into my eyes and smells the crazy. I'm not a boy any more. I am a single-use, one-time-only mousetrap itching to be triggered. 'You ain't worth it.' He spits on the floor and walks away.

People stare at me, unsure whether I deserve respect for standing up to Imran or to be cussed out for hating on the king of Stanley Park. In the end, I hear a mixture of both – the positive voices maybe just a bit louder. Maybe I've tapped into something, made them see that bullies don't always win.

Then a can of Monster hits the right side of my head. Warm fizzy liquid spills down the back of my shirt, and the corridor fills with laughter.

CHAPTER 41

'Ilyas? Ilyas!'

I turn around and stare at Ms Mughal in surprise. 'Sorry, miss. I was a million miles away.'

All around me people are clearing their stuff away, getting ready to go home for the weekend.

'Are you OK?' she says, motioning me over. 'You've been dazed all lesson.'

I stand by her desk and shrug miserably.

'Ready to win the Kablamo! Kon IV competition?' She smiles at me, her eyes dancing with excitement.

'No, miss,' I say, looking down at my shoes, my mind constantly replaying those images of Kelly.

'Oh no, you *must*. Even Idris was blown away by your fabulous idea!'

'He called PakCore a rip-off,' I remind her.

'Only because he thought you could refine it.' She looks at me, frustrated by my lacklustre attitude, then taps her computer. 'Come on, show me PakCore again. He was just the sort of character I wanted to see as a kid. And anyway, Idris won't be a judge on the day.'

Sighing, I drop my bag. She rubs her hands together as I double-click on the latest version of my comic. I think she's just trying to make me feel better. It's working. A faint, wavering glow is awakening in my heart.

'I switched it up,' I explain as the file loads. 'PakCore is now Big Bad Waf.'

On cue, the comic explodes on to the screen. Ms Mughal's hand covers her mouth. *Shit!* I think. Beavering away on the animation for weeks, losing track of the real world, I'd almost forgotten Big Bag Waf was based on my maths teacher. Man, I hope she's down with me basing the character's look on hers.

'Is that Ms Mughal?' Kara asks from over my shoulder, dialling my embarrassment up to eleven.

'You didn't make that!' Ray says. 'Did you?' he adds, a little more doubtfully.

I gape at them, surprised that they haven't already gone home.

'No. Yes. I mean, I guess I was inspired by Ms Mughal . . . Is that OK, miss?' I ask, blushing. 'I mean, I won't be entering the competition anyway, so no one ever needs to see this. I can delete it if you want?'

'Are you serious? This is the most flattering thing anyone's ever done for me,' Ms Mughal says, relief washing over me. 'A superhero – wow! Idris is going to be so jealous.'

'What's this comic about?' Kara asks, her eyes flitting back and forth between the panels.

'Er, I can show you. I made a motion comic . . . a sort of movie out of it . . .'

'Grab the popcorn!' Ray says, perching on his desk.

Kara joins him, ripping open a bag of Maoam. 'Budge up!'

Ms Mughal dims the lights, then sits down on Kara's other side. Kara offers the bag of sweets, but Ms Mughal politely shakes her head.

The presentation begins. I've ripped tracks from a whole bunch of movies and dubbed over them using my own voice. It sounds crap. But although I'm always my own worst critic, even I have to admit the animation is on point. The camera tracks and pans, following Big Bad Waf as she runs across roof tops, faster and faster, her jilbab billowing like a sail in a gust of wind. She leaps and swoops and dances from building to bridge to a radio tower. There's a close-up of her hazel eyes as they flare like beacons, providing her with a magnified visual on a group of bad guys. They've hijacked a research facility and are packing some serious heat. Big Bad Waf's eyes switch to infrared mode, quickly scanning a van parked suspiciously close by, only to discover it filled with explosives. She leaps off the tower, zip-lines along a telephone wire, then thrusts her arms wide. With a clap of thunder, her jilbab snaps open like a parachute, and she glides towards the action.

I glance nervously at my audience, but their expressions are hidden in darkness. My armpits start to leak like taps.

Waf unleashes holy hell on the bad guys, eventually saving the day. I'm not prepared for the rapturous applause that follows. Not one bit.

'Did you come up with that story yourself?' asks a silhouette in the doorway. He snaps the lights on, and I freak because it's Daevon.

I stutter, apologize, and deny everything.

'Look at my dude!' Daevon tells my audience. 'He's a genius, and he don't even know it.'

'I don't know whether you guys know this,' Ms Mughal says, 'but Ilyas was going to enter the Kablamo! Kon IV competition. The winner gets to develop their idea with an industry professional. Who thinks he still should? Say *aye.*'

But I'm already shaking my head. 'My co-creator, Kelly Matthews, helped me develop the character and make the story better. Doesn't seem right to do this without her.'

Kara frowns. 'Kelly Matthews? Isn't that the girl on the sex tape? She was some bougie bitch who hung around Jade and that lot!'

Ray shakes his head. 'My sister found the clip on my phone

this morning and legit thought I'd been downloading porn! Now I'm grounded.'

'That's enough!' Ms Mughal starts up, completely shocked.

'But that's just it!' I say, throwing my palms out. 'Kelly isn't just the-girl-on-the-sex-tape. She was amazing long before that ever happened. And she's still amazing. She's clever, and funny and woke.'

Kara raises her eyebrows. 'Suppose her best friends Jade and Melanie better change their names to Woke-ahontas and Melanin Central.'

'She's *nothing* like her so-called friends, though. Her mum doesn't want her hanging out with a brown boy from these ends, but she does anyway. She sees past all of *this* –' I draw circles in the air around my face – 'straight to *this*.' My fist thumps my heart. 'If that ain't woke, then I don't know what is.'

'That is woke.' Daevon nods in agreement.

'And I don't care that she fell in love with the wrong guy and ended up making the biggest mistake of her life. It doesn't change anything. She's still Kelly. She's still my best friend.'

'Bro, I had no idea she meant that much to you,' Daevon says.

I wait for the ridiculing, to be told how lame I am. Instead, Daevon walks up to me and gives me a hug. Not a bro-hug, but a proper one.

'You boys are gonna make me cry!' Kara says, stuffing her face with Maoam.

Ms Mughal stands up to address us. 'Ilyas is right. Stanley Park may have its problems, but the one thing we do get right is that every student matters. None of us is perfect. Not teachers, not students, no one. What gives anyone the right to assassinate this poor girl, who must be feeling absolutely devastated? Newsflash: people tend to remember the bad stuff more than the good. When I'm the one lying face down in the dirt, you better believe I'm going to pray I was nice to the person standing over me.'

Everyone is silent. Then Ray clears his throat. 'I can't even imagine what's going on in her head right now. So, you know what? I think you should win this competition for her.'

'Yes!' Kara squeals. 'Winning something for me would get me like . . .' She jumps off the table and begins to perform a mesmerizing victory dance.

'I finally get why you been ghosting,' Daevon says, chuckling to himself. 'Ilyas, man, this is your tribe. And Kelly. Not DedManz. Haven't seen you this happy since primary.'

'I don't think you belong with DedManz either,' I blurt.

He glares at me, but my mouth won't stop yapping.

'You're too good for boys playing gangstas, Daev. Amma always said, "Be careful what you pretend to be, cos one day you'll become it."'

He looks away, his shoulders gradually stooping. 'You might be right.'

'So you gonna enter this masterpiece?' Ray asks, directing our attention back to the comic.

I wrinkle my face. 'You guys seriously think this could win?'

Everyone says yes except Kara.

'Honestly?' she begins. 'I think the voices were crap. I go drama school every Saturday, so I know what I'm talking about.'

'So what do you suggest?' Ms Mughal asks, grinning as if she already knows the answer.

Kara stands a little taller and begins to tell us her idea.

CHAPTER 42

Saturday morning, I put my board art in the corridor, leaning against the radiator, as I snag my jacket off the hook. I was up till midnight designing and creating it.

'What's that?' Shais asks. She's dressed in a bathrobe with her hair wrapped in a towel turban.

'This? Oh just a project for a friend . . .'

Before I can tell her not to, she flips it over and glares at it. 'Oh . . .' she says, disappointed. 'This is actually pretty good.'

It's the nicest thing Shais has ever said to me. I want to tell her she looks lovely without make-up, you know, to make her feel better about herself. But I'm pretty sure she's going to twist my words and make out I'm saying she wears too much of it. So instead I take a leaf out of Daevon's book and give her a massive hug. She goes rigid, her face as shell-shocked as *The Scream* (if the dude in the painting was rocking a towel turban and ombré nails).

Grabbing my artwork, I book it out the door.

I'm hot and sticky by the time I get to the Matthews' house. The cold air converts my sweat to liquid nitrogen. Resting the board against the front gate, I wipe my brow. The Ghost of Mrs M hisses in my ear: *If I ever catch you on our property again, God help you!*

My insides shrivel. There's no convincing some people. Mrs M wants to believe I would hurt Kelly so she can justify cutting me out of her life. Being as stealthy as I can, I open the gate and stalk up the long drive. Carefully placing the board on the drive, I scamper away.

From a safe distance, on the opposite side of the street, I pull out my phone and text Kelly.

> Look out your window xx

Her bedroom window remains completely still. No peeping eyes, no twitching curtains.

I get the idea to send her a voice message on WhatsApp. I press record:

I still love you, Kelz. There's nothing you can say or do to ever make me hate you. And I want you to know there's a ton of other people at school who think you're amazing.

On Saturday, Ms Mughal and a bunch of students from my maths class want to come with me to Kablamo! Kon IV. They legit think we can win! Never gonna happen – I can't do it without you. You and me, Kelz; we ain't had things go our way for time. But we have to keep hoping and fighting, right? Nothing worth having comes easy.

OK, I'm gonna go now, cos it's freezing out here. Miss you. But take all the time you need. I'll still be here when you're ready.

I send the message, but end up staying another fifteen minutes, staring up at Kelly's bedroom window, wishing for a sign. Icy serpents slip between my ribs, coiling inside my lungs. Maybe her phone was confiscated? Wiping my leaky nose on a square of kitchen towel I find in my pocket, I resign myself to going home.

The painted board lies under her window: Cassie and the rebels from Project X realized in moody street art. I hope it brings a smile to her face. Hope she sees it before Mrs Matthews reports it to the council.

*

Later that day at Dad's shop, I carry a large crate from the stockroom, struggling under its weight, as I make my way outside. Not the best way to spend your Saturday, but Dad needed an extra pair of hands, and I need something to focus on.

Beneath a tangle of shredded paper lie fresh brown cassavas that have travelled all the way from Ghana. Tipping the hairy buggers into the display tray, one root catches my eye, and I pluck it out. It looks like a Hobbit foetus. For a moment, I'm about to snap a pic and send it to Kelly, but then I remember she's gone off-grid and isn't replying to messages.

'*Beyta?*'

My heart leaps into my throat as I spin round, ready to hug the life out of Amma and beg her to sort out my messed-up life. But standing in front of me is a small lady wearing dark glasses and a pink coat with stains on. She starts speaking to me in what I think might be Gujarati.

'Sorry, Auntie,' I say, placing Frodo's baby on display. 'Could you say it again in English, please?' I offer her a smile, hoping she's not going to call me out for losing touch with my roots.

'Yes,' she says, looking off sadly. 'I am trying to buy kaki, but I am blind. Can you help me find fresh ones, please? I always end up buying the bruised ones, and they go off before I can eat them.'

I spot the white stick she's clasping tightly and wonder how I could've missed it. Ripping off my gloves, I guide her by the elbow round to the fruit stall. Dad is crap at spelling, so it's just as well she can't see the price cards. *Carkey/purssimom/Japinees frut*. Dad's doing them three for a pound.

'Bung any three in,' Yunus whispers, carrying a sack of blushing onions over to the other side. 'Or we'll be left with ones we can't sell.'

I nod, waiting for him to go, then pick the best three I can find. 'There you go!' I say, placing them in the blind woman's basket. 'Not a blemish on any of 'em.'

Putting her basket down, she reaches out and touches my face, cold, dry fingers fluttering over my features.

'You have an honest face,' she finally concludes, picking up her basket. 'May Lord Ganesha bless you with happiness and success!'

I watch her tapping her way over to the till.

'Elias!'

I glance round. Kelly's mum is standing beside a tower of bright yellow buckets of vegetable ghee. With her merino wool coat and periwinkle leather gloves, she sticks out like a sore thumb.

'Mrs Matthews!' I bombard her with a hundred questions about Kelly till she cuts me off with a raised hand.

'I asked you to keep away from Kelly because I knew you were trouble,' she says.

'Me?' I say, pointing at myself in disbelief.

Her lips shrivel like salted slugs. 'Who else? What sort of a boy seduces a teenage girl into performing misogynistic sex acts on him, secretly films it, then sends it to her peers? Do you have any idea what you've done?'

'You think that was me?!' I almost scream. 'Oh my life!'

'Well given that you're the only boy Kelly is friends with of a tan complexion . . .'

'But I'm not!' I say. 'I got lighter skin than the guy on that video. Plus I'd never do anything like that. Trust!'

'What's going on here then?' Dad asks, bustling over and looking at Mrs Matthews with distaste.

My ears burn with shame. Even though I've done exactly nothing, I don't want Dad to hear what she's accusing me of.

Mrs Matthews blinks, turning her hatchet face to Dad. 'Are you Elias's father?'

'What's it to you? Why're you scaring my customers with all your shouting?'

'Your son coerced my daughter into performing a filthy sex act, filmed it and distributed it to the entire school. I want to know why he did it. I want justice for my daughter!'

Dad's face colours. 'I don't appreciate you coming here and throwing around accusations about my boy. He's a good lad, and if he says he didn't do it, I believe him. So either buy a banana or clear off.'

'I shop at M&S,' she hisses.

'Well la-dee-da!' Dad retorts. 'Someone call the press: we have a lady here who shops at M&S!'

Mrs Matthews and Dad glare at each other. Customers goggle like they're being treated to an exclusive performance of Punch and Judy. A few of the aunties give me evils, instantly assuming the worst.

'You may have your father fooled,' Mrs M says stiffly, 'but you don't fool me. My daughter doesn't deserve to have her reputation destroyed by a teenage lothario. If I ever catch you on our property again, God help you! Oh – and that ridiculous sign of yours has gone straight in the bin.'

'You've made your point, now piss off. Nobody's interested in your cock-and-bull story,' Dad growls.

Mrs Matthews ignores him, fixing me with a look that could cryogenically freeze a polar bear. I gulp. She makes a show of adjusting her expensive leather gloves, then marches off, stiletto heel boots shivving up the pavement in a preview of what'll happen to me should I darken their door again.

'All right, show's over,' Dad tells the gathered scandal-mongers. 'And for the record, my son is not guilty, so you can wipe those looks off your faces.'

Two women drop their shopping baskets and walk out. One of them calls me a name that sounds like 'Weinstein'. But right now, all I can think about is that Dad stood up for me.

CHAPTER 43

'Amma, *please* come home.'

It's Sunday night, Imran's definitely going to kill me now I've called him out in front of the whole school, and I can't enter this competition without Kelly. Our plan to win her round clearly didn't work and even though Ms Mughal and everyone want me to do it, Big Bad Waf belongs to Kelly just as much as me. She's my best mate. My life is falling apart, and I need Amma.

There's a pause on the end of the line. I chew my lip, snipping off ragged flakes.

'I'm sorry, *beyta*,' Amma says. 'I'm needed here just a *little* while longer. Sohail is putting on a brave face, but your little cousins – oh it breaks my heart to see them suffer!' Her sobs cut me up, and when she starts to apologize for them, holding it together becomes impossible.

'I miss you, Amma . . .' A tear rolls down my own cheek.

'Give me ten more days. I'll bring a box of *petha dhi mithai* for you and a beautiful *jamawar sherwani*. You'll look so handsome! Is everything OK?'

I clamp a hand over my mouth. Offloading my problems on my already miserable mother seems unforgivable. She's trying to be a rock for Uncle Sohail and my little cousins, even though her big sister just died.

'You know me: same as ever,' I say, giving a hollow chuckle. 'Shaista's doing well. Some make-up company tapped her for advice about launching a line of Asian cosmetics. And Dad's given up smoking.'

'What about you, *beyta*? How's your comic book coming along?'

I smile. 'Better than ever. I have this friend called Kelly, who's full of amazing ideas. Only she's stopped coming to school . . . family problems, innit.'

'Oh dear! Make sure you're a good friend to her.'

'I will,' I say, though I don't know how.

'I better go now. Take care of your dad. He can be such a hopeless buffoon.'

I hold back the ugly crying till she's rung off.

CHAPTER 44

Monday morning, and our year curriculum coordinator, Ms Hinds, directs us into the hall, class by class for a special assembly. With only Year 11 present, the hall takes on a surreal quality, like we're all aboard HMS *Damnation* on a one-way trip to the Island of Lost Souls.

Mr Gilchrist and Officer Pryce are up on the stage, grimly surveying us. Two captains on the bridge, about to whip this motley crew into shape. I hope they make Imran walk the plank.

'Good morning, Year Eleven,' Mr Gilchrist begins. 'I've called this emergency assembly as unfortunately a terrible thing has occurred— WHY ARE YOU LAUGHING?'

Whoever was stupid enough to think this wasn't next-level serious just got the awakening of a lifetime.

'Get up!' Gilchrist orders, making everyone look round.

Noah rises slowly, showing disrespect with every gesture.

'I don't think you quite understand the importance of what has happened here at Stanley Park. I've had to call Officer Pryce away from urgent police business to give you this talk.' He lets that sink in. 'Sit down.'

Noah drops into his seat, his face redder than a mini Babybel.

'Morning, Year Eleven.' Officer Pryce scans the hall solemnly. 'As your deputy principal has just explained, I'm here to give you a timely reminder of the law regarding sharing photos or videos of a sexual nature.'

At any other time, there might've been a few sniggers, but after Gilchrist's outburst, everyone is corpse silent. By now, everybody has seen Imran's evil video and knows exactly what she's on about.

Officer Pryce gives us the same talk we had last year, back when we thought we were all too smart to ever get caught. She talks about evolving technology, about how we might think naked selfies are a bit of a laugh, but by doing it, we're putting ourselves at risk and breaking the law.

'Once you post an image on the internet, you've lost control, and it's out there forever,' she says.

She goes on about sexting and child pornography and how we're all still legally children until the age of eighteen. Then she drops the bombshell about 'joint enterprise' – how even viewing and sharing this kind of video is a criminal offence that we could get prosecuted for.

'A female student at this school engaged in a private moment with a male,' she says sombrely. 'It was recorded without her consent and shared publicly. You cannot even begin to imagine the distress and humiliation she is going through right now. We can't determine if it's a student from this school or another man in the video, but we do know he had tan skin, so was probably of Asian or mixed-race descent. If you know or even think you *might* know who he is, we would like you to do the right thing and come forward with this information. I will be in school all day today . . .'

There's no shortage of compassionate, pitying faces in the hall. Where were these people when the video dropped? Where was the sympathy when mob mentality spread like an infection? Kelly's moment of shock and betrayal slices through my thoughts, nearly choking me. How she pushed me away, like she no longer recognized me, like her brain was too damn mashed up to work. Was it fun watching another human being getting utterly destroyed? Did she get one top grade too many, or was it volunteering for loads of assemblies that got people's backs up?

Did her family's wealth make her fair game to be utterly destroyed? The lion's share of guilt lies with Imran, but all these bastards had a hand in it.

'Over the days ahead, we aim to get to the bottom of this,' Mr Gilchrist says. 'The sooner, the better. At Stanley Park, we pride ourselves on being the sort of school that cares about each and every one of our young people. The right to learn in a safe environment has been violated for this student. When she comes back to school, and we don't know if she will yet, there will not be any – and I mean *any* – mention of the aforementioned video clip. If there is, if she is made to feel unhappy or ashamed, I promise you that I will personally exclude you on the spot. Because if you could be that cruel to another human being who made a terrible mistake that they already regret, you do not belong at Stanley Park, and we are not willing to give you the benefit of our nurturing community.'

I hear sniffling and see Jade crying into a pink tissue. Melanie hugs her, placing her chin on top of her golden head as she strokes her shoulder.

Next Officer Pryce speaks about humiliation and mental health. She reminds us to be careful of what we say, because we can never know how it will affect someone else or what may be going on in their life.

'Trust me – you don't want to make yourself the trigger that pushes someone into hurting themselves.'

I zone out, distracted by the constant need to call Kelly. I don't even care about the competition any more and anyway, I can't enter something that's half hers. I just need to know she's all right.

'When you go back to your lessons, you will do so quietly,' Gilchrist says. 'You will be mature and not share information with the lower school. The following students will need to stay behind:

Rory Petersen, Imran Akhtar, Krishna Patel and Ilyas Mian.'

My stomach bottoms out. Why me?

'Why you making me stay behind, though?' Imran has the audacity to say as students are dismissed row by row. 'This is racial profiling.'

'Calm down,' Officer Pryce says. 'I assure you that's not the case, but we do need your full cooperation. Whoever was on that video has committed a very serious crime.'

'And?' Imran says.

I want to scream.

'Why you picking on me and my bredrin for?' Imran kisses his teeth.

'Because some people have already come forward with your names, and by law we are obliged to investigate,' Officer Pryce retorts.

Yaas, queen! I think, wishing she would really Hulk out and twist him into a pretzel.

Imran snorts. 'So what you want us to do? Get our dicks out so you can match 'em up with that video?'

Krishna and Rory snigger.

'I'll thank you to watch your mouth, sunshine,' says Gilchrist, shooting Imran a warning look.

'Follow me, please,' Officer Pryce says stiffly, and Imran has no choice but to follow her into the corner where he won't have an audience to show off to.

'Sir,' I say. 'Is Kelly OK?'

'Well how do you think she feels?' Gilchrist replies tetchily.

He moves off to assist Officer Pryce's inquiries because – surprise, surprise – Imran is being a prick. Now's my chance. Pulling out my phone, I fire off a text.

Pls let me know you're OK.

I wait, but, just like with all the other texts I've sent this weekend, Kelly doesn't reply.

'You watching that video again?' Rory asks, grinning.

I shake my head, putting my phone away.

'Look at Imran denying it!' Krishna says, gesturing with his chin.

I crane my neck. 'You gonna tell 'em it was Imran?'

'Whose mans is this?' he says derisively. 'Bro Code.'

'Why, you thinking about snaking?' Rory asks, leaning forwards threateningly.

I shake my head quickly.

'Course he won't,' Krishna says. 'They're DedManz. If Imran goes down, he's taking this one with him.'

I gulp.

All too soon, I'm being summoned by Officer Pryce. At least I'm up last. Do I do what the other lads did and deny all knowledge, or stick my neck out?

'Before we begin,' Officer Pryce says, her light eyes staring into my soul, 'it's really important that you remember to tell the truth. OK?'

I nod.

'Do you know the identity of the male on the video?'

Glancing over my shoulder, I spot Imran lurking in the doorway and gasp. Pryce's eyes follow mine.

'Oi, bro!' Imran shouts.

Officer Pryce bristles. 'You've had your interview. Go back to your class.'

'Yeah, in a second.' Imran motions me over, and I get up.

'Sit down,' Officer Pryce instructs.

'Just a sec, miss,' I plead and duck out.

I run up the steps to where Imran is waiting between the aisles of seats so we can't be overheard. He places strong hands on my shoulders and pitches forward till our foreheads are touching. For a moment, I think he's going to kiss me.

'You gonna keep quiet, fam?'

Looking into his dark eyes, I see the universe, and the universe stares back. Only now do I fully understand the power Imran commanded over Kelly. 'You hurt my best friend, Imran. She's the only one who ever liked me for who I am.'

'What you chatting about? I rated your skills from Day One. Why you think I got you to tag up these ends?' He moves his lips close to my ear, his goatee tickling my jaw. 'Bros before hoes. Money over bitches.'

I throw my arms around him and, after a startled pause, he hugs me back. My hand slips inside his pocket.

'What you doin'?' he asks in surprise.

My fingers squeeze his phone. 'Getting evidence.'

'Huh?'

Whipping round, I sprint towards Officer Pryce. Imran swears, and I know he's coming, know he's going to tear me apart with his bare hands and make fritters out of my liver. The very ground shakes with rage, and the promise of revenge hums in the air, and for a moment, I believe Imran can control the universe.

Officer Pryce's confused face switches up fast, her shoulders squaring, her hand reaching out for the phone. Holding it out like a baton, I barrel towards her. Imran's hand snatches at my blazer, twisting the fabric. Gripping his phone tightly, I fling my arms back like wings, still pumping my legs as I slip out of the jacket. And I run like the wind, like the devil is on my heels blasting jets of fire and skunk.

Five metres, three metres, one—

Officer Pryce's shoulder catches me in the side, sweeping my feet out from under me as she intercepts Imran. My bum slaps the polished floor, and I go skidding. Officer Pryce uses Imran's own momentum to swing him round, slamming the side of his face down on to her interview desk. *Snick-snick*. She's cuffed him.

'GERROFF ME!' he yells, bucking and twisting, trying to yank his wrists out of the handcuffs.

'Don't make this worse than it has to be!' she says, pinning him down. But it's like trying to nail down lightning.

His eyes cut into mine. 'You got no idea what you've done. What happened to your dad's shop was *nothing*, fam. Watch.'

Mr Gilchrist rushes in to help Officer Pryce restrain Imran, while she radios for back-up. Heart trying to explode out of my chest, my ears echo with Imran's final threat, as I walk away dazed—

Suddenly, a gag of flesh and sweat slips over my mouth, mashing up my nose, then I'm being dragged out of a fire exit. The next thing I know, I'm flying through the air and kissing the playground tarmac.

'Paigon!' Noah yells.

Pushing myself up on grazed palms, my heart drops when I see the seven-inch Ka-Bar knife he's wielding. My eyes cut to the fire exit.

'Ain't nobody coming for you now, bruv. DedManz had your back. But you turned it. Now you the deadest man.'

Noah's hair gathers round his skull like twisted flames. Red lips curl over razor-wire braces in a grin that belongs in Arkham Asylum.

'You don't wanna do this, Noah . . .' I say backing up, eyes trained on his knife. 'Officer Pryce is just in there, and life in prison ain't worth it . . .'

But Noah isn't listening. His eyes have glazed over, and he's chanting drill lyrics, something about making me 'leak juice' and putting me in a body bag. Gilchrist and Pryce are occupied with Imran. The whole school is busy in lessons. The playground is no-man's land, and I am completely alone.

With nobody else to turn to and nothing left to do, I make the *Sign of Wahid*, hands slicing through the air, cleaving apart one reality, opening up another. Here comes the burn. First in my brain, then in my heart, energy waves like ripples in a pond. Suddenly I am Big Bad Waf and I am PakCore together. I'm that angry nine-year-old in a Superman costume who was told brown boys aren't allowed. I am Ilyas Mian and I am Kelly Matthews. I'm every bullied kid ever. And I am vengeance.

I leap to the right, then to the left, springing into the air with blossoming rage.

Noah's blade whistles past my cheek, splitting light into a spectrum of psychedelic colours. My left leg whips round, spinning my whole body through a wide arc. **BAM!** My heel strikes Noah square in the forehead. **KA-DUNK!** My right foot slams into his chest. **PHWOOSH!** A squall of spittle blasts from his ruby lips.

Then the tarmac is soaring up to meet me, and I know I am in for a world of pain. But just before I crash out, I glimpse Noah stagger like a drunk as Gilchrist rugby tackles him to the ground.

I fricking kicked the moon!

Then I'm just screaming.

CHAPTER 45

Worry, worry, worry.

I wake up with a knot in my stomach, hoping this will be the day Kelly finally comes back to school, or calls me. With Imran and Noah both arrested, I figured she'd make a triumphant return, desperate to talk about how I channelled Big Bad Waf and saved her honour. But nothing. Her story *has* inspired a whole bunch of girls to come forward with allegations against Imran though. Texting her daily gets me mad depressed because there's never a reply. Part of me is still hoping she'll appear in time for us to enter Waf into Kablamo, but I know deep down that the dream is over.

After a full week of silence, I bite the bullet and approach Jade's galdem in the refectory on Friday.

'Hey,' I say, acting like a boss, though I'm low-key shitting myself. 'You guys know where Kelly's at?'

Jade's hostile glare changes to amusement. 'Have you tried the local brothel?'

Her friends crack up. These girls are savage.

'She's definitely dropped her standards,' Melanie adds, appraising me. 'But probably not *that* low.'

My face sizzles but not because of the shade. What these girls think of me doesn't even rate. It's because these ungrateful witches benefited from Kelly's genius. Assemblies, trips, events, the school paper. The girl with the Midas touch made Jade's crew look golden, gave them status. Then the one time she messes up, they turn cannibal.

'Better check in with the Kardashians!' Nicole quips,

provoking screams of laughter.

'Who are you supposed to be, anyway?' Victoria asks, arching her eyebrows. 'Discount Zayn Malik?'

More hooting.

'Hang on,' Jade says, raising a hand to silence the coven. 'This is the boy who ratted Imran out to the police.'

'Did you think with him out of the picture, you'd be seen as a hero?' Melanie sneers.

The greatest comeback of all time sizzles on the tip of my tongue. Then I walk away.

'You owned him!' I hear one of the girls say behind me.

She's wrong. DedManz is over. I finally belong to no one but myself.

When I get home that evening, I consult Sparkle, and we both decide I should try texting Kelly one more time.

> Yo, Kelz, you OK? Man is worried. Hit me back, yeah? xx

I wait with bated breath, staring at my phone screen, as if I can Franklin Richards her reply into existence. That kid has Omega Levels of telepathy; Ilyas Mian has nothing but an old phone with a dodgy signal.

I'll clearly be waiting a long time.

The next day, Saturday, I hear the doorbell ring and only manage to make it to the top of the stairs before Dad answers the door.

'Hello, Mr Mian,' says a familiar voice. 'I'm Ms Mughal.'

'I know you,' he replies. 'You're Ilyas's maths teacher. What's the bugger done now?'

'Oh no! Nothing like that. He's a brilliant student. And a very talented artist.'

'I thought you said you was his maths teacher?'

'I am. The thing is, there's a comic book competition at Olympia London today and we think he has a really good chance of winning. But he won't do it alone – which is why I'm here.'

'Comic books?' Dad says, opening a chasm of sarcasm. 'That's not art. That's the trash kids read instead of doing homework. I should know. Used to get *The Beano*, twelve pence a pop.'

Kara's voice butts in. 'Mr Mian, why can't you be supportive of Ilyas's dreams? My mum's on benefits, yeah? But even she pays for me to go drama class cos it helps me with my confidence and makes me happy.'

What on earth is *Kara* doing here?

'*Kara*,' Ms Mughal says, reminding her of her manners.

'I do want my son to be happy, young lady,' Dad says. 'But it's different for blokes. He can't waste his life doing namby-pamby stuff, else he'll end up getting beaten up for it.'

'Not if you let him hang around people who get his talent,' a boy's voice says, which sounds a lot like Ray.

'What would you know?' Dad scoffs. 'No offence, but some day you're gonna be a grown white man with the world at your feet!'

A finger pokes me from behind, and I nearly fall down the stairs. It's Shais.

'Who's Dad talking to?' she whispers.

I shrug.

'Uncle Osman,' I hear Daevon say.

Exactly how many of my friends did Ms Mughal rope in for this intervention?

'Making comics is Ilyas's talent. I know where you're coming from. Me and Ilyas have been in a gang since we were eleven, so we wouldn't get beaten up. But now Imran's been arrested for revenge porn and Noah's been arrested for carrying a knife. You'd hate it if that was Ilyas.

'Being in a gang is whack. You believe you're a boss, but you're just a worker, crushed by this pack mentality. Ilyas is the only one of us who wouldn't get involved in intimidating other people or taking drugs. And you wanna know why? Cos he had his drawing.'

'Look Ms Maths Teacher,' Dad says, ignoring Daevon. 'I don't know why you care so much, but if Ilyas doesn't want to go, he doesn't have to. He's helping me in the shop today and he's happy about it. He's finally come round to the right way of thinking and I don't appreciate you coming to fill his head with more of this rubbish. '

'Oh, Dad, just support him for goodness sake!' Shais says, making my jaw drop. 'He's probably going to make a fool of himself, as usual. But there's a tiny chance he might win. And if we don't let him go, he's going to be wondering about it for the rest of his life, and it'll be *your* fault.'

'Ilyas! Get down here!' Dad hollers.

Shyness and shame compress me like bookends. Here I am, eavesdropping on all these people saying stuff about me they've never once said to my face, and now I'm expected to look them in the eye. I wish Amma was here to tell me what to do. She wouldn't be standing on the doorstep arguing with Ms Mughal.

Stumbling down the stairs, I act all surprised when I see them gathered on our stoop.

'Your maths teacher and friends are here asking me to let you go to some weird competition in London. You put them up to it, did you?' Dad says.

I quickly shake my head.

'Do you, uh, want to go?' he says with disappointment.

My first instinct is to lie. It's what's kept the peace all these years. But after everything my friends and my teacher have done for me today – not to mention Shaista's eleventh-hour boost – I owe it to all of them to be honest. It's my dream and although I don't want to do it without Kelly, I suddenly realize I owe it to myself.

'Yeah,' I say simply. 'I wanna go.'

Dad stares as if he sees me for the very first time and isn't sure how to feel about it. 'All right, all right. You've twisted my arm, Ms Maths Teacher. But you're taking full responsibility, all right? You drive him there, and you bring him back. And you're buying him lunch too.' He wags his finger. 'And I should warn you: he looks like a Twiglet, but eats like a horse.'

Dad is low-key treating Ms Mughal like she's a kid. I'm half expecting her to clapback.

'Done!' she says with a dazzling smile.

And suddenly my respect for her rockets even higher. Whether it's Mr Gordon (from maths) or Dad, men seem to talk down to her a lot. But she never gets shouty. Just responds with this level-headed dignity. It's what Amma and Kelly were trying to teach me about rising above it.

'We'll all take very good care of Ilyas,' Ms Mughal tells Dad. 'He's Stanley Park's finest artist.'

'Wish I had a teacher like you when I was a kid,' Shais says jealously. 'And you're so *pretty*. You have to let me do your hair and make-up some day.'

Ms Mughal smiles at her, then looks back at me and shrugs. 'Well, with your lovely family onboard, the decision is yours to make. Absolutely no pressure. But if you're up for it, I think it would be a good idea to change into a suit.'

'Ha! Good luck with that!' Dad says waggling his eyebrows. 'Last suit Ilyas wore was to a wedding three years ago. Try squeezing him in, and he'll be singing soprano for the rest of his life.'

Ray steps uncomfortably close, arranging my limbs like a mannequin. 'You're about my size. Miss, can we quickly pop round to mine, so he can borrow a suit?'

Dad blinks in surprise then gives Ms Mughal a dark look. 'Who are you? Snow White with your seven dwarfs?'

Ms Mughal leads us over to a shiny blue people carrier. On the side is stencilled: *Ginsby Mosque, Keeping It Halal Since 1988!* 'Thanks for doing this, miss,' I say in a small voice.

Ms Mughal glows. 'No worries. Your friends were the ones who kept pushing me.' Unlocking the doors, she leaps in the front.

'I call shotgun!' yells Kara, shoving Ray aside.

I open the rear door and am surprised to find yet another classmate hiding back there.

'About time!' snaps Nawal. 'I was literally dying in here. You better win this damn competition, boy.'

'Nawal's got a bet riding on this,' Ray says with a wink.

Ms Mughal drives like the wind, first to Ray's place, where I change into a skinny-fit navy tuxedo – which looks ridiculously baggy – and then straight on to central London. Seeing all the classic landmarks whizzing by – London Eye, Big Ben, Buckingham Palace and the Thames – brings home that this is *really* happening.

'We should've got T-shirts printed,' Kara says. 'Team Big Bad Waf.'

'That woulda been lit!' Daevon agrees. 'But considering we weren't even sure Ilyas would be allowed to enter, I guess not the smartest investment.'

'What's the name of the story you're entering anyway?' Nawal asks.

'*Who's Afraid of Big Bad Waf*?' I say shyly.

'OK, he's definitely winning,' she replies, then promptly starts singing 'Who's Afraid of the Big Bad Wolf', sampling rhymes from Cardi B and making up a few of her own.

Daevon gets in on the action with some old-school beatboxing.

Everyone is hype for this. But in the midst of all the happiness, I can't stop thinking about Kelly. Entering the competition without her seems so wrong. But between her not answering my calls, and Mrs M wanting to slaughter me, I guess there's not a lot I can do. Even after Imran's arrest, Mrs M still blames me for bringing him into Kelly's life. One bad experience with an Asian boy, and she blames all of us. Madness.

We get to Olympia early, since Ms Mughal has GPS traffic updates built into her brain, where Ray elects himself our tour guide.

'My parents are always bringing me to this place,' he says, throwing his arms out. 'Ideal Home, House & Garden, Food and Veg, Weddings.'

'So basically your parents are freaks who take you to all the most boring shows?' Kara says.

'Don't call food boring.' Nawal throws him an angry glare. 'Or weddings.'

Everybody looks at Ray, who looks like he's going to crap himself. We burst out laughing.

'Let's finish our GCSEs before sending out the invites, please!' Ms Mughal says, hushing us as she steps up to the box office to sort us out ID badges.

'We're entering the Breakout Star competition,' she tells the man at the desk.

He gives us a massive form to fill in. I'm panicking so much, Kara has to take charge and fill it in for me. She sprinkles a generous amount of hearts all over it. Then I'm being asked to hand over my USB and art portfolio case. Parting with them is a lot harder than I thought it would be. The man tags both with barcodes and scans them through to be sent on to Level One scouts. They're the gatekeepers who get to decide whether I make it to Level Two or not.

'Here are your day passes,' the man says pushing a tangle of lanyards across the counter. 'Competition entrants should keep their phones on at all times. Between twelve and one o'clock, texts will be sent out to the lucky five picked to present their work before our panel of judges. If you're one of them, you'll need to head directly to the green room for two o'clock sharp, with the main event scheduled to take place at three.'

Eyes watering, teeth chattering, I nod like there's no tomorrow. It doesn't get any more intense than this. Even facing off against Imran and Noah doesn't compare. This time, it's personal. My one true talent being judged by the very people who do comics for a living.

'You got this,' Daevon says, hooking an arm round my shoulder, leading me away. 'Not gonna lie: winning would be sweet. But if you don't, so what? You could try again next year. Or you could go art school.'

'I know you're right. I just feel like this is my one chance to prove to my dad that I'm not the dud in the family.'

'I feel you, bro. Pops gave up on me a looooong time ago. He's always telling Mum I'm *her* son, like he's washed his hands of me. Doesn't help that my brother and sister are both investment bankers. I pretend like I don't care, but it hurts.' He gives the thousand-yard stare. 'Guess being part of DedManz dulled the pain.'

'Exactly! The stuff I did for Imran to get his approval.' I shudder. 'Just cos I never got it from Dad.'

Daevon ruffles my hair. 'Look at us! Coupla nutjobs whinging cos "Daddy never loved us".'

'Know what? We should totally win at life, doing the stuff that matters to *us*.'

Daevon sighs. 'Dunno, fam. Might be a bit late for man . . .'

'We're fifteen. There's time to fix up.'

'Tell you what,' Daev says, unwrapping a muesli bar. 'Win this shit, and I'll start believing good stuff really can happen to good people.'

Hearing this from the friend I thought I'd lost to the cult of DedManz gives me all the feels.

'I love you, man,' I say.

'This bar tastes like shit.' He chucks it in a bin. 'Come on, let's check out some comics.'

The moment we walk through the turnstiles and enter the exhibition hall, it's like sensory overload. Too many colours, a thumping, soaring film score, and hazardous levels of excitement and anticipation.

'It's cray cray in here!' Kara says, pirouetting. 'Omigosh: there's Chris Pratt! Aaagh: there's Chris Evans! Holy Black Jesus: there's Chris Hemsworth!'

'Those are waxworks,' Ms Mughal says, trying to calm her down.

'That's good enough for me!' she says. 'Hey, can someone take pics of me kissing the Chrisses?'

'*Astagfirullah!*' Nawal says. 'I ain't getting involved with your sex-doll madness.'

'Sounds like a new show,' Ray quips. '*Kisses with Chrisses.*'

'Strictly pay-per-view. Adult-channel exclusive,' Daevon says with a suggestive wink.

I volunteer to be Kara's photographer. Honestly it's the least I can do after everything my friends have done to get me here.

So we spend the morning wading through row after row of comics, DVDs and Blu-rays, toys and games, model kits, busts and statues, trading cards and stickers. Ms Mughal buys some limited-edition Pop! Vinyls for her brother. Then we visit the interactive pods set up by movie studios trying to outdo each other with the latest immersive tech.

'Man is in LOVE!' Daevon announces. His dilated pupils seem to be hoovering up a woman in Power Girl cosplay.

I'm about to reply when my phone buzzes. My blood runs cold. 'Guys, my phone just buzzed . . .'

'Well, look at it, you fool! Here, lemme do it!' Kara snatches my phone and reads the text. Then, giving nothing away, she dramatically clears her throat.

'What is it?' I ask, ringing my hands. 'What did they say?'

'Ilyas got selected!' she screams. 'He's in the final five!'

My friends whoop for joy. One minute, I'm covering my mouth in disbelief; the next, I'm at the bottom of a celebratory pile-up, being squashed to death by my overenthusiastic mates. We draw lots of stares; some friendly, others openly hostile. Yet even in the face of this mind-blowing success, all I can think about is Kelly.

'Stop worrying, bruv!' Nawal says as I get back on my feet. 'You'll walk it. For sure.'

Smiling, I let my mates believe my silence is nothing more than regular nerves. How could I even begin to explain what my friendship with Kelly means to me? We're like a single creative soul split apart by an evil troll called Imran. Saying it out loud makes it sound like I'm in love with her so I swallow my words.

By 2 p.m. my panic levels are off the scale. The Green Room looms ahead like the Emerald City.

'You are going to be fine,' Ms Mughal says, slow and steady, like a hypnotist. 'You made it this far, and nothing happens without a reason.'

'*Wallah!*' says Nawal, raising a hand. 'Preach my teach!'

'Can't you lot come in with me?' I ask, wringing my tie.

Ms Mughal shakes her head. 'Only VIPs, I'm afraid.'

'But we're all rooting for you,' Kara says, slapping my back. 'We'll make bare noise when it's your turn.'

'Yeah, and we'll boo for all the other entries!' Nawal adds, snapping her fingers.

'Do it for Stanley Park!' Ray says, smoothing my tie and adjusting my tuxedo.

'Do it to show tramps like Lee Garrison that brothers can have heroes too,' Daevon says, making a Black Power fist.

'You remember that?' I ask in surprise because it was six years ago.

'Course!' he says with a wink. 'I been wanting to slap that fool ever since he started on you with his outdated racism.'

'So why didn't you?' demands Kara.

'Too scared, innit?' he says, making her laugh.

'Go win this thing!' Ms Mughal says with a flourish of her arms, her jilbab sleeves cracking like whips, spurring me on.

I take the deepest breath, say a prayer, then enter the Green Room.

CHAPTER 46

The first thing that hits me is that the Green Room is actually *red*. Red walls, red carpet, red-and-black furniture. The second thing is that every other competitor is an actual full-grown adult.

'Sorry, this place is only for Breakout Stars,' says a very pale man dressed entirely in black. A nest of black hair sits on top of his head. I wonder if he's in cosplay.

'Yeah, get outta here, kid!' sneers an American woman with large Harry Potter glasses and frizzy blonde hair. 'You're making me nervous.'

'Oh, um, hang on . . .' I rummage through my pockets, before remembering my ID is on the lanyard round my neck. 'Here!' I say, holding it up.

'You're the fifth competitor?' says the American. 'Huh. What are you – some kind of Boy Genius?' She chuckles snidely, looking at the others with a sour expression.

I laugh nervously, feeling like a dork.

The other competitors quickly lose interest in me and go back to their private conversations.

'Here, come and sit next to me,' says a lady with a green pixie cut. 'I'm Fenfang. How old are you?'

'Fifteen, nearly sixteen,' I say, as if that makes it any better. 'Oh, I'm Ilyas, by the way.'

The American lady scoffs. 'So I hear diversity is a *thing* right now.'

'Ignore Julie,' Fenfang mutters. 'Companies only care about their bottom line. If you're in the final five, it's because your idea has marketability.'

'Thanks,' I say, wiping sweat off my brow. 'Did I do something to piss her off?'

'I actually wish you had. But no. She's just got a chip on her shoulder because she flew all the way over from LA and apparently her dad was a legend – *her* word – who used to be friends with Stan Lee. She thinks winning is her destiny.' Fenfang rolls her eyes, adjusting her smartwatch.

It turns out Fenfang is a professional sculptor whose work has been included in exhibitions all over the world. Her favourite theme is animal cruelty.

'My work makes people uncomfortable,' she explains. 'I make bold statements, and people get offended.'

Fenfang briefs me on everyone's entry. Compared to them, Big Bad Waf is seriously childish. Their entries are all high-brow stuff, full of political commentary, satire and subversion. Me? I was looking to create a rollercoaster of fun with a little representation. Sitting here, listening to them discussing their comics, it becomes clear that I'm punching above my weight. Nobody asks me about my comic, and it's actually a big relief.

An important-looking woman with a clipboard and a steel-grey power suit walks in and clears her throat. 'Hello, everyone! I'm Geraldine, and I just want to let you know that in about ten minutes, the show is going to start.'

My stomach gurgles loudly.

'Don't go crapping your pants, hon!' says Julie making me blush.

Geraldine goes over the format in excruciating detail. Everything still flies over my head. I need Kelly. If we're supposed to pitch our ideas to the judges, I've already lost. I can barely finish a sentence without slipping into slang. Kelly could make a shopping list sound exciting. If only my pictures could speak for themselves—

Fenfang nudges me.

'Huh? What?' I say, blinking myself back to this dimension. Everyone laughs.

'Geraldine just went over the order of appearance. You're up last,' Fenfang says.

'No fair!' complains Julie theatrically. 'He's going to steal all our best ideas.'

'Then let's switch,' I say, finally losing my rag with her. 'Whoever goes first sets the bar. Going last is like the worst gig.'

'OK, Julie – they're about to introduce you to the panel,' Geraldine says, beckoning her over.

Julie gives me the slow burn as she rises. '*Aquila non capit muscas.*'

'Excuse me?' I say, raising my eyebrows.

Julie swishes through the curtains and is welcomed with excited applause.

'Forget her,' Fenfang says. 'It's Latin for "the eagle does not catch flies". It means an important person doesn't deal with insignificant matters.'

Wow. Shaded by an adult over a comic book competition. Shit got serious.

I try to listen to what Julie is saying to the judges and the audience, but it's just making me psychotically nervous, so I give up.

'I'm going to pray,' I announce. Kicking off my shoes and rolling up my trousers, I head into a corner before anyone can stop me. *This is my protective bubble*, I think. *This is how I deal.*

Pacing up and down nervously, writing and rewriting my pitch over and over on a sheet of paper I begged off Geraldine, I still can't get the words to flow.

I pull out my phone, and even though I know it's the last thing

I should be doing right now, I open a selfie of me and Kelly, grinning like idiots in anime onesies. My heart twangs, and suddenly I miss Kelly so much, I think I might actually cry. Thumbs fluttering over the screen, I type out a text, then hover over the send button. I end up deleting it. How can I go on spamming Kelly when she never replies? Why I can't I just accept she doesn't want to be mates any more and move on?

I'll move on, I tell myself. *But I can't leave it like this.*

I speed dial her and get voicemail.

'Hey, Kelz,' I say, in a thin voice. 'It's me again, hanging around like a bad smell. Sorry.' I swallow. 'Just wanted to let you know I made it to Kablamo! Kon IV. And I'm sorta pissing myself. I got Ms Mughal, Daevon, Kara, Ray and Nawal in my corner, all backing me for the win. Who'da thunk it? Yesterday I had no one.'

Polite laughter filters through the curtains as Fenfang works the audience.

'In a moment, I'm supposed to walk onstage and tell scary-ass judges and a thousand superfans why Big Bad Waf should win. Only I'm starting to think she shouldn't. Don't get me wrong, you made her ten times better than PakCore ever was, but . . . well . . . You ducked out, didn't you? I get it now. You were abandoning a sinking ship, and you didn't want to hurt my feelings. Big Bad Waf isn't anywhere near as cool or sophisticated as Project X. Man, did seeing all the other contestants' ideas make *that* clear! I'm just an idiot with a pocket full of dreams and a brain full of air.

'We didn't get much time together, but thank you for being my friend. You made me feel more important than I've ever felt in my whole life . . . Got three minutes before I'm due onstage. Gonna be making a fool of myself, innit? Should be used to it by now. Goodbye, Kelly . . . You won't hear from me again.'

A tear rolls down my cheek as I terminate the call. I highlight the folder on my phone containing all our moments together then hit the bin icon. All gone.

Sniffling, I walk to the window, pulling the curtain away to stare up at the sky. If I had wings, I'd fly away. Geraldine would have a fit, but I'd be long gone.

'Ilyas!' Geraldine calls, making me jump. 'You're on now.'

CHAPTER 47

I've never had a panic attack before. Apparently you get hot and sweaty, your head starts pounding, and it feels like all your airwaves got blocked.

It's happening to me now.

As I lurch towards Geraldine, my own body turning traitor, her expression switches to concern.

'Are you all right? It's literally just a short introduction about yourself and the idea behind your comic. There's a clicker for you to flick through your images. Finally a brief piece, lasting no more than ten minutes. OK?'

I nod, breathing through my mouth.

'Would you like some water?' she asks, holding out a bottle of mineral water.

I'd rather go home, I think. *Go back to living in the shadows, where it's safe and boring and lonely. Why did I ever reach for the stars, when all they did was burn me?*

Grabbing the bottle, I rasp my thanks, then push myself through the curtains.

I. Am. Not. Prepared.

Calling the auditorium 'big' would be like calling the Taj Mahal 'pretty'. Three thousand people from the furthest-flung places on the planet have come to watch. Sitting on ten levels, they spread around the stage like a two-seventy-degree slice of colosseum. There are cameras everywhere, including one attached to a zip wire. My dumb face is projected on to four IMAX-sized screens. The ceiling has been done up like a galaxy, sprinkled with ice-white stars, glowing planets and interstellar bodies.

Ten metres away stands a ghostly lectern made of clear glass, glowing blue with hidden LEDs. As I lurch towards it, my eyes swim in and out of focus. The applause sounds like a thunderstorm.

Nausea jabs at my stomach, but I keep pushing on. I owe it to my teacher and my friends to see this through. I owe it to Amma, who never quit encouraging me, even when it meant arguing with Dad. I owe it to Shaista, who believed in me for once in her life. I owe it to Kelly, even though she isn't here. But most of all, I owe it to myself. This has been my life-long dream, and I will never forgive myself if I don't give it my best shot.

'G-g-good afternoon,' I stutter into a microphone that nearly blows my eardrums out. 'My name is Ilyas Mian. I'm fifteen, and I go to Stanley Park Academy in south London.'

'South London represent!' screams someone who is probably Kara. Other Londoners whoop it up for our home city.

'I'm here to talk about my comic book character, Superman. No!' I shake my head. 'PakCore.' I slap myself, and the sound of it reverberates through the speakers. Laughter spreads through the hall. 'Sorry, sorry!' I say, blushing so hard. 'I mean Big Bad Waf. She went through a lot of changes to get to this point so . . .' My attempt to explain my confusion clearly isn't working. I change tack. 'Here's the cover for issue number one.'

I hit the clicker, and the screen behind me fills up with a picture I no longer recognize as the one I created on black card with coloured pastels in my dank bedroom. The illusion of bas-relief is brought to 3D life through light and shadow and a whole lot of smudging. Big Bad Waf stands like a statue, arms raised, fingers pointing as she makes the *Sign of Wahid*. Her hijab is adorned by a golden crown of daggers, the uneven spikiness of the tines evoking a crown of thorns, symbolizing her sacrifice for humanity. Her eyes are luminescent ovals of golden-green as she powers up. Vapour seeps from her lips, rising to form the title is wispy font:

Who's Afraid of Big Bad Waf?
created by Ilyas Mian & Kelly Matthews

I yank at my tie as if it's a hangman's noose. Tremors and heart palpitations threaten to bring me down. Jamming the water bottle in my mouth, I slurp for my life. My lips make a smacking noise, and I'm left gasping, rubbing my wet mouth on a sleeve. The audience gawps, unsure what to make of me.

'See, the truth is, I'm no good at this . . . *talking*,' I admit. 'My co-creator, Kelly Matthews, is the girl with the silver tongue and brilliant ideas. Like, if it wasn't for her, my character might've been just another big-boobed, funnel-waisted chick leaping from panel to panel doing a whole lot of sexy poses. And my mum woulda slapped me silly!'

There's laughter and some clapping. I blink, taken aback by this.

'Um . . .' I scratch behind an ear doubtfully. 'So . . .'

I've got nothing. The unexpected positivity has fried my brain. Being hated is what I'm used to. Shit.

'Ilyas is just being his usual annoyingly modest and adorable self,' says a disembodied voice from a universe that no longer exists.

Kelly is sauntering over to me. She's wearing a floaty evening dress in fiery colours and Uncle Fiz's DM boots. She places an arm around me as if to prove she's actually there. But I only start to believe it when I see us, side by side, on one of the HD screens.

'I'm Kelly Matthews,' she says into the microphone without a hint of fear. 'And I'm here to fill you in on all things Big Bad Waf.'

I gape. She speaks. They listen.

Kelly tells the audience that the world desperately needs Big Bad Waf. She talks about the dark times we're living through, how people's mistrust has evolved into hate, how it spreads like a plague. She talks about Big Bad Waf being a character with universal appeal. Someone to unite fans, blast stereotypes and stay true to her faith and culture.

'The news is full of depressing stuff,' Kelly says. 'And we play spin the bottle with the finger of blame. Gotta hate those social-justice warriors for spoiling everybody's fun! And how about those Feminazi bitches? They're on a mission to castrate every last man!

'The truth is it's not a level playing field out there. It never has been. No matter what you tell yourself, the world still isn't a safe place for girls.'

She's not going there. The world is watching. People are judging. Please don't do this to yourself, Kelly!

'I recently had a really bad experience at school,' she tells a deathly quiet audience. 'It nearly destroyed me. I'm a girl who knows her privilege. I'm white, middle class, and I usually get top grades. So life should be a bed of roses, right?'

Silhouettes like sand dunes in a breeze shift about uncomfortably, titters sifting through.

'I fell in love with a boy. A boy who lived and breathed toxic masculinity. My friend here tried to warn me, but I wouldn't listen to him. So I did everything I said I'd never do. I tried to conform to the sexy-gal stereotype Ilyas has just been talking about. I'm not proud of myself, but neither did I deserve what happened. The guy discarded me like trash, and I was slut-shamed by kids at school. So if I'm so smart, why did I do it?'

My lips are as dry as autumn leaves. I lick them, wanting Kelly to stop telling the world her business. I can't bear her being judged any more.

'Why?' she demands, spreading her hands quizzically. 'Because comics. Because TV. Because music videos and movies and toys and dolls and everything else you feed us. You put this stuff out there; *you* should take responsibility for it. If I'd had a character like Big Bad Waf to look up to when I was younger, maybe I would've thought I was good enough just the way I was. And maybe the guy who used and abused me might have thought twice about treating a girl in that way.'

The auditorium is so quiet right now, it's like everyone got abducted by aliens. With Kelly by my side, words stir inside me, rising to the surface, refusing to be denied. I step towards the mic, next to Kelly.

'People aren't born evil,' I say. 'We pick stuff up from the characters we want to be. I never had anyone to look up to. *I* ended up in a gang. Something terrible had to happen to wake me up. But I'm one of the lucky ones. Some people never get that wake-up call. Ladies and gentlemen, the antidote to global madness. Meet Big Bad Waf.'

I press the clicker, the lights dim, and I feel the weight of an auditorium filled with expectations. The motion comic I have bust a gut over for weeks is brought to life across four IMAX screens. Kelly perfected the story, my friends did the voice acting and mixed the soundtrack, and Ms Mughal was my kick-ass muse. As Big Bad Waf leaps about on the screen, bringing the bad guys to justice, she is all of us. The judges stare at the screen – smiling and gawping. Even the sour-faced guy on the end is leaning forward in his seat. The audience reacts to the special effects with wonder and delight, and it's already more than I could ever have wished for. Somewhere in the auditorium, Kara is whooping for joy, and Nawal is shouting '*Mash'Allah!*' with ferocious pride.

My lower lip trembles, my heart thrums, and my head is roaring. I steal a glance at Kelly, ashamed that jealousy made me think the worst of her; that foolish pride and anger stopped me from protecting her. But now she's told the whole world what happened with Imran and set herself free. Whether Imran ends up doing time in prison or gets released, Kelly can never be destroyed.

As I scan the room, I see an international audience reacting to Big Bad Waf in just the right way, and I finally understand my place in the world. I am more than DedManz, the least talented of three siblings, or the kid who ends up working at his dad's shop because nobody wants him. I'm the kid who can go toe-to-toe with adults in the cut-throat world of comics.

Across the lectern, Kelly and I stare at each other for the longest time, eyes misty blue in the diffused glow of the LEDs. We've both addressed literally thousands of people but don't have a clue what to say to each other.

'You're late,' I croak.

Kelly laughs, her eyes filling with tears. Then she gives me the hug I have been missing forever.

KAPOW!

ILLUSTRATED BY AMRIT BIRDI

ACKNOWLEDGEMENTS

To Mama, I love you the most. You are my inspiration, always and forever. And Sheba, the fluffy inspiration behind Sparkle!

Huge thanks to my friend and agent, Penny Holroyde, for guiding me on this amazing journey. Talent and kindness are a rare combination. You are one in a million.

To my incredible editor, Lucy Pearse, who shines like a beacon when I become lost in the detail (and who knows the best place for a biriyani in Edinburgh!) Thank you for championing every teen who appears in my books. Your skills are out of this world.

To Rachel Vale for creating another incredible cover design and Amrit Birdi for bringing PakCore and Big Bad Waf to glorious comic-book life. To Simran Sandhu for slang checking and answering my questions at all hours. Big ups, fam! To Veronica Lyons and Nick de Somogyi for copyediting and being my Time Lords. To Sarah Mehrali and Habeeba Mulla for sensitivity reads and great comments.

To Macmillan for believing every child deserves representation and to Amber Ivatt, Alyx Price, Kat McKenna, and Bea Cross for presenting my books to the world. I am forever grateful.

To the Society of Authors for the John C. Lawrence Award which bought me a little more time to finish my book before returning to teaching maths.

To Patrice Lawrence and Alex Wheatle – award-winning authors who took me under their wing and Fiona Noble for writing the very first article about me. You made my students believe the world is rich with opportunity. Thank you!

To every amazing book blogger & vlogger who supported a very nervous debut author and the fantastic librarians who put books in children's hands, allowing them to experience a multitude of worlds through different eyes. Empathy will save the human race. Without you, there is no me.

To Rebecca Watson and Charlie Langdell for making dreams come true.

And Esther Enaruwe, Agnes Goodgame, Yasmin Mohamed, Lubna Asad, Shamnika Vijayakumar, Durga Jeyasingham, Jane Morris, Medina Ubah, Aminat, Sammy Parker, and M. Caesar – your kindness will never be forgotten.

The UUL crew – Shamz, Dan, Sarah N, Sarah K, Joel, Chris, Rachel, Angela, Steph, Jo, Robbie, Alexis. You guys rock! And Russell Schechter, an inspiring and nurturing lecturer (and the oldest 'Boy Detective' in existence!)

To Devon Cox and Clare Rees for pushing me to the finish line. The world needs your magnificent books.

And last but by no means least, to YOU dear reader. If this book brought you joy or made you think, don't be shy, let me know!

ABOUT THE AUTHOR

Muhammad Khan is an engineer, a secondary-school maths teacher, and now a YA author! He takes his inspiration from the children he teaches, as well as his own upbringing as a British-born Pakistani. He lives in south London and has recently completed an MA in Creative Writing at St Mary's University. His critically-acclaimed debut novel, *I Am Thunder* has been nominated for the Carnegie Medal and shortlisted for a number of regional awards.

ABOUT THE ILLUSTRATOR

Amrit Birdi is a No.1 bestselling comic book artist, best known for illustrating Joe Sugg's *Username:Evie* series.

He and his team have delivered comic art, concept design, storyboards and commercial illustration for international brands and publishers such as Netflix, Square Enix, SKY, Porsche, Universal, Hachette, Pepsi Co, ITV, Ubisoft, Nike, Warner Bros and Titan Comics.

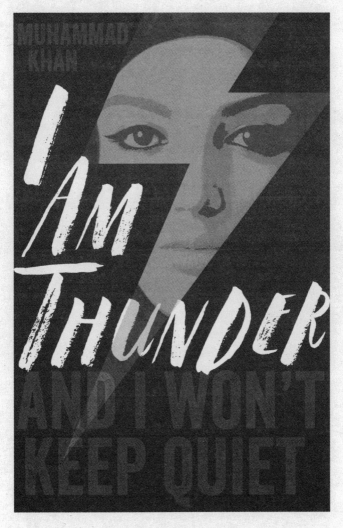

'Funny and clever – a perspective long
overdue in British fiction'

Alex Wheatle, Guardian prize-winning
author of *Crongton Knights*